What the reviewers said .

"At the center of this compelling and superbly crafted novel is the town of Strettam. . . . With incisive insight and compassionate understanding the author plays out the day-by-day, minute-by-minute lives of these ordinary people, interweaving the great and small events that touch their lives. . . . *Strettam* is a powerful and fascinating novel—one of the best you'll ever read."

—*The Pinebrook Bookcast*

"It . . . gripped me in a way few books have. If C. S. Lewis were still alive, I am sure he would be delighted and challenged with the superb account of the Deadlies in their modern dress. . . . The author's insights into human personality are almost inspired. She has an uncommon understanding of a wide variety of human struggles with the seven deadly sins."

—Dr. Lawrence A. Juhlin

"*Strettam* reminds the reader (*this* reader) of Joyce Carol Oates' *them*, Adela Rogers St. Johns' *Tell No Man*, and C. S. Lewis's *Screwtape Letters*—for wildly different reasons. *Strettam* is like *them* in its psychological-spiritual focus, . . . like *Tell No Man* in its depiction of spiritual struggle. And the moral insights and revelations of supranatural dimension remind one . . . of C. S. Lewis. . . . An excellent novel, and I predict it will be bought and read for many years to come."

—Howard A. Snyder
Excelsior

"[Elva McAllaster] certainly tackled a HUGE canvas in *Strettam*, which I read when it first came out. . . . How marvelous to see a truly educated person writing for Jesus Christ. . . . I admire [her] more than I can say."

—Eugenia Price

"Realism at its best; likely to make the reader set a closer watch on temptations coming his way."

—Vera Bethel
Light and Life

"A superbly crafted novel—and yet a book with far deeper meanings than usually found in fiction! . . . Deeply thoughtful pages—some of the best you'll ever read—keep coming back to prick your conscience again and again."

—*Bookstore Journal*

"Satisfyingly different from the usual run of Christian fiction, *Strettam* is about flesh-and-blood people who live, breathe, love and envy. Sometimes, they resolve their conflicts; more often, they do not."

—*The Reveille Echo*

STRETTAM

Elva McAllaster

Zondervan Books
Zondervan Publishing House
Grand Rapids, Michigan

STRETTAM
Copyright © 1972 1987 by Elva McAllaster

Zondervan Books are published by the Zondervan Publishing House
1415 Lake Drive, S.E., Grand Rapids, Michigan 49506

ISBN 0-310-26491-X

Printed in the United States of America

87 88 89 90 91 92 93 / AH / 10 9 8 7 6 5 4 3 2 1

C4680

Contents

"Sleepy Strettam" is the nickname it receives most often. Cadillacs and Buicks and Chevrolets on Highway 37 pause at the blinker light. Drivers glance left toward the smooth, wide surface of the Metonic River, ahead toward the "Speed Limit: 30" sign, right toward the row of storefronts facing Main Street and facing the river. Having glanced at Strettam, most drivers proceed to ignore Strettam; by the time they accelerate at the "Resume Speed" sign, three blocks beyond the Norwich State Bank corner, they could not say the name "Strettam" if three kingdoms depended upon the saying, nor if next year's income tax were thereby to be canceled.

Once, four years ago, a Dodge from Arizona was so attracted by the tulips and lilacs in Simon Wilson's yard that it turned right at the blinker light and drove slowly up the sloping streets, all the way to St. Mark's Episcopal Church at the very crest of Strettam Hill. The Dodge even stopped for three minutes in the graveled parking lot beside St. Mark's before it ambled back down to Highway 37.

Sleepy Strettam. Merest microcosm, Strettam. But a cosmos, though micro-. At the last census, only 1,797 people. But for them, 1,797 different centers of the universe. Everyman lives in Strettam. Strettam is Babylon and Nineveh. Strettam is Gomorrah. Strettam is Oxford and London, New York and Rio.

Strettam is one of the sixty or seventy surrounding towns that metropolitan Keyesport tends to consider as her vassals and outposts. But Strettam is also vassal and outpost for contending eternal cities.

Sometimes a governor or a U. S. senator may have occasion to flash through on Highway 37, but the Seven Deadlies are permanent residents. They like the Strettam climate. They like being kept busy. And they like the comradeship they have with each other as permanent cronies. Each helps the other, often and well. Just as often, all seven will get together for ribald and convivial hilarity. Sometimes they all squat in the graveled parking lot up at St. Mark's. Sometimes they perch on the little bridge where out-of-state cars could turn left at the blinker and cross the Metonic River to Gilson's Garage. (Could, but never do.) Sometimes the Seven Deadlies prefer to convene in the bank lobby. Sometimes they sit like gibbons on the gray-white branches of the sycamores in the woods on the far side of Strettam Hill. Or in all those places at once, and simultaneously in scores of Strettam homes. They can, since they are the Seven Deadlies.

9

"*But go with great caution, for in this wilderness there are many evil beasts: the Lion of Pride, the Serpent of venomous Envy, the Unicorn of Wrath, the Bear of deadly Sloth, the Fox of Covetousness, the Sow of Gluttony, the Scorpion with its tail of stinging Lechery, that is, lust. These, listed in order, are the Seven Deadly Sins.*"

.—The Ancrene Riwle

Before You Enter Strettam...

Before you enter Strettam, let me mention that the people who live in Strettam are entirely the figments of my imagination.

I am a daughter of Adam myself. I have lived lifelong among Adam's children. And I sincerely hope that the Strettam residents—the human ones—are authentic siblings of Adam's various children, but siblings and not portraits.

If anyone in Strettam ever causes you to think of some Adamic sibling whom you know or have known, I hope you will think of him with new insight—and a prayer.

If anyone in Strettam ever resembles your own mirrored image, more or less, or less than less, I hope you will think of yourself with new insight—and a prayer.

But please do keep in mind that the people who live in Strettam are the figments of my imagination.

And so is Strettam town.

Its map started to take shape in my mind one summer as I drove through New Brunswick, Canada, en route to some weeks of writing on Prince Edward Island. As I drove through town after town along the St. John River, I was storing away pictures which later blended and blurred and re-emerged as Strettam —but Strettam isn't in Canada.

A few days after I signed a contract with Zondervan Publishing House for this book, a friend and I were driving across the country on U.S. 70. Once when we left the highway for a meal stop and wandered over country roads to find a country town, I exclaimed with lively interest, "Why, this is Strettam! Strettam has one bank; there's one bank here. Strettam has three churches; I've seen three churches here—"

"Does Strettam have this many liquor stores?" asked my friend as we circled another block. No. No, it doesn't. (Strettam people buy their liquor at Keyesport or Princeville. Joe won't sell it in his diner.) That country town off Interstate 70 is Strettam's sibling, not its portrait. And Strettam town, like Strettam people, is entirely the figment of my imagination.

Of course I can't say the same for the Seven Deadlies. I think it was Christopher Marlowe who first taught me about the ancient classification of the Seven Deadly Sins, as he paraded them in his *Tragical History of Dr. Faustus*. But Marlowe, who died in 1593, did not know about their tricks and pranks and antics in Strettam. That remained for me to tell.

E. McA.

Three

If there had been a better restaurant in Strettam, the three preachers with Strettam parishes would probably have lunched together often. They liked each other. In spite of quips and pretended rivalries, none felt threatened by the others. They liked shop talk and reminiscing about seminary experiences. On their differences in affirmations and procedures, they had cordially agreed to disagree.

With Joe's Diner as the only local restaurant, the three men were not tempted toward ministerial luncheons, but they met often and convivially for coffee.

"Sermon ready for Sunday morning, George? Sermon, homily, sermonette, disquistion?" Tom Williams, the Methodist in the trio, was asking on a Thursday morning.

George McPherson nodded. "More or less. I have a text to work on, anyway—one that correlates pretty well with the New Testament lesson for the morning."

"Good boy," said Dave Yeoman. "What are your Episcopalians going to hear about?"

George took another sip of his coffee. "Want it in King James or the RSV or in Greek?"

"All three," grinned Dave. "How about the Douay and the Cotton Patch versions too?"

"Nope. One's all you get. Let's see which one's handiest in my brief case." He reached for a small black book and turned onion skin paper quickly. "Here you are. King James. Hebrews six, eleven and twelve. 'And we desire that every one of you do shew the same diligence to the full assurance of hope unto the end: That ye be not slothful, but followers of them who through faith and patience inherit the promises.' "

"Not slothful, eh?" said Tom. "You stressed that phrase, didn't you? Well, my Methodists would expect that from me, I suppose, and Dave's Mt. Carmel Baptists would expect it from him. Will your flock expect it from you?"

she knew it, she knew that Mrs. Vincent had misjudged her and disliked her. The whole Metonic River valley seemed pervaded with a faint, unpleasant smell, a murky haziness, she thought.

Metonic River. The small bridge. The Standard Oil station down by the bridge. Maybe I'll go get some gas for my car; I don't feel like reading.

She didn't let herself even think his name, but she knew young Sam Metafield would be working. She knew he would grin and try to get her to linger and talk with him. She knew his eyes would take her dress right off—this dress or any other dress— and fling it into the back seat of her car. She knew that he would not frown at her and disapprove.

Later on, though, he did frown and disapprove: when she got pregnant and he had to marry her, and the school board made no end of trouble about whether she could have a maternity leave.

And the scratch became acutely infected and inflamed; afterward it faded to a livid scar. Sometimes, still, it becomes infected and dribbles pus.

She disapproved of washings that were hung out after eight o'clock on a Monday morning. She disapproved even more of washings that were not hung out in God's good air and sunshine at all, but were surreptitiously placed in automatic dryers in Strettam basements.

She disapproved of all those whose incomes seemed to be perceptibly less than she herself received from the insurance policies of the now long-deceased Mr. Vincent; she felt them somehow guilty of indolence and faulty management. She disapproved even more strongly of those whose incomes were visibly greater than her own.

She disapproved. She disapproved. She disapproved. Daylong and yearlong. She wouldn't have said so, even under hypnosis, but she counted herself a superb standard of excellence, and any difference of any sort from her own codes was utterly suspect.

But Kathleen Morion did not know, when she stopped to buy ten stamps on a September afternoon, that she was meeting such a master craftsman in the art of disapproval. Kathleen saw two observant eyes glide over her hair, down her hips, and across her toes. She saw the eyes narrow a little, the mouth tighten a little, the forehead lines deepen a little. She saw the eyes sweep back up: shoes, hemline, hipline, bodice, hair. She felt the inaudible "Hmpfh!" as Martha turned from the stamp window and jabbed the screen door open.

"Is my slip showing?" wondered Kathleen. "Or has she heard something unpleasant about me? The children have seemed to like me, and the parents I've met—"

Newest and most timid of the teachers in the Strettam Elementary School, Kathleen had wondered all week what impressions she was making. Although she did not look visibly different when she left the post office and stopped at Martin's Rexall, a close observer might have noticed the faintly flushed cheeks, the faintly anxious eyebrow line. No Strettam citizen could have seen a jagged scratch across her psyche, but a scratch was there. Old Pride saw the scratch and grinned. "Nice work, Martha," he said to Lechery. "Very nice work. If that woman knew how well I have her trained—. She's like a puppet when I pull the strings."

"And she doesn't think she even knows you?"

"Right. Now let me flip some dust into that oozing scratch. If I can get a nice infection going in Kathleen—"

"She'll have a handsome scar, eh, if not a permanent oozing ulcer? Go ahead. I have my own intentions."

Kathleen sat brooding, magazine in hand. Without knowing

Martha Vincent

Undoubtedly Martha Vincent's greatest skill was in disapproving. She had a thorough training for it, since her mother and her four maiden aunts each had special skills of the same sort, and each had passed the nuances of her own technique along to Martha. And Martha's apprenticeship with them in her teens and her twenties had been matured by some five decades of further practice. By the September when she started disapproving of Kathleen Morion, whom she had just met in the Strettam post office, it was well over five decades.

Kathleen was wearing an orange dress and raffia sandals. When Martha looked at the dress and the sandals, the crows' feet deepened in her own parchment-flaked face. Martha disapproved of orange or fuchsia or cerise for young women. When she saw poppy colors, the disparaging nouns that her aunts had whispered about girls during the twenties always lingered at the back of her mind.

Actually, Martha automatically disapproved of anyone as young as Kathleen. She also disapproved of bouffant hair styles. Her own hair, thin and paste-colored, was skewered into a flat bun on top of her head; the skewers were the same tortoise-shell hairpins that she had been using for forty-two years.

Along with what her aunts had whispered against, Martha disapproved of all Strettam citizens who were not Baptists and Republicans. She disapproved of everything against which any preacher at the Mt. Carmel Baptist Church had ever warned her, and the composite list had become both long and complicated.

Through the years, Martha had also disapproved of those same preachers, one after another. "Talks through his nose," she would say contemptuously. "Fidgets like a chicken when a body tries to talk with him." "Spends altogether too much time a-visiting at Mrs. Thurston's place." "Quotes too much Scripture when he preaches. Doesn't he think anybody else ever reads the Bible but him?" "Doesn't use enough Scripture when he preaches. My land, his sermons don't even sound like sermons."

Ross Killoran

Murky. Floating in cotton wool. Miles away, a bird starting to sing? Murky. Back into thick, warm darkness. Walking in warm molasses. Walking through caverns. Wrapped in grave clothes. No, it's the blanket twisted around me.

Grave clothes. Easter morning. Should get up now and have devotions. Read a chapter today for sure. Murky. Blanket furry. Kitten fur.

So sleepy. Good firm mattress. New mattress. No good for camping trips. Trout stream. Water swirling around my ankles. Um-m-m, dreaming again. So sleepy.

Pillow soft against my jaw. Gotta shave. Should let it grow. Get ready quicker. Murky. Half a snore. Me, snoring? Fuzz in my throat. Sleep: fuzz two inches thick. Sleep: a white bear to roll up against.

God, bless this day and everybody. Gotta get up. Told the guys I'd read John's gospel. So sleepy. Feel all disconnected. Ankle bone disconnected from the—from the leg bone? Leg bone. Chicken leg. Good dinner at Thurston's last night. Promised Jim Thurston I'd teach his Bible class. So sleepy. Left eye twitching. Too much work on the wholesale orders at night lately. So sleepy. Eyelids stuck together. Elmer's Glue. Old song: "Only five minutes more, give me five minutes more."

God, You know I start snapping at people if I don't get enough sleep. You'll understand if I don't pray this morning, won't You? M-m-m. Tired. Murky.

Like under thick, brown clouds. Nice sheets, nice pillow. M-m-m, blankets. Feel like a football dummy, jointless.

Uh, what? Shut up, alarm clock. Gimme five minutes more. I'll dress faster today. So sleepy. Weights on my eyes. Weights on my brain. Carrying sacks of bran to the barn for Grandpa. Old Prince barking at the horses. Bran sacks piled behind the manger. There. Uh. Smells like bacon, though, not bran. Bacon and coffee. Hey, mom, why didn't you call me? Good night, I'll never make it on time. Another ticket for speeding? Should get a job closer than Princeville. Where's my blue tie?

No, just a cuppa coffee. Well, okay. Hot in my throat. Egg dribbles from fork. Yawn. Ouch. Scald the tonsil scars. Comfortable in my stomach, though.

'Bye, mom.

Didn't even read one verse. Sorry about that, God. Tomorrow for sure. Kind of a cozy feeling, though, y'know. Like going to algebra class without having the problems done and not getting called on. Now let's see. The wholesale orders. . . .

Tommie Millard

Each of the Seven Deadlies has his own set of personal mottoes. Some of their slogans are interchangeable. One that Sloth especially likes: "It's never too soon, and it's never too late." Pursuing that motto, Sloth lolled on top of Mrs. Millard's new avocado green refrigerator on a Saturday morning and watched as Tommie pouted over his pancakes.

"Grandma, I wish you had a TV," he muttered.

"Do you, now? Seems to me I've heard you say that before. Grandpa, Tommie wishes we had a TV."

"It's good for your eyes to have a rest," said Mr. Millard.

"Aw, grandpa, that's what you always say."

"Good for your mind, too, I should think," said Mr. Millard. "From the announcements I see in the Keyesport *Herald,* I still don't think we're missing much."

"Aw, grandpa—"

"Well, there's no TV in this house, Tommie, and that's that. Want to try for some fish in the Metonic today? The garden's full of big, fat worms."

Tommie twirled his fork on end. "I'm still tired of fishing from last summer," he said. "There's gonna be baseball on TV today, and all the guys I know at home will be watching baseball. Who wants to sit around with a fishing pole?"

"You're only here for three weeks, Tommie," said Mrs. Millard. "There'll be other TV programs waiting for you when your folks get back from Europe."

"Yeah, but—grandpa, I'll bet you could rent a TV for a while. There's a TV rental place in Keyesport, I betcha."

"There's a moon in the sky, too."

"Tommie," Mrs. Millard said from the sink, where she was starting to rinse the breakfast dishes, "when your daddy was about your age, he spent hours and hours with grandpa's books. You used to like the pictures in the travel books when you were just a little tyke, four or five years old. You're old enough now to read the ones your daddy liked so much."

"Oh, nuts."

"Thomas Edward, you are not to speak to your grandmother in that disrespectful way. Tell her you're sorry."

Tommie glowered, then shrugged. "Okay, I'm sorry," he said in a tepid voice. "Now can I go over to Johnny Wilson's for a while?"

"Well, yes, I guess you may," Mrs. Millard said. "Why don't you go look around in grandpa's bookcases for a while first? Three weeks will soon be over if you find some books you like."

Tommie's lips clamped shut. All of his facial muscles were still saying, "Oh, nuts." Aloud, he muttered, "Do I have to?"

"It won't hurt you," said his grandmother mildly. She poured granules of Dreft into the sink and swished the water through her fingers. "Don't be rough with them. Some of grandpa's books are pretty rare and valuable."

Tommie snorted softly. "I wouldn't give ten cents a dozen for all the books in the world. 'Specially when we'll have to read so much junk in seventh grade next year."

But he moved to the long living room, where he peered and prodded among the hundreds of volumes that lined shelves on three walls. Ten minutes went by. Mrs. Millard shook out her tea towel and spread it over the rack.

"What are you finding?" she called.

"Uh, nothing much."

"You might look at the Dickens set on the top shelf by the fireplace," she suggested.

"Mom doesn't ever let me say 'dickens,' " said Tommie. "How's come you do?" He had opened a lower cupboard and was peering into it absent-mindedly.

"Oh, Tommie, you silly boy. Charles Dickens, the English writer. Your daddy started with Dickens when he was eight— *The Old Curiosity Shop*. You might like *David Copperfield* better, though. Or *Oliver Twist*. Or *Nicholas Nickleby*. It has lots of boys about your age in it."

Tommie reached deeper into the cupboard. "Hey, grandma, here's my old comic books. Did I leave these here? I had these when I was about in third grade!"

"Yes, you left them. Nobody else. Can you imagine grandpa going out to buy comic books?"

No answer. For twenty minutes, no answer. For more than an hour, no answer.

Mrs. Millard finished dust-mopping the bedrooms and came to the door of the living room. Tommie was sprawled on the rug with his head against the couch, a comic book propped against his lifted knee.

"Did you find the Lewis shelf, dear?" she asked. "I remember that your Murphy cousins talked about liking *The Lion, the Witch, and the Wardrobe.*"

He wasn't listening. "Hey, grandma, these old comic books are sorta neat. Better'n my new ones. I think I'll read 'em all two or three more times while I'm here. Now can I go over to Johnny Wilson's for a while?"

On top of the avocado green refrigerator, Sloth watched Tommie fling himself out the back door. Then Sloth settled flabby jowls against a hairy paw and burped smugly. Very smugly.

Nadine Welch

"Di-a-a-a-na! Di-a-a-a-na! Di-a-a-a-na!" Nadine Welch pushed a wisp of hair back from her face and stepped into the kitchen again, pulling the back porch door shut with a snap. "Cathy, where is your sister?"

"I don't know, mother. You told her after lunch that you wouldn't need her for a while, didn't you? I thought she asked you." Cathy picked up another white shirt from the laundry basket and slid it over the ironing board.

"Well, I didn't mean she should take the rest of the summer off! The guest room floor needs waxing before your Aunt Susan comes next week, and she could wash the kitchen shelves. But first I need to try this dress on her if I'm going to finish it tonight."

"Do you have to finish it tonight?"

"I don't have to do anything but die, as your Grandma Mac-Inness always says! But you know I don't like a piece of unfinished sewing hanging over my ears when I start preserves, and Mr. Wildeman has a flat of nice apricots he's holding for me—if your father remembers to bring it home this evening. Maybe I should send Diana down in the car, if she'd ever show her face. I'll be glad when you're sixteen, Cathy; maybe I'll have one driver around for errands when I need them!" She stepped back to the kitchen porch. "Di-a-a-a-na!"

An alert pixie face with expressive green eyes and sandy blonde hair appeared in the living room doorway.

"Did you want something, mother?"

"Well, rather. Do you think I stand here screaming your name just for practice? Where have you been, anyway?"

"I was—uh—I was out for a little walk."

"Out for a little walk? In the middle of the afternoon, with sewing and cleaning and ironing going on? Diana Welch, you are the limit, the absolute limit."

"But you did say, after lunch, that you wouldn't need me for a while, mother. I asked you. Didn't I, Cathy?"

"Well, I didn't mean for you to have a week's vacation! Peel your dress off so I can try this dress on you and mark the hemline."

Diana pulled off her dress as commanded, managing to dab her eyes with the hem of it before she placed it on a chair. Turning to pick up the new garment, Mrs. Welch didn't see either the moistness on Diana's eyelashes or Cathy's sympathetic glance.

"You've been taking an awful lot of little walks this summer, Diana," she said through a mouthful of pins.

"I wish I could take a few big ones," said Diana. "Mrs. Overton is on a hiking tour of Norway with some other P. E. teachers; I wish I were there too. When the moon is full, like it was on Sunday night, I'd like to walk and walk and walk. Sometime I'd like to walk all night—"

"Well, don't you ever let me catch you trying it, Diana! The very idea! You always were a silly little dreamer, ever since you were two years old; I thought high school would cure you, but it's just making you worse. That or your MYF. You have an awful lot of Youth Fellowship committee meetings any more. You haven't gone and got a boyfriend without telling me, have you?"

A tear dripped down each cheek, but Diana kept her hands in place, knowing that any motion would bring her a tart rebuke and pins repinned.

"No, mother," she said.

"There. Take it off and put it on the sewing table." She picked up a spool of yellow thread and a needle. "Now you may put on your jeans, miss, and wax the guest room floor. And try to do a good job of it, Diana. Your Aunt Susan notices everything, you know. If it doesn't look nice, I'll be sure she knows who did the waxing."

"Yes, mother."

"I never thought a daughter of mine would be called lazy," Mrs. Welch reflected as she twitched her chair into place beside the sewing machine. "Cathy, I'm glad you know how to work."

When both girls were putting up their hair that evening, Cathy stopped abruptly with a roller between her left thumb and little finger. "Boy, I wish mom would quit buggin' you so much, Diana," she said. "She was really smoky this afternoon, wasn't she?"

Quick tears welled up in Diana's eyes. When emotion was already throbbing under the surface, to receive anger sometimes made her cry; to receive sympathy invariably did. "I wish I didn't make her so mad," she said in a voice that tried to be

23

matter-of-fact. "I never seem to know when she's going to yell at me next, or why. You know, when I have a home of my own, I'm absolutely sure that it's going to be a place to live in and not to live for."

"To live in?"

"Um-hum. We don't *live* here. We just stay here. Sometimes I feel as though the house were a big stomach that is trying to dissolve us and digest us into itself."

"Oh, Di, how awful! What do you mean, we don't *live* here?"

"I don't know, Cathy; that's what I'm trying to figure out. We eat here and sleep here and keep polishing the place, whether it needs it or not, but that's not living. I s'pose I'm sorta starving for what Mr. Hinman kept calling 'the eternal verities' in English class last year. Don't you ever feel as though you were stubbing your toe against forever, and if you give it the right kind of a kick you will sorta know more about God than the Old Testament guys did?"

Cathy stared.

"Like this afternoon. I felt so pent-up I was just about ready to pop. Like the Metonic when it's at flood stage, up over the banks, and some loose logs come down banging against the bridge piles, and it tugs and tugs until you wonder if the whole bridge will go out—whoo-om. When you stop to realize that you're a person, a human being, with this one teeny lifetime to be *you* out of all the centuries—"

"Di-a-a-a-na!" A strident voice floated up the stairs.

Luminous green eyes and a luminous face turned suddenly drab. Her pixie chin dropped into her hands, and her fingertips pressed her lips together firmly for long seconds.

"Di-a-a-a-na!"

"Yes, mother."

"There's work to do tomorrow. You girls quit your chatter now and get to sleep. You hear me?"

Outside on the porch, Sloth grinned. "Keep at 'em, momma, keep at 'em. I love you, momma darling."

"Whaddya mean, *you* love her?" asked Pride from the porch swing. "She's all mine, from her toenails to her eyelashes."

"Sure," said Sloth, rubbing his hairy belly with pudgy paws. "Sure. All yours, and ol' Anger has a claw in her, too. But, y'know, all that tearing hurry around the house is just the routine I've been teaching her to keep her flabby soul from doing any push-ups. When it comes to anything the Enemy wants most of all, she's about the laziest in three states. Isn't she? She puts a good flavor on my tongue, chum. Mighty good. Sorta like the juicy ones friend Nero kept sending us in his day."

"Nice lad, Nero," said Pride, idly pushing the porch swing into motion. "Nice wench here, this Welch creature. But that whelp Diana is going to take some watching. From all of us."

At Bartlett's

Sloth always likes to go to the parties in Strettam. You'd think he'd rather not. At first glance, you'd expect the person-hood of sluggishness and indolence, which he is, to be repelled by party verve. But Sloth is, after all, not slothful about making people over into his own image, and he knows his goals. What he can accomplish during office hours is all to the good, but some of his nicest nudges, some of the kneadings he wouldn't want to miss, occur when Strettam puts on party clothes.

Like the cool Friday evening in June at the Bartlett's, when he had something of a tussle with Mannie Mitchell.

The Bartletts had five other couples over for the evening. The Kendricks and the Mitchells from Strettam itself. The Thurs-tons and the McMahons from Mill Creek, ten miles up the Metonic valley. And the Mermanns, who live in a split-level brick house on a hilltop two miles south of Strettam.

The same crowd has been together often. They were all young marrieds together, and they still feel themselves to be young marrieds at forty-five and fifty-one and fifty-three. Old jokes have accumulated, worn threadbare, been patched at the elbows. Sloth encourages the old jokes; he knows the pervading threat of Grace and how it can slip in through fissures in habitual old routines.

"'Lo, Janet. 'Lo, Tony," Jimmy Bartlett greeted the first-arriving McMahons. "Bring me any blackbird pies?"

Tony guffawed. "It isn't your birthday this time," said Janet. "And we don't have any more music boxes I could use, anyway."

"Well, come on in, pie or no pie," said Jimmie. "Boy, that was one of the neatest jokes I've ever had pulled on me, though. Your wife is a corker, isn't she, Tony?"

"Sure is." Tony laughed again, and his "haw, haw" bounced off the Bartlett fireplace mantel and reverberated against the windows.

"Hi, kids," said Sue Bartlett, looking in from the kitchen.

"Choose the chairs you like the best, as long as you're here first."

"Any Duncan Phyfe for Tony to break this time, Sue?" asked Janet.

"No Duncan Phyfe," said Jimmie. "Boy, Tony, I never will forget the way you looked that night when the chair collapsed under you. Not if I live to be a hundred."

Tony chuckled, but no sound bounced off the mantelpiece this time. "Hey, there's Ray and Martha in their new Buick," he said. "How about that chrome? Some buggy, eh?"

"Yeah, how about that?" said the host, moving toward the front door. "Come in, come in." He held the door open for Ray and Martha Kendrick. The Kendricks might have sat for a portrait to be entitled "Study in Blue and Gray." The gray in his suit precisely matched the gray in her hair; her blue dress matched the color of his eyes, his tie, and his neatly folded handkerchief.

"Some buggy you've got there," Tony McMahon said.

"You like it?"

"Sure do."

"What kinda mileage you gettin' with it?"

Then the Mitchells and the Thurstons arrived together, followed soon after by the Mermanns, and scrutiny of the new Buick was reiterated, amplified, and re-reiterated.

From car to weather. Sue Bartlett thought it was the coolest June she could remember. Gracie Mermann thought housework went a lot easier when the days were so cool. Tony McMahon thought the Boy Scouts weren't very happy about it, with their camping trip over at Junietta State Park last week. Well, maybe it wouldn't be a long, hot summer, said Sam Thurston. Sure hoped it wouldn't.

A fine mist of tension diffused itself through the room. "Hot summer" to "Harlem-Watts-ghetto" was a short step. Easier not to. Martha Kendrick's fingers tightened on her cigarette lighter. Don't lose your temper this time, Ray; please, please. Across the room, Sloth touched Jolene Thurston's arm softly. "Sue, you've got a new slipcover on this couch," Jolene cried. "Look, Gracie, isn't this a cute fabric? It looks almost Oriental—"

"Should be cute," said Jimmie with jovial pride and pseudo-wrath. "Man, what that woman does to our bank account when she gets in a mood for something new around the house! Shouldn't happen to a dog."

"Speaking of dogs," said Gracie Mermann, "what can you do about a neighbor's dog that barks at all hours? George just lies there and snores through it all, but I'm getting worn to an absolute frazzle—"

"Serves you right," said Sue Bartlett. "You're getting due

retribution for that big hound you used to have. My dining table still has claw marks."

"Interesting idea, retribution," said quiet Mannie Mitchell. "Did you notice in the papers—"

Sloth was tapping Jimmie Bartlett's shoulder. Tapping very firmly. "Oh, hey, I just thought," he interposed. "Is it cool enough so's you folks would like a fire in the fireplace? 'Scuse me, Mannie, you were starting to say something. Whaddya think, Sue? Shall I make a fire? It's all ready for lighting."

Nods. Smiles. "Nothing like a fire in a fireplace," said Ray Kendrick.

"Mannie, couldn't we have a fireplace built into our living room?" wondered Linda. "I get downright jealous whenever I come over here, Sue. We have that big east wall—"

"Sure, you could have one built in. Easy." Jimmy Bartlett was moving the kindling slightly and tipping a match to a twist of paper. "My cousin Al does a lot of fireplace and patio work during his evenings and weekends. Shall I get you his telephone number? He lives over Princeville way. He'd give you a good bargain. Course, it wouldn't be any song, with costs the way they are."

Fireplaces and patios, with sundry adjacent topics, were good for half an hour, during which the women made excursions into recipes for green tomato pickles and sprayed the aphids in their respective gardens.

"Mrs. Finch always used to have the nicest roses in three counties," Linda Mitchell said. "I haven't been up the Princeville Heights road for over a year, I guess. Did the new people vow to love, honor, and cherish the roses when they bought the Finch place?"

"Oh, my dear!" Sue Bartlett's bouffant hairdo quivered at the vigor of her voice. "Hadn't you heard?"

"Heard what?"

"About the Finch place? They're Arty people. Capital A. He does sculpture—anyway he calls it sculpture—and she paints. They've made the old garage into a studio, and the neighbors say they keep the craziest kind of schedules. Real bohemians, you know."

"Or hippies, Sue?" asked Tony McMahon.

"Oh, I wouldn't go that far, I guess. I haven't seen them myself. But they must be pretty far out for our Metonic valley citizens. Heaven knows why they chose to settle on the Finch place."

"Heaven knows, and I thought all of Johnson County knew,"

said Ray Kendrick. "You mean, Sue, you didn't know that this sculptor inherited the place?"

"Oh, really?"

"Sure. Mrs. Finch was his great-aunt. She didn't especially like him, I guess, but the property is his. She'd turn over in her grave if she knew how her roses need pruning, believe me!"

"Maybe she does know," said Mannie Mitchell. "Maybe she does know and is glad. Did you ever think—"

On cue (those last four words from any speaker were always a cue), Sloth touched four or five people simultaneously. Jimmie Bartlett reached for the fireplace shovel and tongs and started readjusting the glowing coals.

"It's smoking a little, Jimmie," said Sue. "Is there something you can do with the draft? Are you warm enough, everybody? Too warm? I'll get you some coffee in a minute."

Tony McMahon looked up from the magazine he had been leafing through. "Did you say Mrs. Finch was this sculptor's great-aunt, Ray?" he asked.

"That's right."

"Then it's young Matt Heiler. Any of you remember him? Stayed with his aunt for a while and went to our high school. My kid brother knew him. Bert used to laugh at him to a fare-you-well. Boy, was he a dreamer. Had the craziest ideas. Yeah, he would be a sculptor or something like that."

Coffee. Blueberry torte or fresh apple pie? More coffee. More coffee, anyone?

Then good night, and good night, and good night. "Great party," said Janet McMahon. "Thanks loads."

"Even without a blackbird pie?"

"Even without a blackbird," said Tony, and laughed so hard that Janet said, "Sh-h-h, you'll wake up the neighbors. See you, Jimmie, G'night, Sue."

In his own living room again, Mannie Mitchell sat down heavily and stared at the rug for five minutes. Linda came back from the bedroom and looked at him with annoyance. "Well, Manfred, aren't you going to bed?"

His lips tightened. Suddenly he lifted his right hand, clenched it, brought it down on the end table beside him with a harsh thud. Linda thought she heard the wood crack softly. "What's the matter, Mannie?"

"Linda, I don't want to go back to their house again. Not for the next million years."

"What on earth do you mean? It was a nice party—as nice as always."

"That's the trouble. When, in ten years, has any one of us   29 said anything worth saying or thought anything worth thinking when we were together at the Bartletts? Or anywhere else?— though I think it's worse there."

"Well, for heaven's sake—"

"Precisely. It's about time we did some thinking and talking that had something of heaven's sake about it. Some faint flavor of heaven, anyway. Don't you feel as though an evening like this leaves you with a head full of feathers instead of a brain? Really, don't you?"

"You'd better go to bed," said Linda shortly. "Do you have a temperature?" she cupped her hand across his forehead. And Sloth stood close beside her, adding suede gentleness and velvet weight to her touch.

"Go on to bed," said Mannie. "I'll read for a while." He picked up half a dozen books, one after another. He touched tooled leather bindings, tracing the designs absent-mindedly. His eyeballs felt hot, and he was numb with drowsiness. "And so to bed, like old Pepys," he murmured bitterly. "To bed, to bed, to bed. Lady Macbeth, and all. To sleep. Perchance to dream. We are such stuff as dreams are made of. Such stuff." He put down the collection of essays he was holding and opened the bedroom door.

"There now," said Sloth. "Easy does it. Nice party, nice Bartletts, nice conversation. Sleep on now and take your rest." He grinned, a malevolent grin. "And take—your—rest."

Mannie Mitchell's face settled into his pillow, while Sloth and Night walked through the streets of Strettam.

Janice Wilson

She picked up another little price tag, wrote "98¢" on it, touched it to her tongue, and jabbed it against the next hand towel in the pile. Then another. And another.

Gray-haired Alice Benedict, straightening slips and nightgowns into firmer nylon rectangles at the next counter, paused to watch Janice for a moment. "You could use that little sponge thing to lick 'em, you know," she said mildly. "You don't have to use your tongue."

"I know." Jab, write, lick, jab.

"You *like* the taste of that glue?"

"Not especially." Jab, write, lick, jab. Janice pushed the pile of hand towels to one side and pulled forward a higher pile of bath towels.

"Well, it's your tongue that will taste like a kettle of paste, not mine," said Mrs. Benedict, moving on to adjust the black-numbered size markers on a rack of housedresses at the back of the store. The bookkeeper, Mary Odette, caught Alice's eye and shook her head about two-fifths of an inch. Alice knew that motion of the head and the accompanying primming of the lips. After twenty-two years together in Dacey's Dry Goods they hardly needed spoken words, but Alice soon found a sales book to check at the bookkeeper's little oak cage.

"What's eating her majesty this morning?" Mary Odette half-whispered.

"Beats me. Maybe she has a headache."

"She didn't say?"

"She doesn't ever say what's wrong when she's in a sour mood. She just goes around like a thundercloud. And if you try to give her a suggestion, she acts insulted."

"Well, she'd better not snap at the customers today. Tom Dacey's going to be here part of the day, and he'll have an eye on everything. And you'd better get ready to open the doors. It's five till."

Alice went back toward the front of the store. Now Janice

was marking a small mountain of washcloths. Jab, write, lick, jab. Jab, write, lick, jab.

Actually Janice could not have possibly told Alice Benedict, nor anyone else, why her red corpuscles were carrying on such violent warfare with each other, why there were even more bombs and machine guns and land mines inside herself than usual. Hating Joy McNair had become so habitual to her that she did not always identify new episodes of hate as being new. Anyone probing—as Alice Benedict would have been willing to probe—would have received an honest surliness in reply: "Nothing's the matter. Nothing special."

In fact, as Janice walked to Dacey's that morning she had seen Joy McNair pause at the blinker light and then drive north on Highway 37. (Joy, with her smooth tan and her smooth blonde hair. Joy, with her father's car to drive while I walk to work at Dacey's dumb old store. Joy, probably going to Keyesport to shop for college clothes while I sell denim overalls to all the farmers of Johnson County. Or maybe she's going to the courts at Junietta for another of her tennis tournaments.) And seeing Joy at the highway blinker left Janice feeling like a river into which some new factory had just emptied a conduit of refuse.

Sometimes, when she became introspective—when she would sit in a study hall, for instance, and see Joy's face in and around and through her geometry problems for a whole period—it seemed to Janice as though she must have started hating Joy prenatally. Or envying, for of course the envy part always came first. It annoyed her and amused her to visualize herself curled up inside her mother's body: "And I'd kick and squirm and think to myself, 'Yeah, I'm pretty uncomfortable, but Joy's mother is so much taller, and she's got a lot more room to kick in.' And I'd feel my face growing into a human face and be mad at it because Joy's was prettier. And I'd hear my folks talking, while mother bumped her stomach against the table with me in it, and I'd feel like squalling because Joy's folks were smarter and more handsome and more fun."

For all of their eighteen years, if not prenatally, Joy always had what Janice wanted, what Janice longed for. Not that Joy was the only one whom Janice envied. In first grade, Ellen's patent leather shoes. In third grade, the Johnson girls' bicycles. In seventh grade, the others who sometimes had boys carry books home for them, as Janice never did. As a sophomore in high school, Kathy's easy grace in Drama Club, and Jimmy's A's on Spanish tests, and Carol's beautiful clothes, and Karen's riding horse. As a high school senior, the ones on the honor roll. The ones who had nice dates for the prom, when she was stuck with stupid, freckled David. The ones who were casually sure they were going to college.

But through it all, Joy was the one she envied most and hated most. From kindergarten onward, when Joy came to school with a flawless new dress, the muscles in Janice's middle would tighten up until she felt nauseated. When they were eight and Joy got to be the madonna at Sunday school, Janice kicked every tree on the right-hand side of the street between the Methodist Church and her home—and afterward kicked her dog until her father spanked her and threatened to give the dog away. Whatever Joy got—a new tricycle or riding boots or flute lessons, a tennis racket or a trip to music camp—Janice wanted, and wanted with a desperation that sometimes frightened her placid mother. Janice soon learned the diplomacy of not saying, "But why can't I? Joy's folks got one for her," after hearing (at age four and five and six), "Joy's father is a banker, Janice, and your father is not a banker. Now be quiet." But the silenced "Why can't I?" was a subterranean fire.

From junior high on, that smoldering "Why can't I?" pushed Janice into dazzled worship of all the goddesses in Hollywood's pantheon. Imagination easily believed herself the equal and rival of those faces on the magazine covers. In a favorite daydream, talent scouts would finally discover her (she never quite decided how they would locate Strettam and the Wilson residence), and she would become a superstar. In due season she would return for a world premiere at Keyesport, and there would be a gala motorcade to Strettam, and she would sweep past Joy McNair (who would be standing on the corner of Main Street just across from her father's bank) with a faint, haughty smile and a slight wave of her gloved hand. A very slight wave.

In high school, that same silent but relentless "Why can't I?" pushed her—more than she would or could have admitted—toward identifying herself with some of the ego-driven women she read about. Wanting a new knit cardigan like Joy's, she walked over the Wessex moors with Eustacia Vye or climbed other moors toward Wuthering Heights. She gave counsel to Lady Macbeth. Wishing she had Kathy's skirts or Ellen's legs or Karen's trip to Florida, Janice was Amber, and forever. And gone with the wind.

After which, Dacey's Dry Goods. (Jab, write, lick, jab. Jab, write, lick, jab.)

She felt personally affronted by the mediocre and unimaginative dresses that Mr. Dacey stocked, and by the drab, shapeless hats that sat like lumps on his one millinery shelf. Even so, it twisted something inside her when anything moderately pretty would go off the racks and into the waiting hands of a customer. If the world were hung together better, she told herself darkly, she would have been the customer, but in far more genteel shops than Dacey's Dry Goods. Meanwhile, Karen or Kathy or Ellen would carry away a brown paper bag or box with Dacey's ugly blue-brown advertisement stenciled on the outside, and for the rest of the day Janice would carry an ugly blue-brown flavor on her tongue.

"When you get the towels done, Janice," said Alice as she came back from unlocking the front door and putting up the fly-specked shade, "you might bring some more of those seamless hose in from the stockroom. People seem to like the sale prices."

"Okay."

Alice looked annoyed. "You could smile, Janice. It's a brand new day."

Janice shrugged. "So why should I smile about that? It's gonna be a day like any other day, isn't it?" Later, at the funeral home, she would remember that question, and her throat would get even drier.

Until five o'clock, it was like any other day. Almost ten after, by the time she signed out on her timecard and walked down Main Street. Past the Rexall drugstore, past Mr. Wildeman's grocery, almost as far as Joe's Diner. Then, simultaneously: Joy McNair crossing Main Street toward her at the blinker light. (Joy back from Keyesport, or wherever, then? Joy in a sleek, slim cotton dress, with her blonde hair pulled back and tied in a little-girl blue bow.) Joy, tossing a too-quick glance up Highway 37 but not really looking because Kevin Thomas was just bicycling past and she was calling to him about the Junietta tennis tournament. And a red convertible (Is that an MG? Is that what an MG looks like?) that apparently didn't even see the Strettam blinker light. The driver was slouched low in his seat, laughing hard, holding a lighter to a cigarette with his right hand. The dark-haired girl beside him was laughing hard, too, until their brakes started to skid and her face went pasty-white and she shut her eyes and screamed.

Janice saw Kevin and his bike, saw the blinker, saw the convertible, saw Joy not see the convertible. "Watch out, watch out, *watch out!*" her mind screamed. At first her tongue didn't scream. Her mind was whispering as well as screaming. "Let him hit her," it said. "Let her die. Or she'll be crippled. And she'll never outclass you again, not in anything."

Then his brakes started to skid, and the windblown girl beside him started to scream, and Janice screamed too. And felt

34

such nausea that she sagged against the windowbox of Joe's Diner. She realized later that she had vomited on the sidewalk. Her dress was stained with the slime of it, and she kept tasting the horrible sour-flavored stinging in her throat and nose. But Joe never told her that in her hysteria she pulled up all of the petunias his wife had just planted three days before.

At the funeral home on Thursday Janice felt totally numb, as though she were another kind of corpse. To be a murderer. Really, I am a murderer. If we were Roman Catholics, I'd go confess it to a priest. I won't ever forget her body sprawled on the curb across from Joe's. Her blood, Joy's blood. There is a fountain filled with blood. Well, anyway, nobody knows. Would it be better if somebody did know? If I'd go talk with her mother? No, she'd just hate me, and it wouldn't help Joy. One second of warning would have—I wonder how much people know when they're dead? Does Joy know I killed her? She never knew how I felt. Or I don't think she did, anyway. That one time at the Girl Scout camp-out when we were twelve, and she said—what did she say?

If I could have leveled with her then and asked her to forgive my horrid feelings. If I could talk to her tonight and tell her I'm sorry. "Hello, Joy? Look, this is Janice, and I've killed you, see, but I didn't really mean to, see?" "Hi, Janice," she'd say. "But you did mean to, you know. That's the point. And under all this guilt act, you're sorta glad I'm gone. Aren't you?" And I'd have to say I don't really know. Maybe so.

Janice asked her mother about staying away from the funeral. She asked carefully, evasively.

"No, dear, I think you'd better go. Take plenty of Kleenex. I know it's hard, when you were right there and saw it happen, but you and Joy have always been such good friends. You'll always be sorry, and afterwards you couldn't change your mind, you know."

Always such good friends, ha. But the murderer is supposed to revisit the corpse. And afterwards you can't change your mind; you can't stand in front of Joe's Diner again for one tiny second and yell, "Wa-a-a-atch OUT!" Do most people feel about some-body the way I've always felt about Joy? Does everybody murder somebody a little bit? Did I really start aiming that MG toward her when we were in kindergarten? Always such good friends.

During the funeral itself, up at St. Mark's Episcopal Church, Janice's numbness almost turned to hysteria, and her mother was not the only one who wondered if Janice really should have come. She bit her lips until they bled and filled her big purse with crumpled, soggy tissues and mopped her cheeks with angry, dabbing motions. After the hymns and the ritual—which Janice heard but didn't hear—and after solemn words by the rector, the long, mauve coffin was wheeled into the narthex while discreet ushers with white carnations on their lapels nodded departure permission to row after row of Strettam and Keyesport and Princeville citizens.

Shall I look at her again? Janice wondered. I know what they've done with her. I saw her over at the funeral home. I'll just shut my eyes or look at the floor. But when her mother paused beside the coffin, she paused too, with unwilling compulsion.

Joy's hair had never had a silkier sheen. Her pretty face was tranquil and composed. "Like a princess," someone behind Janice was breathing. They had put a dress on her that Janice had never seen before: powder-blue and trimmed with exquisite lace. She does look like a princess, thought Janice. All she needs is a crown. And I s'pose, according to the ol' Sunday school hymns, she really has that, too, if she wants it.

Ludicrously, bitterly, she thought of the contrast: here I am, with my face all splotched from crying, and with—with this guilt of being a murderer like a monkey on my back for the rest of my life. A misery I can't even talk about. And there she is, looking like a princess. That's the way everybody will always remember her. Janice crushed a handkerchief to her lips and ran for the stairs. Her knees felt rubbery, but she made it to the ladies' room before she vomited again. Never, ever, since before they were born, she thought, had she envied Joy McNair so desperately.

"—really worried," her mother was saying to inquisitive Mrs. Benedict, just beyond the outside stairs to St. Mark's. "She and Joy have always been such close friends, you know."

Charlie Wright

"Well, I suppose every congregation ought to have one real character," said the Rev. Mr. Williams as he watched cream turn brown-amber into whited-amber inside his coffee cup. "But sometimes I wish one of you guys had drawn Charlie Wright instead of my getting him."

"A real character, with a capital K, isn't he?" agreed George McPherson. "You can keep him, thanks; that's what you Methodists get for letting John Wesley start ordaining laymen a couple of centuries ago." His slim face was quizzical, humorous, alive.

"Oh, come now," Williams protested. "You sound as if I had been there in person, shaking Brother Wesley's hand and giving him my individual blessing." He chuckled. "Now that would be old Charlie's fondest daydream—to have talked with John Wesley in the flesh!"

"Wouldn't it, though?"

"Slow down, you guys," interposed Dave Yeoman. "Clue a poor Baptist into your mysterious allusions, will you? I thought Charlie Wright was one of your best pillars, Tom. What are you beefing about?"

"Oh, he's a pillar all right. It's the kind of granite he's cut from that's a trial to the flesh."

"Your congregation sent him to represent you at that big Methodist meeting in Kansas City last summer, didn't they?"

Williams shrugged. "Sure, who else?"

"Come on, don't be so mysterious," prodded Yeoman.

"Oh, he's a good guy," said Williams. "He's a retired farmer, you know, moderately wealthy—"

"You object to that?"

"Shuddup. You want I should tell you something, huh, you listen while I tell you something, huh?"

"As an Italian guide you're a great Dane, Tom," grinned Yeoman.

"Yeah, Hamlet himself. Well, anyway, Charlie Wright used to have two strings to his fiddle—Hereford cattle and Methodist history. Or three—cattle and Methodism and his grandchildren. He's a doting grandfather. Well, now the grandchildren are all away, he's retired from the farm, and he saws at that one string like a monomaniac. He reads piles of books, makes scrapbooks, and corresponds with librarians and editors to a fare-you-well. He can just about tell you where John Wesley slept during every single night of his whole preaching career!"

"I humbly repeat, sir, you object to that? You're a Methodist preacher, aren't you? He sounds like a great guy to have around. Here I've been saying 'Good Morning' to him for two years and didn't realize I was greeting a scholar."

Williams shrugged again. "I could have worse tribulations. If his obsession could be carved up in about twenty little portions and scattered through the whole congregation, or through twenty congregations, it would be mighty good seasoning. But—" Williams looked at his watch. "Look, Dave, I should go up to Wright's this morning anyway. His daughter Marian—that's Mrs. Bill Willeford, you know—has some Vacation Bible School stuff that I'm supposed to pick up before my committee meets this afternoon. Wanta come along and meet the old lion in his den?"

"Just don't cherish any thoughts of snaring him into your Mt. Carmel flock," warned George McPherson with a grin. "That would really be one for the books, now, if you could proselyte Charlie Wright into becoming a Baptist. They'd give it headlines in the Keyesport *Herald!*"

"In the *New York Times* would be more like it," said Williams. "Coming, Dave?"

"Well—okay, sure. I'm way behind with my own calling, but —yeah, sure." He flipped a coin toward the counter where Joe Bynum was washing cups and plates and followed Tom toward his green Pontiac.

"Mr. Wright lives with the Willefords?" he asked as they drove along a graveled road northwest of Strettam.

"That's right. His big farm was about fifteen miles on out in the country."

"Sue Willeford is his granddaughter, then?"

"Yes, she is; you've probably never heard her full name, have you?"

"I doubt it. Why?"

"Well, listen to this. Don't ever let her know you know, but on her birth certificate that girl is Susanna Annesley Wesley Willeford."

Yeoman stared. "How's come? Is Annesley a family name?"

"Oh, my stars; I keep forgetting that the man is an ignorant

Baptist." He grinned amiably. "Susanna Annesley, my dear David, was John Wesley's mother's maiden name."

"And you mean—"

"I do mean. Marian Willeford told me that they argued about it all during her pregnancy, but she and Bill finally gave in—and grandpa has always made a special pet of the child. So when Sue finishes up at Northern State—when and if—I suppose her name will be there on the official diploma lists for all the world to see: Susanna Annesley Wesley Willeford."

"That's enough to make a junior decide to be a dropout," said Yeoman darkly. "Though from what my Karen says, Sue might have other reasons to be a dropout. This is the Willeford place?"

"This is the place."

Dave's lips twitched a little when Williams presented him simply as "My friend, Dave Yeoman," but he didn't comment. Charlie Wright welcomed them into a cluttered big living room where he seated himself again beside an old roll-top desk.

"I'm glad you've come, Brother Williams," he said, smoothing a ruffled crest of white hair with his right hand. "I've received such a wonderful letter this morning from one of my correspondents in England. He has just been at Westminster Abbey and has written me a nice paragraph about the Wesley brothers' plaque. You know the handsome plaque they finally put in the Abbey, don't you? Wait a moment, I have a photo of it here somewhere. I was just looking at it to savor Mr. Richards' description all the more. There we are—"

"Yes, I've seen it," said Williams. "Mr. Yeoman may like to have a look." Mischief flickered across Yeoman's face under his crew cut. His friend's toneless "I've seen it" clearly said that he had seen the photo approximately a thousand times.

"It has always seemed to me such a pity," Wright was going on, "that the British nation didn't put a full-size statue of Wesley in the Abbey. It would have been so much more deserved than the memorials to poets and statesmen, you know."

"Is Mrs. Willeford in?" asked Williams. "I'd like to ask her about our Vacation Bible School materials, if I may."

"Of course, of course." The old man raised his voice. "Marian, oh, Marian. Brother Williams is here." His elbow dislodged a magazine, which fell to the floor. "Um-m-m—what—oh, yes. I've been keeping this to show you, Brother Williams. It has a fine article on Wesley's methods of preaching in the open air. A very scholarly article. You must take it along."

"Thank you," said Williams. Yeoman, watching him, thought that an odd fire was beginning to glow behind Tom's brown eyes. "That reminds me," Tom went on crisply, "did Simon Wilson tell you that we have an opportunity to have our Sunday morning services broadcast during the autumn months? Over the Keyesport station in this series they're carrying. The Board of Evangelism will be talking about it tomorrow night."

"Um-m-m. I don't recall—yes, maybe Simon did speak of something of the sort. It would cost a tidy sum, I suppose? More than a little church like ours can afford, I daresay."

"No, I think not." There *was* a fire behind those brown eyes, Dave told himself.

"Uh—I see. You really plan to go ahead? Well, I suppose we might get used to a microphone in the church, though I can't say's I like the idea. It's a pretty good church as it is, without any microphones in it. Don't you think so, Mr.—ah—"

"Yeoman," supplied Dave.

"Mr. Yeoman. Yes, to be sure. You haven't been here before, have you, Mr. Yeoman? Ah, I thought not. Mr. Yeoman, wouldn't you like to see my little library? I'm sure Marian's in the kitchen, Brother Williams. Maybe you'd like to step out and speak with her? This way, Mr.—ah—um—"

He led the way to an adjacent room. Used to be a guest room, probably, Dave thought. There was another roll-top desk, smaller than the one in the living room, and a rocker or two. Old-fashioned bookcases with sliding glass fronts lined two walls. The other two were nearly covered with framed documents, framed photographs, framed postcards.

"Here we are," said Wright.

"Well, you've made quite a collection!"

"Oh, I have a few things. One ought to have a certain pride in the heritage of his church," said the old man. His hand was smoothing the ruffled white hair again. "Nothing here is really valuable, though. I keep inquiring, but the Methodist museums are very greedy, I must say. I would like to get hold of one thing that Wesley himself handled. A lock of his own hair or one of his own books. Wouldn't that be wonderful?"

Yeoman looked dubious. What to say that would please the old man? "What is your greatest treasure, Mr. Wright?"

Ah, the right question. The wrinkled old face lighted up with pleasure. "That's hard to say. That's really hard to say. I do treasure this big photograph of his rooms at Lincoln College; it took a bit of doing to get that, but I managed, through one of my correspondents in England. And this new book of early Methodist hymns, which the editor kindly autographed for me—"

Tom Williams reappeared in the doorway with a manila folder

under his arm. The fire behind his eyes was getting a lot brighter, Dave thought.

"Ah, Brother Williams. You found Marian, I trust. I was just mentioning this book of hymns—"

"Marian's just been telling me the wonderful news about our MYF retreat grounds," said Tom.

"Uh—yes, indeed, I presume Marian would wish to speak with you about the project. Now, in this bookcase, Mr.—ah—"

Charlie Wright's pastor needed an immediate ally, Dave told himself. "What's the great news, Tom, if I may ask?"

"We've been talking for months about getting a conference center for our high school kids," said Williams quickly. "Now a fine piece of ground just eight miles down the Metonic is up for sale, and a woman Marian knows over at Iroquois is willing to pay half the cost as a memorial to her mother. I wish we could have had this retreat center when Sue was still in high school, Mr. Wright. The MYF has really needed something of the sort."

The old cattleman stiffened perceptibly. "Susanna found enough places to play as it was, I believe," he said tartly. "You know it has always been a real grief to me, Brother Williams, that the youth group no longer dignifies itself by the title of 'The Epworth League.' That was a name with real dignity and character. MYF is pretty nondescript, if you ask me. As I've always said, a church ought to take great pride in its historic heritage."

"Wesley grew up in the town of Epworth," Tom said aside, in response to the quizzical look on Dave's face. "All our youth groups used to be Epworth Leagues."

"Oh, yes." Dave glanced from one to the other and tried to speak to both. "Look, will you be able to raise the funds to buy this property now that it's available? The donor is giving only half of the costs? And there'll be construction to do?"

Wright's wrinkled old face was impassive. He picked up a paperweight, a model of some church, and turned it over and over. Tom shrugged a little and smiled a little. "We'll manage somehow," he said. "We've got to. With kids like Diana Welch and Kevin Thomas and Sue Willeford—"

A long, long pause. And Sue Willeford's grandfather could pay for the thing, I suppose, Dave thought. But he couldn't care less.

"How is Sue?" asked Tom. "She doesn't get home from the U. as often as she used to, does she?"

"Susanna is doing very well, I believe. Oh, you were asking about my greatest treasures, Mr.—uh—Mr.—"

"Yeoman."

"Um—yes. I would like you to see one object which I do take great pride in owning. A rather personal sort of pride, which I trust is merited. It's a small scale model of Gwennap Pit." He opened a bookcase and took from the shelf a dark, square object which made Dave think of an oddly ridged volcano crater.

"Gwennap Pit?"

"Yes, Gwennap Pit. It's one of the great centers of Methodism, really. Not much known in this country, I believe. I was able to secure a photo, and Susanna was very clever at building this model for me when she was in ninth grade. There we are."

Dave touched it with a curious finger. "Gwennap Pit. I'm sure I've never heard of it. What is a Gwennap Pit?"

Tom was looking at his watch. "There's only one. It was a caved-in mine, originally," he said tersely. "Became a natural amphitheater. In Cornwall. Wesley preached there—"

"On seventeen occasions, with thousands of the Cornish miners gathered around him," said Wright. "Cornwall was a great center of early Methodism, you know. Wouldn't it have geen great to hear the miners singing Charles Wesley's grand old hymns there in the out-of-doors?"

"I'm afraid we must be going," said Tom. "Greet Sue for me when you write her, won't you?"

They walked back to the Pontiac without speaking, and Tom turned the car from the driveway onto the graveled road toward Strettam. Suddenly Dave started to laugh, almost uncontrollably; Tom joined him, and they laughed for two miles.

"Sorry, old man," said Dave finally. "Remind me of this morning if I ever seem to doubt your word. I still don't believe him. Talk about monomaniacs! You didn't tell the half."

"But wouldn't about one-twentieth of him be a good dose for any congregation?"

"I suppose. As he himself has always said, a Methodist church ought to take great pride in its historic heritage. Do I quote accurately?"

"Right on the button. And you've only heard him once. You're amazing."

"No, he's the one who's amazing," said Yeoman. "A fraction of him would be good seasoning, as you said. But all in one piece, he honestly isn't of much use to the twentieth century, is he? How does he get on with the granddaughter? I've never gathered from Karen that Sue Willeford was particularly known for her piety."

"How could she be? I value my heritage, I really do, but he always makes me feel the way I felt when Catherine and I had that summer trip to Europe and they would show us the reliquary containing the chin of Saint So-and-So in some cathedral. Actually, I'm worried about Sue, and her mother didn't particularly reassure me this morning."

"Oh?"

"Says Sue is going around with a first-class hippie up at the U.; I gather Marian is afraid that Sue has already been living with the guy, but Marian doesn't know what to do about it."

"That'll be a classic—when grandpa and the hippie meet head-on for the first time. S'pose she will bring him to Strettam sometime?"

As a matter of fact, even while the preachers were driving from her home and wondering about her, Sue Willeford was on a fast motorcycle cruising toward it. She was helmeted and in a dark leather jacket. Now and then her chin touched the uneven ends of Rickie's hair which edged below his helmet. Behind her big sunglasses, she squinted at familiar landscapes without seeing them. When the motorcycle had circled into the Willeford driveway and its noisy wake was receding down the hillside, Sue sat for a long moment without moving. Then she tugged off the helmet and swung herself off.

"Thanks, Rickie." She took his left hand in both of hers, somberly.

"Sure you don't want me to come in?"

She shook her head. "Not this time."

Scowl shadows brushed across his forehead and down into his reddish-yellow beard. He looked almost ready to say something harsh. "You're gonna get back to campus okay without this horse to ride on?" His yellow-stained fingertips tapped the motorcycle.

"I told you a million times, Rickie; the bus still runs, and my dad still has a car. And I can hitchhike, if it comes to that."

Again he looked almost ready to say ugly words, but he didn't. "Well, okay, then, baby doll. I'll be shoving along. Parting is such sweet sorrow and all that jazz."

"Rickie—"

"Yeah!"

"Rickie, take your helmet off and kiss me first—"

"Or kiss you last? Your mom's probably watching, you know."

"I don't care. I don't care if the whole universe is watching."

"And all the archangels, too?" He smiled, but without any humor or kindness in the smile. He pulled his helmet off, perched it on his right knee, and put nonchalant arms around her. Her face was contorted and she clung hard, but without tears. Then

43

she released him and ran quickly up the back stairs into the kitchen.

"Sue, you're home—"

She laughed harshly. "Nope, I'm still back in Hacklett Hall studying for a psych test."

"Are you—"

"I'm starved, yep, I surely am. What's the quickest way to keep me from utter starvation? Anything good for a sandwich?" She opened the refrigerator door.

"Will you be here over the weekend, Sue? It's only Wednesday."

"I don't know. I honestly don't know. Mom, I'm here, but I'm not in a talky mood. Can I just grab some food and then sleep for a year or two?"

Her voice is like creek ice that cracks and sags when you step on it but doesn't quite break through, thought Mrs. Willeford. "Of course, child. Your bed is made up. And the house will be quiet. Dad's in Keyesport for the day, and right now gramp is napping."

"Right-o."

"Good thing you didn't get here a couple of hours sooner, though, if that's the way you're feeling," Mrs. Willeford went on companionably. "Grandpa had two preachers in to visit him a while ago."

Sue snorted. "Mind if I smoke?"

"Of course I mind, Sue. I always will. But you're a big girl now, and I won't forbid you."

"How's gramps?"

"Oh, about like usual. Getting more puttery about his hobbies all the time."

"More puttery? He couldn't be!"

"He is, though. You used to keep him in touch with things, you know. Strettam things. He'll be glad to see you."

Sue stretched and yawned. "Not for a while. Don't tell him I'm here, will you, mom?"

"He'll know it, child. He has a nose."

Sue stubbed her cigarette out in a china saucer. "Maybe not. He'll think some naughty neighbor of yours came to borrow sugar." She stretched again and climbed the stairs with slow, sagging steps.

Across the hallway she could hear her grandfather snoring: *whuff-umm, whuff-umm, whuff-umm.* She sat down on the bed, chin in hand, and stared at her shoes without seeing them. Hearing him snore, she thought of his farm and summers there and hay-making and how he had taught her to milk. And the silly model of Gwennap Pit that had pleased him so much. Maybe talking first with gramp would be the easiest. She blinked, but the tears came anyway. And more tears. She huddled on the bed and pushed her head between the pillows, so that her mother wouldn't hear, and let the sobs shake her. Finally she slept.

When she wakened, the room was full of April twilight. Good. Gramp will be settled in his library for the evening. I'll go in and say "Hi" and see what happens.

Mild surprise happened. "Why, Susanna, my dear, I thought you had already had your spring vacation."

"Um-hum. This is extra."

"You aren't sick, are you?"

Well, now, there's a lead, she told herself. "Maybe I am, sort of."

"Speak up, child. Can't hardly hear you. You do look sort of peaked. Been studying too hard?"

"Uh—no, not really."

"Better have Dr. Bailey check you over. We can't have my girl getting too thin and run-down."

Sue smiled wretchedly. Too thin? Or too fat, in the wrong segment of her anatomy?

"Grandfather, I—" She looked at the pattern made by the pigeonholes in his desk. "I—gramps, do you mind if I smoke?"

"Susanna Annesley Willeford! Nobody has ever smoked in this library of mine, and nobody ever will. You ought to know that!"

"Sorry, gramps." Right, gramps, I should know. You always were fond of me, but you were fonder of the library. Too bad you couldn't have seen me blowing smoke rings around John Wesley's ears when I first learned to smoke when I was a freshman. Anyway, I didn't throw away the bronze Wesley you gave me, as most kids would've. Wonder where it is. In my trunk in the dorm, I suppose. At least I didn't stick it up on the mantel at Rickie's place. And this isn't getting the grim news out to my lovin' family. Do I have to?

"Well, you ought to be sorry." His bushy old eyebows thickened in a frown. "No wonder you're looking so peaked, when you keep on with those coffin nails."

"Grandfather—would—would you like to take a walk with me? Then I could smoke without smelling up your books while we talk."

"Um-m-m, well—oh, let me show you something first, Susanna. Mr. Bimes just brought it by, from the store in Princeville where I got it framed."

"Oh?" I don't want to see it really, gramps, but go ahead. I don't want to see anything or anybody. I want to know what to do about Rickie's kid that is growing in my belly.

"It's in the living room," he said. "Just a minute till I get it."

Just a minute. Just a lifetime. Shall I have an abortion? Shall I take my exams and have the kid and put it out for adoption?

He bustled back with a parcel, pulled brown paper edges apart, and brought out a handsome walnut frame. "There, now. What do you think of that?"

She stared. "Is it some kind of a symbol?" Symbol. Rickie was always finding symbols. Hindu poetry. Yeats and Eliot.

Mr. Wright chuckled. "It's the market cross at Epworth, my dear. I had it enlarged from a postcard. They did a nice job, didn't they?"

Epworth. Hang Epworth. Grandfather, it's Rickie's baby, and Rickie's furious. Says I must've been sloppy about what I used. And I wish I were dead. Her voice was husky, but controlled: "What do you want with the market cross at Epworth, gramps? Was it something like Gwennap Pit?"

"Ah, Gwennap Pit. I do treasure that model you made for me, my dear. Um-m-m. Yes, it was rather like Gwennap Pit. When John Wesley went back to Epworth, where he grew up, you know, and they wouldn't let him preach in the parish church, he preached from this market cross. From these stone steps, right here." He looked at the drawing fondly, turned it from the light and toward the light. "Now where shall I hang it, would you say? The walls are rather full by now."

Hang it. Exactly. Hang it. Hang everything. And meanwhile I'll go hang myself. Shall I, Rickie? The baby would die too, but you don't want the baby anyway.

Early on Friday morning, David Yeoman put down his electric razor to pick up the telephone. "Tom Williams here," it said. "Dave, you'll want to know this, even though you won't want to know—"

"Yes?"

"You know we were talking about Sue Willeford on Wednesday?"

"Yes. Bad news?"

"Very bad." Tom's voice was controlled, very controlled, and Dave heard in it the chords of funeral music.

"What happened?"

"She came home that same afternoon, without letting them know ahead of time, and without any explanation after she got here. Her mother says she seemed horribly depressed. And this morning they found her dead in her room."

"Does the coroner have any verdict?"

"Nothing official yet. But there was an almost empty bottle of sleeping pills on the bedroom table."

"Any messages?"

"Not really. Some scribbled pages in the wastebasket that look as though she had been trying to write poetry. Her mother let me bring them home, but there's no connected sense here. The only line that's legible is 'Now crucified on Epworth's cross.' Or maybe it's 'new-crucified.' Whatever she meant by that. Apparently she was trying to rhyme it with another line; off in the margin are 'dross' and 'toss' and 'gloss' and 'loss.' "

"Well, my Karen will want to know; though as you say, she won't want to know. The family is pretty overwhelmed, I suppose?"

"Her parents especially. Her grandfather seems to be getting an odd consolation from that obscure allusion to 'Epworth' in these scribbled pages. He's sure it was an accidental death and that her last hours were in some way hallowed by a drawing of the old market cross at Epworth in England. He just got it on Wednesday and says he talked to her about it."

"Which puts her still in the Epworth League for him?"

"I guess you're right. Well, I'll see you, Dave."

"Sure thing."

"Well, what's the scoreboard? How many tantrums did you rack up today?" asked Gluttony. They were lolling comfortably on the ridgepole of St. Mark's, scuffing at the shingles with their heels.

"Depends on how you count," said Anger. "In Strettam only?"

"Oh, make it metropolitan Strettam while you're at it. Downtown and the suburbs. The highways and the byways. That gives you a little more leeway."

"Okay. Though Strettam itself is a plenty good plot of earth to spade in. Well, let's see. Full-blown tantrums, now, or the ones that were kept buttoned down inside?"

"Count 'em all. Count 'em all. I know you have a special appetite for the juicy ones that other mortals never get to see."

"M-m-m-m. Delicious. Exquisite flavors." He rubbed his shaggy belly like an overfed baboon. "Well, let's see. I wasn't keeping very careful accounts today—"

"Leaving that to the Enemy and His recording angels, huh?"

Anger shrugged. "It's all recorded, don't worry. It's all engraved, right in their own sniveling human psyches. Whatever the Enemy does for records. I have my fun with 'em, and I leave my claw marks on 'em."

"Nothing new about that. We all do. Always have, ever since the very first one. Come on, how many?"

"What would you say to ninety-seven?"

"Paltry. Paltry. You've done a lot better."

"Oh, better sometimes. Worse sometimes. I don't feel undernourished." He rubbed his shaggy middle again and grinned.

"Well, how about a rerun on some of your tasty nibblings? Waggle your finger around over the town and think me in."

Anger's grin broadened, and they both dissolved to yellowish haze. Yellowish . . . graying . . . nothing. . . .

Tony McMahon

"Janet, for heaven's sake, can't you make a decent cup of coffee yet? After twenty years of practice—"

"That's good coffee. You just have a foul taste in your mouth after whatever you swilled with the boys last night."

"I do not. And it is not good coffee. It tastes like cold dishwater."

"You've let it get cold, mooning over the sport pages. Anybody would think you'd have the scores all memorized in the evening, but, no, you have to read them all over again in the morning. Sure, your coffee gets cold. Dump it out, and I'll pour you some more."

He reached for the sink, flung coffee toward the center of it, and banged the cup in passing against the hot water faucet.

"Tony! One of my best cups! Why don't you watch what you're doing?"

"One of your best cups, ha. No more yours than mine, woman. My sister gave the set to us, didn't she? And I'll break every one of them if I please." He looked morosely at the broken piece of cup which he still held in his hand. Deliberately he slammed it against the floor; he picked up the saucer, aimed it neatly at the handle-fragment of the cup, and slammed it down also.

"Good show. A very good show. Well, Mr. Cave Man, do you want some more coffee or don't you?"

"I want some coffee, but I don't want any more of that—that brown dishwater. Dump out those grounds and make some real coffee, willya, while I shave? Well, don't just stand there."

The oak floor quivered under the linoleum tiles as he went from kitchen to bedroom; it quivered under the looped nylon carpeting as he went from bedroom to bath.

Janet's face registered storm warnings as she picked up the polished steel coffee pot. Brown dishwater indeed. After twenty years of practice. Not what the girls said last Wednesday when I had the bridge group here. Even when I was out here and not in the living room with them, they were talking about my flair with food. Cold dishwater, is it? Well, this'll be strong enough to choke you. Her hand shook as she filled the basket to the brim with brown granules, to the "ten-cup" line, and then sloshed water to the "four-cup" line of the coffee pot itself.

Broken china fragments crunched under her feet, and tornado warnings flashed across her face again. She swung open the upper cupboard door, and her eyes flicked across the row of small, bright canisters. Nutmeg, cinnamon, mace, turmeric. She picked up one small blue box and one red box, jabbed a tablespoon into each, and flung the powder into the coffee. And if I had some rat poison here, you might get some of that too, you rat. Curry and cayenne will give you a nip you'll notice, anyway.

She left the percolator bubbling, walked into the living room, and picked up a magazine. Ten years ago I might have done it just for a joke, and he'd have thought it hilarious. Like my blackbird pie for Jimmie Bartlett. Only I wouldn't have put in so much for a joke. But his temper has just about burned out all of our laughter. And I hope that coffee scalds the everlasting skin right off his tongue.

She listened grimly as she heard him stride back into the kitchen. Clatter. That would be one of the big plastic mugs. Good. Fill it clear full and gulp it all at one swallow. Plunk. That's the coffeepot, back on the table. Her hands felt a little moist. Will he laugh, the way he'd laugh if the Bartletts or the Mermanns were here, if he were playing to an audience? A soft swish, a slurpy gurgle. He's drinking it.

A-a-a-rgh. A horrible, strangled choke. He wouldn't really choke on it, would he? She had a momentary vision of his dead face against the pillows in their bedroom. Then she heard a sputtering splash at the sink as he spat, roared, and spat again.

"Janet! Janet, where are you?" He stood in the doorway, scarlet-faced and raging. Like any bull, she thought, tearing the sod with his front hooves and making big noises. "Good grief, woman, are you trying to poison me?"

"I thought of it, but there was no rat poison on the shelves. Remind me to buy some, will you?"

He strode across the room and snatched her magazine from her hands. "Reading *Better Homes and Gardens,*" he said bitterly. "What a splendid magazine for my wife to be reading." He snatched it from her, ripped it in two, and flung the crumpled halves in a chair. Then, slowly, he picked one half up again, smoothed it out, and rolled it into a tube. Janet watched him, her scalp prickling and her lips taut across her teeth. Maybe it was a good thing, she thought afterward, that she had stiffened her lips; otherwise they might have bled more. Without speaking again, he stepped toward her and struck her once on each cheek with the rolled pages. Only once, but very hard.

Then the front door banged behind him. She heard the motor of his car, and she went to sweep up broken china.

Roger Metafield

"No, Roger," said Kathleen, coming from the backyard with her arms full of sheets and diapers. Why couldn't Sam realize how much she needed a dryer? "No more cookies now. It's almost lunchtime, honey." Her blond three-year-old backed away from the stove top which he had been reaching toward.

"What is in your hand, Roger?"

"Nuffin."

"Here, let me see." She dropped the pile of laundry on a chair. Roger looked cross and backed toward the door. "Hold out your hand, Roger."

"My cookie," he said.

"Roger, mother said 'No.' Give it to mother, darling."

He glowered at her. As she bent over to take hold of his arm, he kicked her ankle smartly.

"Roger! Will mother have to get the ruler?" She reached for his arm again, but he ducked under her reaching fingers and ran to the middle of the floor, crumbling the cookie into tiny fragments and tossing it around him. Like a little flower girl tossing petals, but such a stormy flower girl would curse any wedding. His small jaw was set and his baby-soft lower lip was pouting. Just like his father's, when Sam is mad. Was there a time, centuries ago, when Sam's anger wasn't the boundary of my life?

"Why don't you run out to play until lunchtime, honey?"

"Won't." He sat down abruptly in the midst of the cookie crumbs. "You're a naughty mommie."

"Roger, get up, now, and let mother sweep the floor. It's almost lunchtime."

"Won't."

She took hold of his arm and tugged gently. "Up, Roger, up with you."

But he flipped free from her grasp, turned over on his stomach, and glared at her. "Leave me 'lone," he said. "You're a naughty mommie. I don't like you."

Kathleen glanced at the clock, at the heap of laundry, at the cookie crumbs, and at her son. Couldn't you have inherited your father's black eyes instead of his nasty temper? At least this time you aren't screaming. She picked up the laundry, carried it into the living room, and started folding sheets as fast as she could. If the baby will just stay asleep for another half-hour. Suddenly she felt Roger at her knee. He pulled her right hand away from the sheets and held it firmly for a second in his two small fists. Then, knitting his small eyebrows, he bit fiercely into the edge of her palm.

After she had spanked him, Kathleen went for the bottle of iodine and dabbed brown liquid over the oozing red moisture of the small tooth-marks. Wonder if it will leave a visible scar, she thought.

Robert C. W. McNair

Penny Atkinson thought it was a good day when she swung her Mustang into the employees' parking lot behind the Norwich State Bank. A very good day. September breezes were light and warm. Wispy tumbleweeds of cloud were rolling southward above the Metonic, incredibly white to their fringiest edges against the clear September sky. Across the highway, she could see a network of ripples glinting on the river surface. She paused for a moment at the side door of the bank on Chestnut Street, breathing the September briskness and vitality, before she put her passkey into the lock.

For several months, Penny had been driving over from Iroquois to serve as an extra teller in the afternoons. Sometimes, now, she worked whole days. In most weather, she liked the drive through the hills. She liked being back among adding machines and ledger sheets. She liked the efficiency and decorum of a bank. Both she and Jeff liked the new freezer and the new rugs 'that her checks from Norwich State were paying for.

Awfully quiet today, she thought as she tossed her jacket on the coat rack. Must be short-handed. No, they're all here. Just happens that nobody is talking. She walked briskly to the teller's window where she usually replaced Lottie Evans. "Gorgeous day," she started to say, feeling half-inclined to sing a phrase or two to Lottie: "Oh what a beautiful morning, O what a beautiful day." But she only got as far as "Gor—" when Lottie turned with a small frown and a warning finger at her lips. She ought to wear lipstick and nail polish that match better if she's going to go around sh-h-h-h-ing people, thought Penny with mild annoyance.

"What's the matter? Somebody's baby asleep upstairs?"

"He's not asleep," said Lottie, hardly moving her lips. "I wish to heaven he were."

"Who?"

"His Nibs." Penny looked perplexed, and Lottie nodded toward the oak door which was handsomely lettered in gold: ROBERT C. W. McNAIR. "Him," she said.

Penny stared and felt some of the September vitality ooze from her knees and elbows. "What—"

"The usual, only worse."

"I don't get it."

Lottie tapped a pile of blotters into place and deftly switched the nameplate at the window from "Miss Charlotte Evans" to "Mrs. Penny Atkinson." "You're still pretty new here, aren't you?" she asked finally.

"I started in June."

"Well, hold on until coffee break, and I'll clue you in. Meanwhile, walk on eggs, just like everybody else is doing. And if any customer asks about seeing His Royal Highness, tell 'em to forget it."

"Until when?"

"Until the wind changes. Maybe tomorrow, maybe next Tuesday."

Penny felt as though it were suddenly November. A deposit slip was being pushed toward her, and she gave attention to it. Then another and another. An hour later, Lottie's final instruction came back in focus when she heard an earnest little man at the next window telling Freddie Farless, "But I'm going out of town for a month, Freddie. I'm leaving in two hours—"

"Well, okay, Bill," Freddie said reluctantly. "I wish you wouldn't, though. Couldn't you write him from Omaha?"

The little man looked doubtful. "I'd better see him, Freddie."

"Okay. If you must, you must, I guess. I'm sure he's free, but tell Mary to buzz him for you, will you?"

Lottie counted bills more slowly than usual as she half-listened and half-watched. The little man paused at the last window, and Mary evidently touched the buzzer, for a small green light flicked on beside the gold-lettered door. He looks like a very small Christian who is going to be chewed by a very big lion, thought Penny. She pushed bills to her waiting customer and dabbed the purple-inked Norwich Bank stamp on the backs of his endorsed checks.

Oh. The small Christian had left the cage door open a little. She could hear a subdued masculine murmur. Small Christian apologizing? Asking for an extension on a mortgage or something? Thwa-a-ack. Big lion hitting his mahogany desk with his paw? "—and we certainly *will not* on *this* occasion—" Big lion roaring. I didn't know Mr. McNair's voice could be so loud. So fierce. So mean. You'd think it was an old melodrama and somebody's about to hold up a sign for us to hiss the villain.

But this is for real. Penny felt as though September were a long, long time ago. As though icicles were forming on the eaves and the Metonic were freezing over. *And me with no snow tires on the Mustang.*

She jotted numerals in a savings book, counted bills, stamped a check. The little man's voice again, soft and pleasant. A little desperate, though, or did she imagine that? And another roar, even louder. "—absolutely *no*—my *final* answer—do whatever you can to meet our terms—no, I will *not* give it further consideration—"

Penny turned her head slightly to see the door open. Small Christian looked chewed all right. The little man's face was dusty-pale, and Penny was sure the hat trembled in his hand as he walked quickly toward the door. She glanced at her watch. Ah, good. *I can do with some Maxwell House.* She turned her brass nameplate around to "This Window Closed" and picked up her purse.

In the upstairs lounge, she was glad to see two or three bookkeepers just leaving and Lottie just arriving. She selected a plastic mug, measured instant coffee from a jar, and sat down on one of the big hassocks. "All right, Lottie, what gives?"

"Everything gives when the big storm starts to blow."

"Oh, quit being mysterious. What's the scoop, really?"

"You haven't known that our Mr. McNair has his very own kind of binge?"

"No, I guess not."

"I'm surprised you've been here this long and haven't known. Of course the McNairs were away all during July this year, weren't they? And I guess August was a good month for all of us. Well, it's just that when something sets him off he gets into a roaring temper for a day or two. Then he calms down again and is the Great White Father to all of us until the next binge. He's kind of a Jekyll-Hyde person, you might say."

"And—and people still like to work here? *You* like to work here?" Penny felt as though she were shoveling snow from her driveway. Big drifts of it. Heavy, clinging snow. And a cutting wind that drove it against her face.

Lottie shrugged. "I hate him with a passion when he trounces somebody; I really do. Though he has never trounced me, yet. Hearing him rumble almost makes me sick. Sometimes when he really flares, I do go home with a migraine. But any job has its drawbacks. Good pay, good hours. And when he's Dr. Jekyll we all get along fine. Wouldn't you say?"

"Well—I guess. I've been telling Jeff all summer about what pleasant associates I have here. I've felt pretty lucky—" She shivered a little in spite of the temperature of her coffee. "Has he always been like this?"

Lottie shrugged again. "Search me. I've just worked here for eight years. You might ask his mother sometime. Prob'ly it started when he was in his crib. I'll bet he was the kind of baby that will hold its breath to get what it wants. I do think, though, that the last couple years have been getting rougher for him."

"And for the rest of you? Any particular reason?"

"Well, he took his daughter's death pretty hard. I did tell you about that one time, didn't I?—how Joy McNair was hit by a careless kid in an MG convertible?"

Penny nodded.

"She was a beautiful girl and the light of his life. Naturally. And some of the controls have seemed to be burned out for him ever since. Then—well, it's wild gossip, but I have heard a time or two that people thought Mrs. McNair was going out with another guy. Don't mention that to any of the newspapers, though."

"Natch. I get interviewed so often."

"Sure. Don't we all? And then—"

"Yes?"

"Well, it's really none of my business, but while I'm shoveling out the dirt—well, I'm sure there's pretty grim friction between him and Ray Kendrick. Ray's been on the board of directors for over a year now, and I'm sure he needles Mr. McNair quite a lot. I've had to handle a few telephone calls that weren't all sweetness and light. Like this morning. I was sure the gale warnings were out when I took some papers in to the file in the board room and found it reeking with cigar smoke. Directors' meeting last night. Fireworks there between McNair and Kendrick. Bango, the storm winds blow today. Call me Sherlock, kiddo."

Penny was glancing at her watch. "We'd better get back to the salt mines, Sherlock, if you don't mind. What about the customers? Isn't it pretty bad PR?" She thought of the little man scuttling toward the door with his hat in his hand.

"Well, sure, it hurts; hard to tell how much. If there were another bank of any stature for thirty miles in any direction, we'd be in worse trouble. But most people around here know that when he's good, he's very good—"

"So they stick it out when he's horrid?"

"They have, thus far."

"Think he'll ever change, really change?"

Lottie rinsed her plastic cup and turned it upside down on the rack. "Can a leopard change his spots?"

Penny walked slowly down the stairs and back toward the teller's cage. Very slowly, even though she knew she had been gone longer than usual. There was sleet in the snow now, and she was walking along a dark country road, and it was night.

"Entering Johnson County," said Myrna. "Now that would be a good spot to have the Strettam band out to greet its returning prodigal."

"Strettam doesn't have a band," said Hank shortly.

"I know. One of the many things it doesn't have. But now it will have its famous Hank Jarvis for two or three days."

"Whaddya mean, two or three days?"

"Four at the outside."

"You know mom's planning on our being here for a week."

"Sure, Hank, I know. She's always planning on your being here for at least a week."

"What are you getting at? Just because Tom sent me an SOS from the studio last summer and we had to go home earlier—"

"And your throat got so bad at Christmas that I had to take you home, and there was a sudden executive meeting at the studio two years ago in August—"

"What are you trying to say?"

"Just that you don't need to pretend. You want to come home, sure, and she wants you to come home. But within minutes after we get there you'll be simmering inside, and in two days the simmering will come to a rolling boil, and then you'll start throwing things back into the suitcases."

"You think so?"

"Well, this time might be different. But the odds are against it. This is Tuesday. What'll you bet? Will you take me out for T-bone at the Carleton if we're gone again by Saturday morning?"

"Might take you out anyway. And if we do stay the whole week?"

"Let's see. I'll bring you breakfast on a tray for a month. How's that?"

He grinned. "And require me to eat it? How long has it been since I ate any breakfast?"

"Not since you started doing the Press Club program live, I s'pose. Sometimes I wish Milt and Charlie didn't like your inter- *59* viewing quite so much. If you got home on the 5:40 local like the staid, suburban burghers we know—"

"Look, doll, I know I'm a ham, but who wants to be a hamburgher?"

"Oh, Hank! A pun like that from you? How are the mighty fallen! Now I know you're on vacation."

"There's Strettam now, hon—down there in the valley," he said. "Is there one new house? Same grade school, same bridge across the Metonic, same everything."

"Same geraniums in the same corners of the same yards. Same dogs." She glanced at his profile. No, she thought, I won't say it: same old anger waiting in your room at the top of her staircase. She'll be just like always, and you'll be like always, and she'll make you furious.

He braked at the blinker, turned right and then left and then right, and coasted to a stop under the big catalpa tree. He glanced up at it. "Needs some trimming," he said. "Put that on the list, kitten."

"For you or for me?"

"You can supervise. There's mom." He pulled off his dark glasses and untangled his long legs from the convertible. She was half-running, half-waddling down the walk, drying chubby hands on her kitchen apron.

"Well, Edward, honey, here you are, finally," she said. "You didn't have no accidents, huh? Honey, I wish you wouldn't drive them open cars. They're so dangerous if anything was to happen again, like that time down on the bridge when you was in high school." She looked disapprovingly at the slim green sports car.

Myrna, watching wryly, thought she noticed a flick of tightening muscles in Hank's jaw. Thirty seconds here and he's starting to simmer, sure enough. Why *does* she keep on calling him "Edward" when she knows he hates it? He's been "Henry" or "Hank" to everybody else ever since he was in the army. And within three sentences she's lecturing him and reminding him of old failures. Easy now, Hank.

"Hi, mom," he said, brushing her cheek with his lips. "How are you?"

"Well, better now than I was last week this time," said Mrs. Jarvis. "I did think you might have to visit me in the hospital over to Keyesport, the way my stomach was behavin'—"

Please, dear lady, spare him the organ recital, thought Myrna. That way madness lies. For sure. She clicked the car door firmly behind her. "Hello, Mom Jarvis," she said briskly. "What a wonderful bright blue sky in Strettam today." She kissed a cheek that had been awkwardly smudged with rouge. "Hank, unlock the trunk, will you, so we can get the suitcases out?"

His car keys jingled in his hand. "Edward," said his mother, "did you stop at restaurants along the way?"

"Why, sure, mom. We had breakfast and lunch. But we'll be ready for some of your homemade bread when it's time for it, don't worry."

"I wasn't about to feed you yet. Did your wife wear them pants into eating places where you stopped, then?"

"Oh, mom, for heaven's sake. Of course she did. Lots of women wear slacks when they travel. You—"

"Here, Hank," Myrna said with her head half inside the luggage compartment. "Take this little suitcase, will you?"

"Your old room is all ready," said Mrs. Jarvis. "It's a mite muddy here in the driveway. Wipe your feet on that old rug on the porch there, Edward."

He wiped his feet, managing to give the rug several vicious little kicks as he did so. He carried in the luggage. And he swore under his breath each time he reached the landing and left her clucking below: "Don't carry too much at once, Edward. You'd better stop and rest for a minute, Edward. Watch that torn place on the carpet, Edward."

"That's it, Myrna. The lot," he said, pulling the bedroom door shut behind him. "Myrna, I can't stand her. Hearing her say 'Edward' is going to drive me out of my mind before we have one meal under her roof."

"Under your roof, too, darling. It's still your own old home, Hank."

"Sweet, sweet home!"

Downstairs again, he assumed a cheerful voice. "Well, what's for supper?" His cheerfulness wore thin over chicken and dumplings as Eliza Jarvis described the moral defects of the "nigger-ohs" of America in general and of Keyesport in particular. It became even thinner when she cross-examined Myrna on her methods of cooking the vitamins into or out of vegetables and lectured at length on the merits of vinegar and honey as a health tonic. When she started on fluoridation of water as a moral menace, he said abruptly, "Mom, I'm going to run down to the drugstore to get an evening paper. What to come, Myrna?"

"Not this time," said Myrna. "Watch out for the traffic at State and Madison."

"Likewise Times Square and Hyde Park?"

"Oh, Edward, do be careful at the highway corner," burbled his mother. "They ought to put better stop signs up. You want to watch for them fast cars on Highway 37; they just whiz right through sometimes and don't even look. You will be careful, won't you, sonny?"

Splotches of red moved up Hank's neck. "Mother, will you stop it?" he said sharply. "I'm thirty-two years old, and I do know how to drive a car. In Strettam, of all places—"

Her puffy, faded face looked hurt and perplexed. "You could have an accident in Strettam, same as any place else," she said defensively. "I told you, didn't I, about the McNair girl getting killed down there at the blinker light? And you always did drive too fast, Edward. You know how you mashed the fenders on your uncle's Chevrolet that time on the bridge—"

"Oh, mother—" He banged the door so violently behind him that neither woman heard the rest of his ejaculation, although Myrna thought she recognized one of his more colorful pieces of profanity.

The next morning there was no doubt of it. He decided to trim the old catalpa tree and assembled saws and ladders. Myrna came to the porch to watch him, and quips flew back and forth between them. "We ought to have the cameras here," said Myrna finally. "Too bad for you to waste your nonsense on an audience of one." She glanced around. "Within some seconds, you may double the numeral in the last remark," she said.

Hank groaned. "Well, thanks for the tip." He felt trapped. His mother would call instructions to him, discuss the merits of the tree in measureless detail, and caution him at every motion of his right elbow. The muscular pleasure he had been feeling drained away with every motion of his saw as the old resentments from scoldings shouted to a treehouse when he was eight and ten and thirteen boiled up inside him. He gritted his teeth as he realized, suddenly, that it would give him a savage pleasure to hurl the saw right at her chattering mouth or to kick the ladder over and let it bang against her. He turned his back to the porch as he sawed the next limbs, but Myrna heard the profanity clearly.

That afternoon he made a point of visiting friends instead of lingering around his mother's home. Well, you can call them friends, he told himself as he drove off. None of his high school buddies still lived in the Metonic valley, but one could exchange the time of day with Sam Metafield at the Standard station, and Gracie Mermann remembered him, and Joe Bynum's stolid admiration didn't hurt a fellow's morale. More substantial admiration from McNair at the bank. McNair wasn't very fond of me when I was a grade school brat wanting to play baseball with the older fellows in the summertime, but now he's mellow enough.

In the evening, he schooled himself to ask questions about the cousins and the great-aunts, and then to think about something else with most of his attention while her monologues flowed along. His control disappeared, though, when she wound the alarm clock and started rolling up her hair at ten o'clock and also started describing to him the ominous peril of his own nocturnal habits—habits which she had ascertained by questioning Myrna relentlessly.

"Myrna," he said grimly, "how long will it take you to pack your suitcase?"

Eliza Jarvis stared. "Pack her suitcase?"

"I am thirty-two years old," he said in the same grim voice. "I am a grown man, and I am managing my own life very successfully. I am not required by any law I know about to stay here and listen to your insults."

"My insults?" Her wrinkles and rouge contorted themselves into odd patterns. "Why, Edward, honey, who's insulting you?"

"Don't mind him, Mother Jarvis," said Myrna. "He's a little tired tonight. Hank, why don't you go on up and find a book, and you can read to me for a little while. That little brown suitcase has the books in it." Then she talked smoothly about hair styles and face creams for a few minutes.

When she reached the bedroom, Hank was pacing and fuming. "Myrna, I can't take it. I just can't take it. Why does she do this to me?"

"I wish I could tell you, Hank. You're not so fierce with anybody else we know. I wouldn't have known that you had such a capacity for anger if you had never brought me here. Sorta scares me, when I think what you might do to our kids, if and when."

"Myrna!"

"Well, you have to face it. There's a king-size generation gap between you and your mother."

"Generation gap? Holy cow!"

"Well, isn't that what it is? She sees things with her sixty-ish eyes, and you see them with your eyes that are precisely thirty-two, as you have been informing her rather regularly."

"It isn't that she's older, Myrna. Some of our best men at the studio are in her age bracket. She sees things with—with the eyes of a blithering idiot."

"And you're a clear-thinking, rational, young intellectual, Hank? Your reactions to her are emotional, if I ever met an emotion in my life."

"Go ahead, Madam Freud."

"Well, really, why can't you be at least a little objective about her? Other people we know have their oddities and quiddities, and you don't see red and paw the earth with your mighty hoof-beats over them."

"They're not my mother. Not my stupid, dictatorial, uncomprehending, narrow-minded fool of a mother."

"Easy, Hank. It's yourself you rip apart when you talk like that. You aren't pawing the earth now; you're goring your own ego, flipping it around on your horns."

"Yeah?"

"Yeah. Listen, Hank. I think I'm just figuring something out. I think—"

"Well?"

"You won't like this very well—"

"Go ahead, shoot."

"Well, I'm no psychiatrist, but—well, look. Granted your mother isn't exactly what you'd write into the script if you had a chance. That's just it. You like yourself pretty well, and you feel, down deep, as though you deserve to have had a dowager duchess in diamonds and lace for a maternal parent. Being you. You don't see her as a person, which she is; you just see—or feel—the bruises on your own ego. And you holler bloody murder."

"Well, you're right on the last point, anyway, Madam Freud."

"Can't you just love her as she is, without measuring her all the time against what you wish she were?"

"Rouge spots and all?"

"Rouge spots and all the rest of it."

"I do love her, Myrna; you know I do. I don't like her, but I love her. I must, anyway, or I wouldn't put myself through the purgatory of these Strettam trips. Maybe I'd be better off if I didn't ever come."

"No, you wouldn't. Not you."

"When I'm not here I feel fond of her; then I drive into Strettam, and I feel as though she were a big, blobby parasite sucking the very juice of life out of me, Myrna. I'm not myself here. She doesn't want me to be myself. She wants me to be about seven years old, right on to the end of the script."

"Like I said, we've got a king-size generation gap on our hands."

"To which assertion by his comely wife, the renowned Hank Jarvis was heard to reply with one vigorous monosyllable. Namely—nuts."

"Look, Hank. You love her, but you don't like her very much. You don't respect her very much. Okay. Does that entitle you to spit flame like a pocket-sized Vesuvius when she bugs you? Now, really, does it?"

"Oh, lay off, Myrna. Let's get some sleep." He sat down,

took off one shoe, and dropped it with a thud. Then the other shoe. "Myrna, my stupid mother would try the patience of any living saint. Now, wouldn't she? And heaven knows I'm no saint."

"Not yet, anyway?"

"Go to sleep."

She slept, soon and soundly. He dozed. Wakened. Dozed. Wakened. The next morning his mouth tasted like a root cellar and his head felt as though it were about two feet in diameter. He listened groggily as he heard a woodpecker. No, someone knocking. Someone knocking.

"Who's there?" he growled.

"It's me. It's mommie. Edward, we've got pancakes for breakfast. Hurry now; they're almost ready." He rolled up on one elbow, looked at his wrist watch, and turned the air blue with surly language. Myrna watched him sadly and reached for her shoes.

At the table, Eliza chattered. Hank glowered. Myrna looked apprehensive. "What's the matter with my boy this morning?" Eliza finally murmured toward the coffeepot. "Did he stay up till all hours, Myrna? Shall we have Dr. Bailey come down and take your temperature, Edward?"

"My temperature is fine."

"Bodily temperature, that is," Myrna told him. "More needs he the divine than the physician."

"You're misquoting Shakespeare."

"Well, you wouldn't want me to call you a 'she,' now, would you?"

He grunted and sipped coffee. "Thursday," he said thoughtfully. "I wonder if I ought to call the studio. I sorta thought Charlie or Milt would be in touch yesterday about the new series on sportsmen."

"Oh, Hank, we're on vacation. Remember? And you really just left them two days ago," protested Myrna.

"There's a number over there on the phone table for you to call, Edward," said Eliza cheerfully.

"There is? They called already this morning?"

"Oh, no. Yesterday. Pretty soon after you went out."

"Yesterday? Mother!"

"Hush, sonny, they'll hear you clear down to Joe's Diner."

"Where is the number? Why didn't you tell me yesterday?"

"Turn about is fair play," Eliza simpered. "They keep my boy up until all hours of the night when he's at work; they can just wait a while when he's at home. Here. Here's the number."

Hank looked apoplectic, but he gulped and went to the telephone in the living room without further words. They heard him dialing, speaking with operators, and then in a long discussion during which the word "contract" occurred often.

"Well, now, you had a nice, long talk," said his mother when Hank returned. "I just hope you reversed the charges."

"I reversed the charges," said Hank, "and I am not sure that I am ever going to speak to you again." Both women looked startled and alarmed. "Go pack up our stuff, Myrna. If I stay here today I'll break up the furniture or do something worse. Mother, that was a phone call about a business deal that may run into millions of dollars. Millions, do you understand? Not reaching me yesterday caused the other men more trouble than you could possibly comprehend. Last night I told Myrna that I don't really like you. Right now—right now I hate your guts. And I wish I had been spawned in somebody else's belly instead of yours."

Eliza sat down unsteadily. Her face, except for the glowing rouge spots, was like a corpse's.

"You go do the packing," said Myrna firmly. "It will do you good. You couldn't drive now, could you?"

He looked at her furiously, but he turned without a word and climbed the stairs. Myrna stepped over to her mother-in-law, who was starting to cry hysterically. Myrna patted her flabby shoulder. "He doesn't mean it, Mom Jarvis. He loves you very much."

"You—you heard—you heard what he said!"

"Yes, but I know better. He loves you, mom. He loves you very much."

"My own son. My baby Edward. To talk to his own mother like that—"

"He doesn't mean it. When he was a baby, didn't he ever hit you with his fists and say naughty, sassy things?"

"Ye—yes." Eliza reached for a dishtowel and blew her nose. "Yes, and I washed his dirty little mouth with soap for what he said, too."

"Of course. And now I wish I knew where to get some soap to wash his dirty big soul! Listen, I'd better go now, mom. We'll be back, I promise you. And he does love you. He really does." She kissed a soggy cheek and patted a still-heaving shoulder again.

Once on the highway, neither spoke for twenty miles. Finally Hank sighed.

"You sound as though your lungs are stiff and sore," said Myrna.

"The understatement of the year," said Hank. "I'm sore all over. The umbilical cord is a noose, and I'm choking in it."

"And what about her?"

"Massive hemorrhage, to say the least. Well, kitten, I guess you get your T-bone at the Carleton."

"I don't want it," she said. "Oh, Hank, I don't want it. It would make me sick."

And then, finally, she started to cry.

Strettam, Seeing Gordon

It was a cloudy, drizzly weekend when Gordon McVey returned to Strettam for his first visit in some seventeen years. Fuzzy patches of white-gray clung to the upper slopes of Strettam Hill. Thinner wisps of white-gray fuzzed through the trees and curled themselves along the metallic surface of the river. Half-iced slush collected in footprints and in tire tracks at the edges of driveways.

"Sorry, Gordon," said Mannie Mitchell as they swung in at his own driveway on Friday evening. He squinted through the fog and eased his old Dodge into the waiting carport. "You know that Strettam can have brilliant days, even in February."

"Sure, I know. And I'm not holding you responsible for the weather, Mannie."

"You hadn't better. Though in that case you could thank me for letting your plane come through. Linda was sure the flights would all be canceled. She must've called the airport about five times since noon."

"Hoping I wouldn't come and she could save you a trip to Keyesport through this pea soup?"

"Man, no. Come on in and let her tell you how glad we are to have you. One suitcase, one briefcase; that's all, isn't it?"

Linda was waiting. The gloomy night outside brightened the red-gold glints in her hair in contrast, Mannie thought. She's very alive this evening.

"Well, Gordon. The prodigal returns and all that," she smiled. "After much too long. Here, Mannie, take his coat, why don't you? How long is it, Gordon, since you honored Strettam with your presence?" They were moving from entrance hall to the white-paneled living room, where two walls were lined with Mannie's books; a third was dominated by Linda's handsome new fireplace, where logs were burning into networks of rose and vermilion.

"What a pleasant room, Linda. The fire almost matches your

hair. Well, Mannie and I were just trying to pin down a few events. My parents were still here when I was in college, but I'm not sure I've been back since before I left for law school. And that would be at least seventeen years."

"You didn't have to settle down in Kansas, did you? Just because you went to Washburn for law——"

"Don't knock Kansas, lady. Between the oil fields and the wheat fields, there's plenty to keep a lawyer from getting bored."

"Even before you landed in the state senate?" asked Mannie. Gordon smiled.

"Senator McVey," said Linda slowly, weighing the title as though it were metal in her hand. "Senator McVey. Tell me now. How does one introduce you properly to one's friends? The Honorable Senator from Whatchacallit County?"

"Don't be ridiculous. After our twelve years in public school together in Strettam? I'm still Gordon, of course. Or Gordy." He grinned. "Or Julius Caesar."

"Hey, that's right," said Mannie. "How did we start calling you Julius Caesar anyway?"

"Search me."

"Freshman English with Mrs. Derwent," said Linda. "She bawled you out for something or other when we were studying Julius Caesar, didn't she? That reminds me. Mrs. Derwent would like to see you while you're here, Gordon, if you have time to stop by. The village grapevines told her you were coming, I'm afraid, and she has been telephoning about every hour on the hour."

"She's still living then? She seemed like a contemporary of Martha Washington when we started high school."

"Nobody was really as old then as we thought," said Mannie. "I'm sure we weren't as old as we thought ourselves to be, either. Look, Gordon, what are your desires about the weekend? We won't let you do a Rip Van Winkle act, but aside from that— do you want to look people up for auld lang syne, or just sit here by the fire? Or play it by ear without planning ahead?"

"We weren't sure how much partying you'd want," said Linda. "Mannie was so pleased to get your call last night that he didn't ask very sensible questions, I'm afraid."

"Sorry I couldn't give you more notice," said Gordon. "The clients I'm seeing in Washington on Monday——"

"Oh, don't apologize!" cried Linda. "We're just glad to have you. Thrilled to bits. But since it's only for the weekend, shall I make like a social secretary for the Honorable Senator from Whatchacallit County? Mrs. Derwent does want very much to see you——"

While the fireplace glowed and Linda's hair glowed back, other plans were also being formulated.

"A little midwinter amusement," Pride was saying to Envy. "Want to work with me on this, old man? I'd be glad to have a hand."

"What's up?"

Pride chortled. "They won't know it, of course, but a fine number of our Strettam customers are going to be splotched with rare and special dyes before this weekend is over."

"Such as?"

Pride rubbed furry paws together and then curled the long ape-tail he was wearing into a flexible swivel chair. "A mild experiment which the Captain is letting me try," he said. "This flea McVey is here for the weekend, see, and I have permission to invoke some special lurid stains in every one of these mortal vermin who will respond to my tickling when he comes around. By Sunday night the February fog will have some gorgeous color splashed all through it, I promise you. Wanta help?"

"Sure, I'll help. Always do help you, don't I?"

"I know he's in," said Mannie as he held the heavy glass and aluminum door at the bank for Gordon. "I checked yesterday before I left for the airport, and Mary put you on his appointment schedule." They crossed to the receptionist's desk. "This is Gordon McVey, Mary," said Mannie. "I mentioned him yesterday—"

Mary touched the buzzer. "Yes, go on in. He's expecting you."

Robert McNair stood behind the mahogany desk. "Well, Gordon, how have you been?" He motioned them to padded leather chairs and reached into a drawer for a slim cigar. Cigars always helped when he was annoyed, and he had a premonition of more than usual annoyance. "Care to smoke? They're imported and rather good. I picked them up on my last junket to New York."

Both declined. Well, let them. I made my point; I get to New York often enough, if I'm not a senator. Who'd have thought that quiet little guy—. He was second string jayvee when I was captain in high school basketball. When I was student body president he was a nobody minus. "Well, who'd have thought," he said affably, exhaling expansively. "Who'd have thought when we sat together in the old high school assembly hall—" That I'd be a kingpin in Strettam but you'd be a state senator, and a kingpin for a whole state. And Lucy says you were mentioned in *Time* as a coming man in the big time. Maybe governor, maybe U. S. senator. You—you little toad.

"That's right," Gordon said. "They had us all alphabetized,

didn't they? McMahon, McNair, McVey. We could have had a Scotsman's glee club, couldn't we? I never thought then about the number of Scottish immigrants that Johnson County was blessed with."

No, I suppose you didn't. Nor about how mighty and noble you would become.

To Gordon and Mannie, the banker still looked the same. Expensive suit, a distinguished silver frost in his hair, manicured nails holding the imported cigar. Maybe a slight flush, thought Mannie. Hope nobody has lighted any slow fuses on his temper this morning. No, I don't think so. No, he looks just the same as when we came in.

But to Pride and Envy, watching, McNair had changed. All of his skin was now a hideous phosphorescent sulphury orange in color, and the same lurid orange glowed through his suit, on his necktie, over his shoes. His cuff links and his glasses were a little more sulphur-colored than his clothes, a little more lurid. "Beautiful," said Pride. "Marvelous. It even smells, you know. The authentic odor of Home, isn't it?"

The watchers were alert as Mitchell and McVey walked back across the embossed carpet to the bank door. Mary was calm and appraising. No color change. But Lottie Evans was like litmus paper in a laboratory, and a faint decayed-looking chartreuse glow moved right from her hair to her brown suede pumps. And at the next teller's window Freddie Farless was like a mannequin in neon on a garish billboard. Little wavelets of magenta stain pulsed through him, lighter and brighter, lighter and brighter.

"Jolly good," said Pride. "Jolly good. I thought it might happen. Push 'em against someone they consider a little better or richer or luckier or more famous, and I can really tweak 'em. This one, now. I'm always nudging him to compare himself with somebody else, but here's a better chance than I've often had."

"McNair's a better specimen," said Envy. "Much better. Why such different dyes, anyway?"

"More interesting. You would like McNair's hue better," said Pride. "There's a lot more of your fingerprinting mixed into his color. For the moment, Farless is my boy, through and through. I think he's gorgeous."

"George and Gracie Mermann live two miles out," Mannie was saying. "How about dropping in there next?"

"Fine. Mind if I leave the window down for a minute to let the wind have some of the cigar smoke from your boss's office?"

"Go ahead."

"Oh, I say, isn't that Mrs. Vincent? I used to do her sidewalks in the winter and mow her lawns in the summer."

"That's the lady, all right. The one and only Martha Vincent." Mannie put his gear indicator back into neutral and rolled down his window also. "Oh, Mrs. Vincent, here's someone who would like to greet you."

Martha paused. A curious old-fashioned hat covered her bun of hair, and its wings of brown felt drooped down over her cheeks, but her sharp nose and sharper eyes were clearly visible.

"Remember Gordon McVey?" continued Mannie. "He used to work for you, he says."

"My land, yes." Mrs. Vincent stepped briskly to the window of the Dodge on Gordon's side. "Mrs. Derwent told me you was comin' back to Strettam this weekend," she said. "So you've gone and got famous, have you?" She peered at him as though about to reprove him for some glaring fault.

Gordon laughed. "Not so terribly famous," he said. "Awfully busy, though, I'm afraid."

"I s'pose you are. Otherwise you'd come back to Strettam a little oftener. I s'pose you're too far up in the world to bother with the likes of us very often, though."

McVey didn't parry. "Do you still have that coal furnace I used to feed?" he asked.

"Land sakes, no. I changed to gas a good dozen years ago. Lots less work."

"Well, it's nice to see you," he said. Mannie flicked the gear indicator back to "R," and the Dodge moved away from the curb.

Nice, humpf. Nice for you, Gordon McVey. Coming back to make us all feel like mice beside you. Coming back to consider yourself high and mighty among us. I gave you a good broad hint about putting on airs, anyway. Hardly time to warn you as your soul deserves. The Good Book has plenty to say about them as is great in their own eyes. Anyway, you know now that I'm not just in the hovels of poverty; I can afford a new furnace if I want one, Gordon McVey. So you're a senator out in Kansas, huh? Must not take much to be a senator these days, if a snot-nosed kid that shoveled off my sidewalks for twenty-five cents an hour can be a senator. Anyways, the Scripture talks about you. 'He hath put down the mighty from their seats.' Your turn will come.

She walked on toward Dacey's Dry Goods, giving her brown felt hat a twitch and a poke as she walked. And close behind her Pride and Envy were embracing each other with guffaws. "Superb," chortled Pride. "Oh, marvelous. I've always had my fun and games with that one, but yow-e-e-e!" Mrs. Vincent was like a grotesque parody of the aurora borealis. Carmine and orange and purple and blue, in shades that any mortal would have called weird or obscene, flickered through her galoshes, through her sturdy coat, through her brown felt hat. Her sharp nose was a flowing orange cone; her chin was wildly and hideously purpled.

The Mermanns. The Bartletts. The McMahons. "Want to call it a day?" asked Mannie. "It's getting on toward four o'clock."

"And I was just thinking about your pleasant fireplace," said Gordon. "I can see some old-timers at church in the morning, you know. And if Linda is having some neighbors in for dessert tonight—"

"Right you are. Home, James. Over the river and through the woods to grandmother's house we go. Without any snow, though. Just this perpetual fog."

"I keep telling you, I like fog. After a dozen summers in that dry Kansas heat, I take pleasure in fog wherever I find it, believe me. Oh, say, though. 'Over the river and through the woods' makes me think of Mrs. Derwent. I really should stop there for a minute, shouldn't I? You know what Linda said."

Mannie shrugged. "You really want to? She's like she always was, if not more so."

"Oh, well. When I get to be crabby and senile, I'll want someone to come and see me. Remember that now, Manfred Mitchell."

"Aye, aye, sir. Let's see. Second street over, I think."

It was a shabby little house, covered with synthetic brick surfacing. February fog clung to the withered stems of daisies and delphiniums.

"This is the place," said Mannie. "There's still time to change your mind."

"Oh, it won't be that bad," said Gordon. "I do wish I had brighter recollections of her classes. Some of the teachers we had here were superb, Mannie; they really were. But Mrs. Derwent did her best to make us hate school, didn't she? Oh, well." He reached for the handle of the car door. "I wonder if I will recognize her."

He did recognize her. She wheeled herself to the door, and her position in the wheelchair was oddly like her position at the battered old school desk.

"Well, Gordon. Sit right there in that green chair, Gordon, so I can have a good look at you."

His face smiled, but only his face. The very same voice. More quivery and cracked. Dormant emotional reflexes stirred. She'll scold, the reflexes said. And the scolding will be an unfair tirade.

She doesn't like any of us, but she sneers more at me because I'm poor.

He sat down quietly. "How are you, Mrs. Derwent? You are retired now?"

"For ten years, Gordon. Ten wretched years. You know how I always loved being with the children—"

No, Mrs. Derwent. I do not know that. I know that you were sadistic with your sarcasm. That time you gave me such a verbal flogging in front of the whole English III class. Over what? Over a book report I couldn't finish when I had the flu, wasn't it?

"—am so forgotten now. I seldom see anyone—"

The same voice, but maybe more whining. More petulant? The same voice in which she inoculated us against great books. One more semester with her, and I would never have gone to college. Nor to law school.

"—but I do get such a satisfaction from knowing that I had a part in putting some of you children on the path of knowledge," she said. "You especially, Gordon. You always were my treasure. And Georgie Joe Bailey. You know he's our doctor now. Who would ever have thought, when he was such a sorry little ragamuffin? And even Matthew Heiler. Do you remember Matthew? He's a sculptor and has his studio over on the Finch place. From what they say about him, I wouldn't give a dime a dozen for the kind of work he calls art, but it is still such a pleasure to know that I made some of you what you are."

Mannie was watching Gordon alertly. Mannie's right hand was across his face, but little muscles were twitching around his eyes.

"And are you able to do your own housework?" McVey interposed with a steady voice.

Neat question, thought Mannie. He won't have to listen to what she says. And I'd better get her claws detached. He stood up. "Linda will be looking for us, Senator McVey," he said casually.

"—so proud of you," Mrs. Derwent was saying. She held Gordon's hand firmly when he extended it. "To think of Manfred actually calling you Senator McVey. I always knew that you had great abilities, my boy—"

"Good-by, Mrs. Derwent," Gordon said firmly.

His voice is still pleasant. All that good legal training helps him keep his cool, thought Mannie. "Sorry, old man," he said as they walked past frost-blackened clumps of dahlia stems. "She was never what you'd call sweet, but I'm afraid she's getting rancid in her retirement."

74   "Also imaginative," said Gordon brusquely.

"You know, I didn't remember that you were her pride and joy," said Mannie.

"Anything but. She was hideous to me. Really malicious. I think any objective viewer would have to say that, with all due allowance for the thinness of my adolescent skin. You know," he went on as Mannie started the motor again, "I've met pride of many kinds and sorts, in my office and in the courts and now in the senate. Wholesome pride and pridey pride and silly false pride. But I can't think right now of anyone else I've ever known who was so infernally proud of doing what she *hadn't* done."

"Infernally?"

"In all honesty, yes. It's a lie of a proportion that has to be straight from the pit." The car was edging through the damp foggy twilight and into the Mitchell driveway again. "Until I heard her voice again, I really had forgotten just how horrible she used to be. A school with a staff psychiatrist would never use somebody like her now, would it? She really hated all of us, I think, and tried to dominate us to feed her own ego. Now she has to get some other kind of garbage for the old ego to chew on. So she comes up with these—these preposterous fantasies her own pride has invented."

Back at the house with the synthetic brick covering, Envy and Pride were standing among the frost-blackened dahlias and watching her. It was easy to see her, right through the synthetic brick surface and the wall behind it. The dye was lewdly yellow, smoky and sulphurous. She was smiling broadly, and on her lips the yellow darkened into ocher. "Beautiful," said Pride. "Looks like gangrene and pus and scabs, doesn't it? Well, what did I tell you? The February fog is getting handsomely splashed, isn't it? And there's the party yet to go that she is giving for him tonight."

"With some appropriate tints for the hostess herself?"

"That's my intention." He frowned, and a passer-by thought that the twilight had deepened with an odd suddenness. "I don't know, though. Her worm of a husband has not given us a flicker of color all day. Had you noticed? The Enemy has been doing some sneaky work on that one. But I say, look back across the town from up here." As he spoke, he had somersaulted high above the treetops, like a huge amorphous skylark. "Not bad, not bad, not bad."

Spots of luminous phosphorescent dye glowed through the February fog: orange, purple, carmine, scarlet, chartreuse, ocher. To mortal vision, each hue would have seemed tainted and noxious, tainted and putrid. But mortal vision never saw those dyes, and no mirror on earth would have reflected them.

Adelle Fiedler

It wouldn't be quite so bad, Adelle thought for the ten thousandth time as she polished the copper bottom of a Revereware saucepan, if there were someone I could talk with about him. Anyone. Maybe I ought to catch a plane for Georgia and look up one of my college roommates. As if I could catch a plane anywhere. He's the one who makes all the trips, with his everlasting Glo-brite Cookware sales meetings. To which some of the other salesmen take their wives. Please, Glenn, take me just once. This one's in Denver; next time in Chicago? I've never been in Chicago.

She rinsed the tough little scouring pad, dried the dull copper sheen, and placed the pan on its rack.

If I could talk with someone. If there were a psychiatrist in Strettam. Glenn would never let me go to Keyesport to see one. He'd laugh like a crazy comedian.

But I will not go around discussing him with the local citizens, the way that loathsome Cullison woman used to discuss her Toby. There are nice women all over Johnson County who would listen kindly—but what nice woman wants to hear about him? And I'd see it in her face every time I saw her afterward, at the grocery store or the post office or wherever. And the ones I know best are the very ones who tried for two years to keep me from getting into this—this purgatory.

Is it a purgatory? A purgatory would be making me cleaner and better, by very definition. But every time, I get angry with him, and it burns something down inside me. Burns and burns. But it doesn't do any purging. What did the Greeks call it when their drama supposedly purged your emotions? Catharsis. If I could go to the drugstore and get a $3.95 bottle of "Catharsis" every time.

A young married woman ought to be able to go home to momma and talk things over. Wouldn't momma purr and lick her whiskers? She warned and begged and scolded and cajoled.

And I didn't hurry into it. I had my misgivings even before I dated him once. The way he surveyed every visible inch of feminine flesh that night at the 4-H picnic, when he first came here to work, while he was theoretically having lemonade with me. Mother and Aunt Martha did their lugubrious duets right up till the wedding. Maybe if Aunt Martha had kept out of it I'd have listened a little more to mother. You really expect anything Martha Vincent dislikes that much to have some merit.

Adelle put away the last piece of stainless steel and folded the tea towel. Well, he's on the way to Denver. For five days. At least I won't have any occasions for five whole days to see him doing his everlasting girl-watching here in Strettam. If those women at church had any idea how he talks about them afterward. Your husband is so handsome and debonair, Mrs. Fiedler. Your husband is so jolly. Your husband paid me the funniest compliment. Yes, of course, girls. So you sparkle at him and ooze a little sexiness at him, all very innocently. And you never know he's playing pornographic games in his mind the whole time. Or most of you don't. If he really took Lucy McNair to Keyesport in January, as he said he did, then Lucy McNair isn't all that innocent. Of course he wouldn't have been flirting with Lucy at church anyway, since McNairs go to St. Mark's.

But did he take Lucy McNair anywhere, ever? I don't know. I just don't know. He lies to me so much that I don't know when he isn't lying. A good half of the lipstick on his handkerchiefs and shirt collars is there because he puts it there, I'm sure. Sheer malice. He knows I'll be hurt and angry and suspicious. And I always am. Adelle the Gullible.

If I had married him when he first proposed, would he have been less spiteful? When I was so dubious, and he knew it, did he start hating as well as loving? So he keeps dabbing on the lipstick in order to get some revenge? And finding his fancy women in every town he visits. Or telling me he does, anyway.

If there were someone I could talk with about him. And about me. If every cubic inch of me didn't love him so achingly much. To love what you despise. To be putty in such dirty hands.

If we had children. Would being a father change him any? It would give me a lot more to live for, but—but, anyway, there's today to face. Curtains to hem. Aprons to mend. Oh, yes, and a hair appointment at two. I'm glad Mona Taylor finally started a beauty shop in her back bedroom. As coarse as she is, it's accessible, anyway. And in a one-car family, that really helps. Wonder if all of the Glo-Brite Cookware salesmen do as much daytime selling as he does. He says they all go out almost every night. He says, he says, he says.

If I could talk with someone about him. But I will not. I will not. It takes some quick maneuvering, sometimes, when old biddies like my own Aunt Martha are just panting to get some information or to give you some. I don't know which is worse.

Let's see. Hair appointment at two.

As always, Adelle relaxed in cocoon-like tranquillity while warm spray trickled across her scalp, while Mona's blunt fingers massaged and lathered. Peacefulness. Almost gladness. If I could just stay here for about two solid days without moving, maybe I would start healing at the edges. Like being a little girl again and having mother do my curls. Centuries ago. Before Glenn.

Still relaxed and almost drowsy, she handed Mona little white plastic pins for the brush rollers, one by one. The shop was empty and quiet. Usually both sinks were in use, and usually buxom Mona was chattering constantly with her assistant.

"Is Lisa ill?" she asked, rotating a white pin between finger and thumb.

Mona stuck two pins between her teeth, rolled a lock of hair, pinned it, and rolled another. "There. My, your hair's stubborn today, Mis' Fiedler. Lisa sick? Stars, no, she never gets sick. Jus' decided she didn't want to work for a few days. Lucky we didn't have too much in the book for her. Course some women, like you, Mis' Fiedler, ain't so choosy whether Lisa does 'em or me. I sure do appreciate that."

Adelle smiled a little. The hazy warm drowsiness was too pleasant for her to push the jagged irony against her body, but she felt it: Adelle isn't choosy. Any beautician that's available. Any handsome cad that was available, if he told enough sweet lies first?

"There yuh are, ma'am. If you'll just step into the hallway, please? I've moved the dryers in there. Gives us a lot more work space here. This house wasn't ever built for a beauty shop, that's for sure."

With the dryer whooshing around her ears, Adelle drowsed over a copy of *McCall's*. Wonder if she chose her assistant for her first name? It could have been the Mona-Lisa shop anyway, I guess. More drowsiness. Distant voices. One very loud voice. Dryer's too hot; my ears are almost on fire. She reached for the dial, turned the dryer down from "Hi" to "Med," and then decided for the momentary relief of "Lo." As the whoosh of the dryer softened, the strident voice became more strident. Like a female longshoreman. Who in Strettam talks like that? Oh, maybe the McNair's new cook. Somebody said she sounds like a Billingsgate fishwife but really knows her way around with casseroles and spices.

"Dollar 'n a quarter?" said Billingsgate. "There you are. Course I coulda gone down t' the Rexall fer m' hair soap, but I sorta wanted to see if Lisa wuz here, or if she really did go off t' Denver with Glamour-heels Fiedler—"

"Shut up!" Adelle heard Mona hiss. And she heard faucets turned on full force. Trying to cover up voices? Too late, Mona. She can't unsay it. Who else is in there besides Mona and this horrible woman? Someone else had gasped. A tiny indrawn breath of a gasp, but it could be one that will be heard all over town.

"And why should I shut up?" asked Billingsgate crossly. "Everybody knows—"

Little scuffling sounds. A whispering. A pointing, too, I suppose.

"Oh, I getcha," said Billingsgate, almost softly. "Well, whaddya know?"

Adelle knew that she was about to suffocate with wretchedness and anger, anger, anger. Helpless anger.

Were they the two coarsest women in the whole Metonic valley? How can I face Mona long enough to let her comb out my hair? I could just disappear, through this hallway and out her front door. I could mail the rollers back to her. And a check. No, then she'd know I heard. Now she doesn't know that I know she knows. I've been acting roles ever since my wedding day. Tragicomedy, but more and more tragedy as time goes on.

The door banged as Billingsgate went out, and there were long minutes of harsh silence. "There you are," Mona finally told the other customer. Adelle flicked the dial back to "Hi" and became deeply engrossed in her magazine, knowing that someone would be brought past her to the second dryer. But she had to know. She lowered the magazine ostentatiously and ducked out from under the dryer. "That's a furnace you've got here, Mona," she said with carefully simulated calmness. "Haven't I baked long enough?"

(Baked. Boiled. Stewed. In the flame of anger. Glenn Fiedler, you're turning me into a cinder inside. A common, floppy slut like Lisa Sprague, of all people.)

While she spoke, she tossed a sidelong glance. It was somebody slim and young. Somebody with sandy blonde hair under Mona's drying net. Oh, young Diana Welch. That little innocent. Maybe she doesn't recognize the scent of purgatory when she catches a whiff of it. Purgatory, but with no purging.

Mona's blunt hands touched the rollers. "Better have five more minutes," she said gruffly. "Mebbe ten. Here, I'll turn it down."

"All right. If you say so." Adelle turned to put her head back under the dryer, but first she glanced at Diana again. Diana was waiting for Mona to put the other cone over her head. (Hope that child never gets into worse heat than a hair dryer's, never gets caught walking on such red-hot coals as these. So angry, so humiliated; I'd be glad to die right here. Do hair dryers ever electrocute? Glenn, how could you? How can you?) Diana looking at me. Young green eyes. Comprehending eyes. She knows, all right, but she isn't shrieking and running. She knows, and she knows that I know that she knows.

Adelle gave the green eyes a faint smile and settled herself back under the cone. The warm whooshing began again. Adelle's hands tightened against each other under *McCall's,* and she took long, slow breaths. She knows, but she won't go blurting things all over Strettam. She's only a child, but she's one you can trust with the raveled inside stitching of your soul. I actually smiled at her, I guess. A touch of communication. Which is to say, for the first time in these five wretched years I have tacitly admitted to somebody that I am married to a depravity.

Diana. I'm not going to make you my psychiatrist, but thanks for caring. If you'd like to play tennis sometime, or come over for a coke after MYF. The compassion in your eyes. I won't open the zoo gates and let the whole snarling menagerie that lives inside me come growling out at you, Diana, but seeing you around Strettam from now on may actually tame the beasts a little.

Odd, she thought. What I'm going to carry away from Mona's, besides my frizzy clean hair, is not so much this new pit of anger that I just stepped into, but a thread of strength that I can hang onto. Oh, now. Careful, Adelle. You're imagining things about her comprehension.

She flattened the *McCall's* on her lap and turned a few pages. No need to read them or see them. Mayonnaise ads. Hosiery, girdles, swim suits. Half a glance to her left. Young Diana had taken a small notebook from her flat black leather purse and was jotting something on a page. Suddenly, with a movement as abrupt as a colt's, Diana dipped from under the dryer, put a small square of folded paper into Adelle's left hand, let her own rest on Adelle's for a moment, and whisked back under her dryer just before Mona Taylor came back to flick a switch and say, "All right, now, Mis' Fiedler, let's comb out them curls."

Adelle held the small paper until she was standing on the bridge across the Metonic, halfway home. "Mrs. Fiedler," it said in round, neat penmanship, "there's a great poem in Isaiah. Chapter 43. I read it about five times this morning. Especially verse 2. Maybe it's for you, too? D. W."

What an odd note. What an odd little girl-child she is. After church last Sunday morning, was it, when Kevin Thomas was asking about MYF and the Bates boy said Diana was going to preach about the eternal verities, and they all laughed? But their kidding didn't seem to faze her. Isaiah, huh? She walked on beyond the Metonic with more briskness and rummaged in the bookcase. Oh, here it is. When did I last read anything from Isaiah? Ezra, Nehemiah, Esther, Job. There we are. Forty-three, hmm. Verse two. ". . . through the waters, I will be with thee. . . ." ". . . when thou walkest through the fire, thou shalt not be burned; neither shall the flame kindle upon thee. . . ."

But I have been burned, Diana. For five years. I burn, he burns, it burns. It burns me. I burn, I was burned, I am burning, I have been burned. Is there something new in asbestos for a wife to wear across such burning coals? Future tense: thou shalt not be burned. "Maybe it's for you, too? D. W." While he's in Denver with Lisa Sprague. While a high school kid with green eyes comprehends a little and cares more than a little.

"You're losing out on that one," said Gluttony placidly.

Anger burped and rolled over on his stomach. They were back on the ridgepole at St. Mark's. "Could be. The Enemy is so hideously relentless and tries so many odd dodges. But she's given me some mighty good forage, and I'm not yelling quits. Not by a long shot."

Three

"There's a glitter in your eye, David," said George McPherson. "Someone leave you a legacy?"

"Or there's a new Baptist family moving into Strettam with ten children for your Sunday school?" offered Tom Williams.

David Yeoman sat down briskly, rubbed his hands lightly across his bristly crew cut, and grinned mysteriously. "Keep guessing." he said. "Coffee, please, Joe? And a couple of those chocolate doughnuts?" He poured cream and took a wide bite of doughnut. "As good as usual," he said. "Boy, you did us all a good turn, Joe, when you started getting stuff from that Princeville bakery."

"Well? Did you come in grinning like a Chessy cat just because of Joe's doughnuts?" asked George.

Yeoman put down his coffee cup and looked at the doughnut in his hand as though it had suddenly changed color. "Now there's force of habit for you," he said wonderingly. "And irony, too. I was going to skip doughnuts this morning, for the good of my soul."

"Shall I help you out and eat the other one?" asked Tom. "My good Methodist practicality would suggest that as a possible alternative."

"Well—yeah, I wish you would! This is not the build-up I intended, but it illustrates my point. Boy, does it!"

"Which is—?" Tom pulled the doughnut toward himself and broke it in two.

"Just something I was both amused and not amused to find in Deuteronomy a while ago, and I was going to razz you guys with it when I got here and be very virtuous."

"Deuteronomy?" McPherson's slim, tanned face was quizzical. "You're reading Deuteronomy? I don't think I've read Deuteronomy through in the last ten years."

"Well, you've read a lot of other things," said David. "This is my revenge, see, for all the times you've come in talking about things that I hadn't read within the last ten years."

"We await your gleaming pearls," said Tom, brushing away doughnut crumbs.

"Okay." Yeoman flipped pages rapidly. "In chapter 21. Now hear this. It never startled me before, but I don't know why it didn't. 'If a man have a stubborn and rebellious son, which will not obey the voice of his father, or the voice of his mother, and that, when they have chastened him, will not hearken unto them: Then shall his father and his mother lay hold on him, and bring him out unto the elders of his city, and unto the gate of his place; And they shall say unto the elders of his city, This our son is stubborn and rebellious, he will not obey our voice; he is a glutton, and a drunkard. And all the men of his city shall stone him with stones, that he die: so shalt thou put evil away from among you; and all Israel shall hear, and fear.' Well, gentlemen and brethren, what do you think about that?"

"One way to deal with the juvenile delinquents," said Mc-Pherson.

"Yow-ee," said Tom. "I don't remember ever noticing that bit either. Makes me think of a short story we read when I was in Sophomore Lit. in college. A grim thing about a weird sort of stoning in a modern village square."

"By a woman. Name began with J," said McPherson. "Johnson—Jones—Jeremiah—Jackson. Shirley Jackson. 'The Lottery.' "

"That's right. How often do you suppose the ancient Jews followed this command?" Tom wondered. He was looking reflectively through Joe's plate glass window, and his brown eyes seemed to be coming into focus across centuries and across continents. "Man, that would do something to a guy's paternal guts, now, wouldn't it? 'Here's my worthless son, fellas; I can't do a thing with him. Stone him for me, will ya? Thanks.' "

"As to how often," said McPherson, "maybe it wasn't too rare. From what we read in the gospels, they were pretty trigger-happy about flinging those lethal stones in the first century A.D."

"Trigger-happy?" mocked Yeoman.

"That is the first-class anachronism, isn't it?" smiled McPherson. "Oh, well, it's picturesque."

"And George is right about the flair for stoning," said Williams. "They stoned Stephen, they were going to stone the woman taken in adultery, they were going to stone Jesus. But look, Dave, you said you were going to razz George and me with this Deuteronomy bit. I don't get it. Are you going to accuse us of being evil parents, or evil sons, or what?"

Yeoman grinned. "There's one fascinating word here. One that it sorta surprised me to find here."

"Let's see it." Tom reached for Yeoman's Bible, and Yeoman

pointed to a paragraph. "Stubborn, rebellious," murmured Tom. "Does that pinch you anywhere, George? Disobedient. A glutton and a drunkard."

"So we're gluttons, are we?" asked George. "That's why he was going to skip the doughnuts this morning. Hoist with his own petard, eh what?"

"Yup," said Dave, "whatever that is. Look, this bit has prodded me into some serious thinking, though, aside from the searchlight that it shines back into the sociology and criminology of the old Israelites. Is gluttony a sin or is it not a sin? If a guy could be stoned to death for it—"

"Not just that," reminded George. "He's an outright rebel all down the line before dad and mom give up and haul him to the city gates for execution."

"Yes, but gluttony is mentioned explicitly. Does anybody you know ever talk about it now? Explicitly or otherwise? Any of your seminary profs ever harangue you about it? Any articles on it during the last umpteen years in any magazines you've seen?"

"Better bring us some more coffee, Joe," said Williams. "This Baptist seminar is getting interesting. What do you think, Joe? Is gluttony a sin?"

"Search me," said white-aproned Joe Bynum placidly as he picked up the Pyrex carafe. "I don't mind either way."

"It's all right with you if the gluttons will just come here to be gluttonous, huh? Thanks, Joe." Tom picked up the creamer. "Mostly we do think of gluttony as crude or amusing rather than really evil, don't we?"

"Or stupid?" continued Dave. He was brushing his fingers across his stubbly crew-cut, as he always did when he was trying to sort out his ideas. "Modern Americans jog and diet because the doctor says to or because their vanity says to, and not from any sense of sin in their excess poundage."

"Wonder if our Roman Catholic brothers ever talk about their gluttony when they go to the confessional," said Tom. "Hey, maybe alcohol is a special form of gluttony that trips up people in our day and generation. Wouldn't it be? It destroys and dishonors the bodies that human beings live in worse than overeating ever did, doesn't it?"

"Maybe yes, maybe no, so far as being worse," said George. "My cousin who is a surgeon in Toronto says he would rather work on an alcoholic any day than on a body with globs of lard layered over it. Maybe eating and drinking are both 'worse,' so far as that goes."

"If you're putting in alcohol," said Dave, "how about the cigarettes? How about LSD and marijuana and all that stuff? If gluttony is too much of a muchness, and any smidgen of LSD or heroin is too much of a muchness—"

Thoughtful silences.

"Anyway, Christians during medieval times had no slight doubt about considering gluttony as a sin rather than an amusing foible or as a cosmetic blunder," remarked George. "And a major sin. Not just a peccadillo."

"You and your fifty-cent words," said Dave.

"Nice one, isn't it?" smiled George.

"Was that partly because values were different—because society in the Middle Ages lived closer to the borders of starvation than we do?" asked Tom.

"Or because the Middle Ages had a stronger sense of the impingement of the eternal upon the mortal?" asked George. There was always a faint touch of Harvard and Oxford in George McPherson's voice, and now Tom, listening, had a faint nostalgia for all the early Gothic cathedrals he had seen in Europe. But he thought also of the monasteries.

"And because they feared the body more than we do?" he asked. "Feared it and distrusted it?"

"So they starved it by fasting and sometimes punished it with hair shirts," George said thoughtfully. "We feed it juicy T-bones —and let our souls find a few wild blackberries to nibble when they can. Which is the wiser? An age that doesn't care much about immortality will always gorge itself upon what is most mortal about mortality, I suppose."

Dave Yeoman reached for the black leather book again. "St. Paul was thinking something like that in First Corinthians, wasn't he? Here you go. 'If after the manner of men I have fought with beasts at Ephesus, what advantageth it me, if the dead rise not? let us eat and drink: for tomorrow we die.' If there's no resurrection, then the natural alternative would be to live it up. Or to gobble it up."

"Our friend Paul wasn't much of a gourmet at any time, was he?" asked Tom. "Having food and raiment, et cetera. And my Methodist patron saint, John Wesley, was hand and glove with Brother Paul on topics like that."

"When you come right down to it," said George, "what is the taproot of sin, anyway? That's where your question has to take us, isn't it, Dave? 'Is gluttony a sin or is it not?' Well, the prior question would be, 'What is a sin?' And there you have—"

"Eight semester hours of Biblical Theology in any seminary," said Dave promptly. "And a good three rows of books in my meager library. You must have hundreds."

"Well, for right now, let's just talk about the essence of the essence. Leave Calvin and Luther and the other guys on the shelves. Ultimately, it seems to me, Christians are human beings who say, as our Lord said in Gethsemane, 'Not my will, but Thine be done.' Right? And ultimately sin would be the precise opposite of that, wouldn't it? Sin grits its teeth and says, 'Not Thy will, but mine be done.' *Nicht wahr?*"

"And?"

"And gluttony is still a pretty prevalent way for gratifying the old carnal self. In our culture, we've clipped its horns and polished its toenails and dyed its pelt and applied some perfume, but the beastie has not yet become extinct. I think."

"And meanwhile," said Dave, "our orderly Methodist boy Thomas is inspecting his chronometer. That's my fifty-cent word for this occasion, George. And I guess the seminar is being dismissed. See you, fellas."

the one with the chewy center false teeth out first no just let
it melt

ah choky sweet like Andy bought me first date his first car
shiny first kiss carmel kiss he said Eliza kiss kiss kiss sweet heart-
sweet that thin blue voile that momma made now mind your
manners miss don't care if he did come all the way from Hartman
Junction sweet brown river throat valley chewy caught on teeth
sweet love you Elizabeth married next Tuesday judge in Princeville sweet stuck on uppers sweet tooth sweetheart he's dead Miz
Jarvis doc said everything tried everything too young kleenex
kleenex kleenex soggy puffy ugly face ugly dark artificial green
grass the undertakers preacher Edward crying sweet stickysweet
stuck inside front teeth tongue thirsty thirsty

another carmel no nut one now walnut almond peanut goo
thin chocolate edge

don't be so edgy mother I'm sixteen now can't you go on to
bed sure I'll turn out the lights when I come in no just messin'
round with the guys

walnut tastes brown chocolate nut white

white Chevrolet what does Uncle Milton want with a white
Chevrolet anyway sure I can drive license big boy momma ohoh-
ohoh crunch scream Edward the bridge railing Edward are you
all right blood bruises no yes no white face white ice white Chevrolet white skid marks black fender jagged broken insurance
Milton you let him drive it coulda been just one only one suits
empty shoes empty dust on tennis racket isn't wasn't walnut
chocolate edge

alone

wind in catalpa

where's the old ladder mom yeah while I'm here trim ladder
catalpa needles Myrna

stop don't think don't think mustn't I hate your guts oh quick
more tea a sandwich maybe make it yes thick mayonnaise millions do you comprehend a slice of white meat breast sleep

sleep on mother's breast father will come to thee father will come to his babe in the nest there with lettuce too sweet and scalding
start making noodles

maybe chocolate richest fluffier German no devil's food soft red-brown moist three eggs how many devils

more tea sugar yes please Mrs. Dimmet's silver teapot when I worked there pot kettle calls the pot bellypot too heavy Mrs. Jarvis forty pounds yes doctor yes doctor but I won't other people drown it in drink don't they drowning gulp prickles in my nose gulp ohohoh drowning Andy sand sun on shoulders neck nice ankles Andy sweetheart

letter tomorrow could never Myrna rusty hinge on mailbox black paint rusted no letter no nothing no

and vanilla beat until smooth

take half of it to Marian Willeford can't with no car haven't been since Sue Sue Sue and so many tall redorangewhite purplepinkredyellowwhite carnations glads white whadjacallums big white bows

poor Sue poor Marian poor Sue poor me

not yet I could though telephone somebody would telephone found your mother dead this morning yes sleeping pills yes sorry Jarvis sorry sorry

no car will you come for coffee tomorrow Marian yes three o'clock well she might nobody does well she might too much for me to eat up Marian soft brown fluffy yes of course I understand of course she don't have any appointment don't want to don't want to well if that's the way you want to be Marian Willeford

they used to come Andy ask them new folks chicken noodles maybe taffy pull tomorrow Andy popcorn twenty laughing Andy he's dead Miz Jarvis

noodles drying white floury yolk thin no thin noodles and thick me no oneninety on the scales I reckon oh well

alone

another piece while supper cooks this one with the swirl on top filling strawberry jam

in a jam mom send me fifty haven't got fifty borrow yes Mr. McNair no Mr. McNair them college bills no no I don't know what kind jam yes housework Mrs. Dimmet no of course but Edward Edward and the laundry too Mrs. Dimmet

alone

could go black silk crepe brown ugly nothing new since Andy died bring Edward Sunday school yes Edward you go mother's tired this morning could go harder hardest

with the red strawberry jam in the middle tickle sweet on my red tongue but redder jam pancakes griddle ready oh tomorrow then Edward we've got pancakes they've called already this morning if I stay here I'll break up the furniture he loves you mom spawned in your guts in the center

the one with the chewy center yes oh choky sweet

"I say, Martha!"

"Yes, dear?"

"You're bringing coffee, aren't you?"

"Yes, Ray."

"This devil's food cake is rather good, you know. Why don't you bring me another wedge of it, while you're up?"

"Another piece?"

"Well, I've only had two, haven't I?"

"And three, if you insist." She took his crumb-littered plate and replaced it with another dessert plate. The cake was moist, red-brown, with a flawlessly even texture. Swirls of creamy frosting, darker brown, clung to the outside of the wedge.

"Very good, Mrs. Kendrick. Very good indeed."

"And more coffee, my lord?"

"Yes, thank you, Mrs. Kendrick."

"I don't know, Ray. The next time you run for a county office they will describe you in the papers as the corpulent Mr. Kendrick from Strettam. Or the chubby Mr. Kendrick."

"Good reason not to run for any more offices," he said comfortably. "Anyway, I'm six two. They wouldn't venture beyond calling me 'portly.' That always sounds distinguished for an insurance man, doesn't it? The portly Mr. Kendrick." His fork edged through the moist red-brownness, and he took another bite. "Very good, Martha, very good. My grandfather would have it called positively Lucullan."

"Let's find another adjective. Isn't that one about worn out?"

"If so, my dear, it's a tribute to your culinary skills." He pushed his chair back from the table. "Such a dinner leaves one feeling very bland, you know. Very expansive."

"I'm peddling insurance, too," said Martha. "Insurance against the flaming of your wrath."

"Oh, come now, Martha. Don't take cracks at my temper when you have just finished lavishing such sweetness upon me."

"When you have lavished it upon yourself, you mean?"

"Well, I guess that's the name of the game for most people, isn't it? You might carve it on my tombstone: 'Here lies a man who knew how to lavish sweetness upon himself.' "

"That isn't a very distinguishing epitaph. You could carve the same thing on about twenty million tombstones. Especially American tombstones, I suppose."

"Yep, ain't it wonderful? Instead of 'the land of the free and the home of the brave,' you might call it 'the land of the free spender and the home of the hedonist.' Which suits my Lucullan palate just fine, Mrs. Kendrick. So long as I have the wherewithal to be one of the spenders. Now where have you hidden the evening paper?"

"You're looking awfully smug," said Envy. All Seven, gnome-size, were seated on the Kendrick mantel, kicking it placidly with their heels as heads leaned back against the chimney brick.

"He likes the irony," said Anger. "Tonight this client's language was truer than he thought. He really was eating some devil's food."

"Right-o, right-o," said Gluttony. "And of course the beauty of it is that while I can keep him busy ignoring the Enemy this way, his every bite of anything is really devil's food."

Janice Wilson

"Mother, what's fasting?" asked Johnnie Wilson. He was sprawled on the living room rug in his favorite position for reading. His shoulders were propped against the davenport. His schoolbooks were scattered on the davenport, just behind his head.

"It's something nobody ever does," said Janice.

"Shuddup, I'm not asking you. Mother, what's fasting?"

"You mean you're eleven years old and you don't know a simple thing like that? Mother, he's hopeless. You'd better find a good school for the feeble-minded before he gets any older."

"Shuddup, Janice. Mother, what's fasting?"

Mrs. Wilson flicked the control on her dishwasher. "Janice, I wish you wouldn't torment him. Now you're a businesswoman down at Dacey's—"

"Businesswoman, my eye," said Johnnie. "She's eighteen, and she sells stupid clothes to stupid ol' women—"

"Johnnie, that will do. What were you yelling at me about when I was in the kitchen?"

"I wanta know what fasting is."

"Why?"

"Oh, there's a thing here in the paper about Governor Baines announcing Memorial Day this year as a day of—just a minute —of 'fasting and special intercession on behalf of world peace.' He's appointing a big committee—Catholics and Jews and everybody—and they're gonna make proclamations, it says here."

"You've got a dictionary, haven't you?" asked Janice. "Grandma gave you one for your birthday, if you haven't thrown it away. Make him look it up, mother. He's getting too lazy to live."

"Shuddup!"

"Janice, please. Well, when you fast you go without some foods or maybe all foods for a while. For a purpose."

"Like a hunger strike, huh?"

"Well, not exactly. That would be one kind. Sometimes people fast to prove a point to someone else, and I guess that would be a hunger strike. Sometimes they fast for their own good."

"To reduce, huh?"

"Not always. More like being in training for athletics. Something else is more important than food to a person, you see—"

"Golly. For how long?"

"That depends on the person and what he decides. Apparently the governor is talking about just one day. Memorial Day, is that right?"

"That's what it says here."

"It sounds pretty silly to me," interposed Janice. "Like trying to make a big, fat bargain with God. 'I'll make myself go hungry to please you, God, if you'll do something special to please me.' As if God got His kicks out of seeing people starve. He must get a lot of kicks from watching the people in India then."

"I don't think you really understand, dear. Sometimes it is good for a person to take some action that will reassert what really is important to him. And all through history prayer and fasting have often gone together."

"Besides, it would be good for your figure, fatso," said Johnnie. "All she ever does any more is sit around and grouch and eat. Is there a word that means the opposite of 'fasting'? Like being a pig and eating all the time?"

"Sure, stupid," said Janice. "Don't you know anything?"

"I know plenty," said Johnnie. "Did you see my last report card? Hey, where ya goin'?"

"To get a coke from the refrigerator. What's it to you?"

"Well, whatever that word is that's the opposite of 'fasting,'" said Johnnie with immense disdain, "you're sure it. Boy, the governor is a lot smarter than you are."

"You're not looking very chipper," said Lechery to Pride. All Seven were lolling in the directors' chairs in the board room at the Norwich State Bank. Lechery was coiling and twining as well as lolling, like a vaporous admixture of rattlesnakes and Buddhas.

"Worn down a little," said Pride. "This present crop of mortals plays into my hands with incredible speed. And such charming naiveté. Keeps a guy hopping, you might say. Jolly good thing that the Captain lets us all be omnipresent, don't you know?" He grinned and twiddled with his mustache and with a long silky goatee. He crossed long legs and swung shiny cloven hooflets, ringed with rhinestones, up on the table top.

"You aren't in the doldrums, then?" asked Lechery.

"I am not in the doldrums. Slightly wearied, old fellow, but your charming presence is wonderfully resuscitating. Now, I'll tell you, though, who might be in the doldrums."

"Covetousness?"

"Not him, not him."

"I'd say not," said Covetousness. It was his whim for the moment, since they were at the bank, to be a robot-shaped heap of ethereal safety-deposit boxes. "I've prospered splendidly today. Made me think of some of my best days with the Borgias and the Medicis, don't you know? These are more petty mortals, but they have the authentic flavor."

"Right you are," agreed Pride. "Every heart a space big enough for all of hell to fit into. Big enough for any or all of us to carouse in. Big enough for us to gorge on, too. Well, Gluttony, old man. Are you the one that might need a swig of courage from the rest of us?"

Gluttony yawned like a drowsy lion. "I'm fine," he murmured. "I'll admit it nettled me to have that sneaky Baptist preacher get his friends to talking about me this morning. You know I hate publicity as much as the rest of you guys do, and I don't often have to face it these days. If they don't admit that we exist, it's a lot easier to tweak them into obeying us."

"Oh, well, what's one blithering little conversation?" consoled Lechery.

"It was neither blithering nor little," said Gluttony. "Don't kid yourself. I'm not kidding myself."

"Don't get into a panic. Now me, I like to have 'em talk about me," said Lechery, undulating as though the rattlesnake portion of him were about to uncoil.

"Sure you do. They talk about you and snigger and then start wanting you to come on in and join the party. That's the advantage you have always had."

"Yeah, I guess it is. Well, ol' buddy, we can't all be alike, you know. You in your small corner and I in mine."

"Small corner?" roared Gluttony. The sleepiness of the sleepy lion was quite gone. "You may describe your own area in any way you like, but there's nothing small about my assignment."

"Attaboy, Gluttony," said Pride. "Now refreshments from the Captain." Phosphorescent mugs were steaming beside them on the directors' table and emitting an acrid stench, smoky and rather sweet, to which no mortal would have been attracted. "Cheers," he said. "Cheers!"

Three

"Good morning, Joe. Sorry to splash so much rain water in with us." George McPherson furled his black umbrella and put it on Joe's nicked and blistery walnut umbrella rack. "Here, Mannie, let yours drip along with mine." He put the two soggy raincoats on the pegs that faced the cash register. "Good morning, brethren. You guys know Mannie Mitchell, don't you? I just pried him loose from the ledgers in McNair's establishment up the street."

David Yeoman and Tom Williams looked up amiably. "Sorta moist, isn't it?" said Dave.

"I thought you'd probably decide to have instant coffee in the lounge with McNair's other minions, after all," George said to Mannie. To the others, he added, "Mannie and I have been talking about C. S. Lewis and Tolkien when we get a chance lately, and I've been telling him he ought to come along for one of Dave's seminars. Two coffees, Joe."

"Good idea, Mannie," said Tom. "'Joe's coffee does a lot more for me than what I brew in my own office."

"Joe's coffee and our scintillating company?" asked Dave with amused eyebrows cocked.

"Um-hum."

"I'm writing a book," Dave said histrionically to Mannie. "It's to be entitled 'The Mastery, Practice, and Perfection of Humility.' "

"Are those the notecards for the first chapter you have there in your coat pocket?" asked Tom.

Dave's face became more serious, and his right hand started touching the stubble of his crew cut thoughtfully. "Nope. That's rough notes for next Sunday morning."

"On Tuesday?" asked Tom. "You're way ahead of schedule."

"This one has been simmering for quite a while," said Dave. "As a matter of fact, I stuck these in my pocket so I could pick your brains. I'm glad you didn't let me down and stay in your respective studies this morning."

"See what I told you?" said McPherson to Mannie. His slim face was alert, like that of a volleyball player waiting for a serve. "Yeoman's seminar on practically anything."

"Fine," said Mannie. "That's what I came for."

"Go ahead," said Tom. "Tell us what's on our minds. Something as stormy as the weather?"

"Well, it's like this," said Dave. "I'm trying a sermon series on the Ten Commandments. One of my profs in seminary said you ought to do a series like that at least every other year, but I'm just now getting with it."

"So?" Tom's dark eyes were on his coffee cup, but his attention was not.

"So right now, precisely now, I am thinking about the covets. 'Nor his manservant, nor his maidservant, nor his ox, nor his ass, nor any thing that is thy neighbour's.' "

"So?" reiterated Tom.

"So I've been trying to figure out a little more precisely what 'coveting' is anyway."

"Don't your Baptists know already?" asked George. "It's not a very esoteric word."

"Nor an unknown skill among us Baptists. I know. Everybody knows, more or less, what Moses meant when he carved something onto a piece of stone that we translate as 'covet,' " said Dave. "What I've been trying to figure out—"

"Now wait a minute," said Tom. "You'd better read Exodus again. Moses wasn't a stonemason with a workshop up on the heights of Sinai."

Dave looked blank. "Now, now," said George. "Don't push him off the track. You've been trying to figure out what?"

"Oh, where 'to covet' overlaps with 'to be jealous' and 'to envy' and just plain 'to desire.' I've been giving the concordances a workout—"

"And the dictionaries? Hey, Joe," said Tom, "have you found a dictionary yet to stash beside your percolator? We've been ordering one along with your doughnuts off and on for about six months."

Joe Bynum grinned but kept on washing cups and did not answer. "Tell you what," said George. "I'll bring one of my old dictionaries down and leave it here if you won't pitch it out, Joe. You could use it for little kids to sit on when they're too big for a high chair. Or think they are."

Joe grinned again, even more amiably but just as silently.

"In the meantime," said Tom, "how about it? Are they synonyms? Or nearly so? What do you think, Mannie?"

"Let's hear what Mr. Yeoman has decided," said the book-keeper.

"Well," said Dave slowly, "words are slippery things, and we use them without too much precision sometimes—"

"I say," interposed George McPherson, "have you been reading some T. S. Eliot?"

"No, why?"

"You're faintly close to quoting him right there," said George. "He has a line somewhere about 'the slimy mud of words' and 'the sleet and hail of verbal imprecisions.'"

"Well, chalk one up for the Baptists," said Dave. "Great minds are still running in the same channels. Remind me to mention this moment in my opening chapter on humility, will you? Well, anyway, it seems to me that these words are all overlapping, sorta like fish scales, but you covet when you want the thing itself. Greed and avarice and all that. When you envy, you are mad at somebody else because of what he has that you don't have. You want it, and you hate him. You covet the property; you envy the man. And jealousy is when you are trying to hold on to something that you already have, or think you have, but you're jittery about someone's opposing claim to it. Like a jealous wife."

"So why do you come to consult us?" asked George. "Mannie, might I ask why you are smiling?"

"Am I? Oh, I was just thinking that Mr. Yeoman clearly didn't attend high school here."

"Here? Was there ever a high school here in Strettam?"

"Oh, no, Strettam-Princeville Consolidated, then as now."

"What's your clue, Sherlock?" asked Dave. "How can you tell?"

"Mrs. Derwent would have had your scalp for saying that jealousy is a 'when,'" said Mannie.

"She'd have had my scalp for a lot more than that," said Yeoman. "Well, whaddya think?"

"I think you're right about what we consider jealousy to be, anyway," said Tom. "Othello and Desdemona. Beware the green-eyed monster. I've had some classic cases to counsel with as a pastor, too. I suppose we all have."

"Cruel as the grave," murmured Mannie Mitchell.

Dave nodded. "That's a powerful verse, isn't it? What's the rest of it?"

"Don't you have it there in your pocket on one of your note cards?"

"Um—yes. Just a minute." He flipped a rubber band and shuffled quickly. "Jealousy. Jealousy. Here we go. Song of Solomon. Eight, six. 'Set me as a seal upon thine heart, as a seal upon thine arm: for love is strong as death; jealousy is cruel as the grave: the coals thereof are coals of fire, which hath a most vehement flame.' "

Mannie was looking at his watch. "George, I'd better be getting back," he said. "So long as Mr. Yeoman's parishioners do covet, somebody has to keep books on them, unfortunately. 'O my sweet gold!' Thanks for inviting me."

Both Tom Williams and Dave Yeoman looked a little blank. "Come again; come often," said George. "But first, tell me what you're quoting from, or I'll be restless all day. You were quoting, weren't you?"

"Marlowe's *Doctor Faustus*. Covetousness speaking. 'And might I have my wish, I would desire that this house and all the people in it were turned to gold, that I might lock you up in my chest. O my sweet gold!' Be seeing you." Mannie collected his raincoat from the peg and hurried up the street past the rain-splashed plate glass window.

"Hey, you should have brought him before," said Dave. "I'll have to call him up and get chapter and verse on that. 'O my sweet gold!' See, that's just what I was saying. Covetousness is avarice. Covetousness wants the gold itself; it doesn't care so much who else has it or doesn't have it."

"Like Silas Marner counting his coins?"

"Right."

"Latin *cupiditas*," said George. "You have the 'root of all evil' passage jotted down already, Dave?"

"Yes, it's here. In half a dozen different versions. Though I must say, after looking at all the others, I keep coming back to the King James. The King James has a richness that really rolls along the tongue."

"Go ahead, practice your oratory," said George.

"Trying to make me feel self-conscious?" He looked at the note card thoughtfully and then read slowly. " 'But they that will be rich fall into temptation and a snare, and into many foolish and hurtful lusts, which drown men in destruction and perdition. For the love of money is the root of all evil: which while some coveted after, they have erred from the faith, and pierced themselves through with many sorrows.' Man, that's great. If I could once in my life write a sermon that rolled with one-tenth of that—that—"

"Resonance?" offered George. "Sonority? None of what Eliot called the 'sleet and hail of verbal imprecisions' in that passage, eh, Dave?"

"No, but it's getting toward sleet and hail outside," said Tom. "I was going to call on sick and afflicted Methodists for the rest of the day, but I think I'm going to revise my schedule. Maybe I'll get out my lexicons and commentaries and slosh around behind you in these footprints you've been making, Dave. I think I feel the fingers of half a dozen good sermons reaching out to shake my hands."

"Come on in; the water's fine," said Dave. "Nice metaphorical Baptist water. I warn you, though. I've got dibs on James 3:14 for a text."

"James 3:14?"

"Yep. Well, actually fourteen to sixteen. In the RSV. No, on second thought, go ahead and use it if you want to. If every preacher from here to Keyesport used that same text for all the Sundays in a solid month, we wouldn't exhaust it." He glanced at another of his three by five cards. " 'For where jealousy and selfish ambition exist,' it says. That's one way to define twentieth century America, isn't it? That's Strettam, too. Even our nice little friendly Strettam."

"Our indolent Strettam?" asked Tom, half smiling. "A while back George was worrying about sloth as being rampant among us—if sloth can ever be rampant. Maybe one vice tends to cancel out the other one in actual practice. Trying to keep up with the Joneses reduces our laziness, and laziness reduces our coveting."

"Better send him back to seminary, hadn't we, George?" asked Dave.

"Or just back to my study?" said Tom. "We've spent a fearful amount of time here this morning."

"Just a minute," said Dave. "Let me throw one more note card at you. Um—yes, here you are. They don't cancel each other out. Or anyway Solomon thought they didn't. Proverbs this time. Chapter twenty-one. 'The desire of the slothful killeth him; for his hands refuse to labour. He coveteth greedily all the day long: but the righteous giveth and spareth not.' Okay, now you can go back to your salt mine, and I'll go back to mine. Hey, George, what kind of a trance are you in?"

"Thinking about what you said a while ago. If I could ever write a sermon that probed into human nature the way the Proverbs probe into human nature—. Reminds me of what J. B. Phillips said somewhere, of feeling as though he were rewiring an old house without having the mains turned off when he was translating the New Testament. Now where did I leave my umbrella?"

At the counter, a heavy-jowled salesman tapped cigar ashes into his saucer and blew on his coffee. "Are they for real?" he asked, pointing with his elbow to the three raincoats out on Main Street.

"Huh?" Joe Bynum kept on tossing silverware nonchalantly into a plastic box.

"They always talk like that?"

"Like what?"

Heavy Jowls tapped his cigar again. "Like the Bible is for real, man."

"Oh, sure. Sometimes they stay longer. Sure. They think it's for real."

"Well, I'll be damned," Heavy Jowls said casually, fumbling in his pocket for a coin.

Joe Bynum looked at him thoughtfully. "Them three guys would prob'ly say that's just the point," he said finally.

Millard W. Wentworth

He looked at the luminous dial. The clock was on the walnut bedstand, just beyond his pillow, but it took interminable effort for him to pull his eyes to it. Like pushing against a haystack. Like rowing a boat through fresh concrete. There. No. Yes. There.

When he saw that it was precisely five minutes after three, he knew, suddenly, that he would die, and his head sagged back on the pillow. The luminous dial rode in front of his staring eyes. Five minutes after three. And I will die. The dial turned itself slowly and slid toward the ceiling, and he drifted halfway back into the dream that had awakened him. And the door edged open, and this tall blob, like a big spider with armor on, came oozing through. Didn't say anything. Slits for eyes and sort of a snout puffing up under a visor. And I asked what he wanted, what it wanted, and it just kept on coming. Ominous, horribly ominous. And I screamed for Millie, and the effort brought me to the surface. Wish my heart wouldn't pound like that.

Five minutes after three.

Not yet. Oh, not yet. I'm only fifty-three.

Millie— He eased his hand toward the other pillow. Millie. Millie, I need you. Why did you—? A glimpse of her mauve coffin with his white roses on it superimposed itself on the nearer, darker glimpse of the nightmare's blob.

Not yet. I can't. Johnson is just ready to sell me his ninety acres that I've been maneuvering after for ten years. His glossy big Herefords grazing there in the summer sun. My Herefords to graze there for the rest of my life. For the rest— How soon will it be? Hours? Days? Weeks? In two more weeks I could finish up the deal with Ellison for the new apartments in Princeville. For what? Can I look up through six feet of earth and say they're my apartments?

For the nephews to fight over. Will, George, Tuffy, Sam. My house, my farms, my cars. My bonds. My deposit boxes. Not mine. There won't be any me. Under the Coffin lid. Smothered in that white satin stuff they put in coffins.

I was going to start taking it easy. This year, for sure. South America, Europe. Sure, I can afford it. Maybe find a handsome widow. Go to New York or Chicago and try a little night life. Sell a farm or two. Get a farm's worth of traveler's checks.

To travel in a hearse. Careful, Mac, don't hit the bumps; we've got the wealthiest man in three counties in this hearse today. He won't feel it, will he? Bump, bump, bump. And they let the coffin down, and the undertaker's thingumajig squeaks a little, and they throw clods into my face. Thumpa, thumpa. But it's a hard wax face, like a dummy in the store window. My face.

So who will care if I had three cars and nine farms? Alone in the dark. And scared. Like the time when I was six and got lost in the south pasture. Dark, dark. And tall grass all around. Gopher holes to stumble in, and the nighthawks calling overhead. Somebody, come find me. Somebody, come find me. Somebody, come find me.

Always scared underneath? Always wanting. Getting one farm helped, but not enough. Wanting, wanting, wanting. To foreclose a mortgage on the Simpson place. He'd mortgage his own bones, they said at the bank. I would, too.

And now they're going to foreclose the mortgage. Final. No new investment of it, ever. It's five minutes after three.

He opened his eyes to keep from seeing the armored, spidery blob, and the darkness he looked into seemed like weighted fingers pushing him down.

Not yet. Not yet. Just about to buy that new house out by the lake. Almost decided. Smooth sloping roof, handsome split shingles. Landscaped so well— Smooth sloping clods of new brown earth at the cemetery. The only roof I'll ever need. Land-scaped around tombstones. Millie's grave already.

The coffin goes there. But my real self. Do I go out whimpering through the big south pasture of space? Somebody, come find me. There's no me left. I paid myself out. All bills, by the tenth. Checks and currency and silver dollars. Hollow. I'm not a me. Nothing left to pay with.

Why did that obscene black thing walk into my room tonight? Why mine? And why tonight? How did it get through the front door? Dogs asleep outside, like always. Door latched. It just nudged the bedroom door and oozed in. If the door hadn't swung, it would have oozed through. I wanted—I wasn't—I'm not—

The luminous dial hovered above him, wavered, slid softly from side to side. Then it widened horribly and became intolerably brilliant. Each numeral, each fleck was like a separate flash of jagged lightning, each one breaking the whole sky apart.

Somebody, come— Oh, my God— Oh, my God—

Davie Gilson

"No, Al, she particularly said in her note that she would like for *Mr.* Gilson to stop by," said Eileen patiently. "I'd be glad to go, though goodness knows there's enough to do if I get anything more planted in the garden this week. But she did say *Mr.* Gilson, not *Mrs.*"

"Stupid woman," grumbled Al. "Everybody and his brother wants a rush job this week. 'Specially these farmers and their trucks. I'll go see her next week or the week after."

"School's out the week after, Al," reminded Eileen. "And she was pretty urgent. You should have gone Monday or last night."

"Well, I didn't. Want me to go up there in my work clothes?"

"She'll be in her work clothes."

"Oh, sure. Chalk dust and a smudge of ink on her pinkie from writing her comments to the parents."

"She won't mind your clothes, Al. You can take off your coveralls and clean the worst grease off your hands, can't you?"

"Oh, I suppose. Drat that woman, anyway. Couldn't she have talked to you on the telephone?"

"You ought to be glad she takes an interest in Davie."

"You mean she meddles. Never saw a school teacher yet that had good common sense. What time did she say?"

"Any time between quarter to three and five."

"Well, okay. If I gotta. What's on her mind, anyway?"

"That's what we want to know, Al."

At 4:15 when he wheeled his tow truck into the asphalt parking lot behind the grade school, Al had stubborn little lines around his eyes. Himself a tenth grade dropout, he felt old frustrations yipping inside him as he clomped down the corridor. Room 10, huh? Miss Beth Ann Frankel. Silly name, Beth Ann.

Not a silly-looking woman, though. Late thirties. Friendly, businesslike. Not the kind to crumple a fender against a garage wall. But the room had the old resented smell of any schoolroom: paste and chalk and floor wax and children's clothes.

"—appreciate your coming." You'd better, woman. If you

knew the kind of jam I'm in at the garage this week, you sure would.

"I've been watching Davie with keen interest all year. He's a fine boy with a great deal of potential—" Yeah? Blah, blah. You say that to all the parents, don't you? "But he has been showing a tendency that concerns me very much—" Sure. Hates school, I suppose. Don't blame him. Who doesn't? "—not in his classroom work, which is quite acceptable, but in his recreational patterns. It may seem trivial now, Mr. Gilson, but his future character is being formed—" Okay, okay, out with it.

She looked at him directly. Her face was still almost smiling, but her gray eyes were somber. Like she thought I owed somebody a bill I wasn't gonna pay. "Mr. Gilson, has Davie shown you his collection of marbles recently?"

"Marbles?"

"Yes."

"Uh, well, no. I guess he plays marbles a lot with the other kids now that it's spring. Seems as though they're always at it, out in our backyard or someplace else. Why?"

"But he doesn't show you his winnings?"

"Gosh, no. Do little kids like Davie play for keeps?" The rascal. My folks never let us. Well, why not? He's smarter than I knew he was. Make his way in the world all right.

"Davie does. I've wondered how you'd feel about it. But it isn't just that he plays for keeps, Mr. Gilson. It has become a kind of passion with him. He teases the other boys into playing, even when they clearly don't want to, and then stays at it—well, rather ruthlessly, until he gets the marbles that he really wants."

"So?" His tone was belligerent.

"I think he's getting to care more about the agates he can win from his friends than he does about having friends, Mr. Gilson. It's not an attitude one would like to see him carry on through life."

"Well, I'd like to know why not. Nobody's gonna hand him anything on a silver platter when he's grown up, that's for sure. Let 'im play marbles and get all he can; maybe it'll make a big businessman outta him someday. I don't 'specially want 'im to be a grease monkey all his life, like me."

"To be a ruthless businessman is not exactly what I would hope your David could become," she said. "I'm fond of David. He's a little fellow with real potential as a person. And people need people. When he's forty, he'll need friends as well as dividends. Right now he needs warmer friendships with the other boys more than he needs another sack of marbles to put under his bed, or wherever he puts them."

"Says you." The stubborn little lines had deepened around his eyes. His hands were fidgeting with his denim cap, and the bits of dark grease that outlined his fingernails seemed to be small individual frowns.

She nodded quietly. Afternoon light from the west window made her look a little more tired, a little more patient. Al Gilson wasn't thinking about how she looked, however. He was seeing small Davie as forty or fifty, seated behind a big desk in a big office with dictaphones and typewriters and secretaries all around him. Davie, with a face like his own but cleaner and handsomer; Davie wearing clothes like the best ones in any department store window. Sic 'em, Davie. Shoot for keeps.

"Yes, says me," she said, without annoyance. "A few times, out on the playground at recess or after school," Miss Frankel went on, "I've watched his intense concentration when he was aiming, or his rather aloof pleasure when he wins, and he really makes me think of a professional gambler in an old-time melodrama. He really does."

"Oh, come on!" Well, that's the way it goes. Some people win and some people lose. Me, I'm not much of a winner. If you are, Davie boy—

The clock face at the back of the classroom gave an electronic "tick-buzz" and the minute hand jerked obediently. "Say, it's getting late," he said. "I told the boys at the garage I'd be back by 4:30 sure." Vague pleasure bounced in his heels as he strode back down the linoleum tile of the corridor. The shaver's only seven. He'll make his way. Go ahead, kid. Take your chances. And cheat a little if you have to.

As he pulled open the door of the old tow truck, his eye caught a ring of small boys in blue jeans and T-shirts in the empty lot behind the Wilson house. At it now, I'll bet. He smiled a little as he cleared the schoolroom taste from his throat and spat noisily onto the asphalt. In the truck, he swung down toward the empty lot and drove past it slowly. There he is, down on his knees. Doesn't see me. Doesn't know the world exists beyond that ring and his shooter. Little puddles of color: red, blue-white, green. Wonder which one he's after this time.

Beyond Wilson's, Al glanced at the rear-view mirror beyond his left elbow for another view of Davie. Davie, crouching, aiming. For a moment it seemed to Al that he was Davie: spring grass crunched under his knees, warm loam odors in his nose, sun on the back of his neck, the round hard shooter poised in front of his springy thumb knuckle. Thunk. There it goes. Click, spin. Yep, it's mine. Whichever one I want. I want, I want, I want.

"You women get excited about nothin'," he told Eileen loftily over fried potatoes, ketchup, and beer. Play it cool, man. Don't get her on the kid's neck. "She—uh—she thinks I oughta take more interest in Davie's 'recreational patterns.' How does that grab you?"

"Well, maybe you should."

"Sure, I'm gonna. Hey, Davie. Davie!"

Jeans and dirty sneakers came back from the living room to the kitchen. "I said 'scuse me," he protested. "Before you ever came to supper. Mom said I could go." He looked back at the ragged comic book in his hand.

"Listen, son. Down at the garage I got a glass case. Supposed to be a display case for bike accessories, see, but I never used it. I been thinkin'. If I'd fit some pieces of lath into it, you could have a purty good case to keep some of your stuff in. Marbles, maybe. Whatya say?"

Davie looked at him tentatively, warily. "How many would it hold?"

"Oh, I don't know. Quite a few. We could try it out." Al stood and stretched, then walked to the living room door and looked out across pitted grass, broken toy fragments, and rusted auto parts. Davie followed him and sat down on the porch steps, comic book in hand. Water was running in the sink. Eileen wouldn't hear, Al knew, and Miss Beth Ann Frankel wouldn't hear him. "If it isn't big enough," he said casually, "maybe I could make you a better one sometime. After you win enough more."

David looked at him carefully and then perched the comic book on the frayed denim of his right knee. "Okay. If you want to."

The little cuss, thought Al. The woman is right. He does look at you like a pro gambler in some old movie.

Lottie Evans

"Good morning. How's everything?" Penny Atkinson put her new beige coat on the rack and tossed a flat pouch of tapestry fabric on the shelf above it. "You should have seen the blossoms in the black locust trees between here and Iroquois this morning," she told Lottie Evans. "They're really lovely."

"Are they?"

"And the spring green in the hills is just superb this year."

"Um-hum."

"Something wrong? Storm winds blowing from the throne room?"

"Not that I know of."

"What's on your mind, then? Or should I ask?"

"Oh, quite a few things," said Lottie brusquely. "We'd better get to work. McNair doesn't pay us to babble."

"Well—oh, all right."

At 10:15 Penny hesitated but finally went up to the lounge for her coffee break as usual. Lottie was already there and was jabbing her spoon dourly into the jar of instant Maxwell House.

"I didn't mean to snap this morning, Penny," she said. "I'm in a foul mood. And I s'pose it's going to get fouler. But that isn't your fault."

Penny looked at her steadily. "Something wrong?"

"Oh, no more than always."

"Oh?"

"Well, maybe. More or less. Memorial Day I hate with a dark purple passion. Especially a Memorial Day weekend."

"Oh?" Penny searched through files of recollection. Did Lottie lose a fiancé in World War II that I never heard about? Iwo Jima, Corregidor, the Battle of the Bulge?

Lottie put her spoon on the stainless steel drainboard. "Family reunion," she said flatly. "I hate 'em."

"Oh?"

"The Evanses and their cousins come for miles around. Last year there were ninety-seven of us, from four states." She stopped abruptly, as though she were applying power brakes inside herself.

"Is that—is that so bad?"

"For me it is."

"Well, do you have to go? Where is it? In somebody's back-yard?"

"No, over at Junietta State Park. Every year my brother Charles reserves the place before he leaves so we can have the big pavilion for the following year. And yes, I have to go. Mother would scold me for the entire year if I skipped. And I do mean for the entire year. Got any migraine headaches or tonsillitis germs in your purse that you could loan me for the weekend?"

"Well, no, but—"

"Oh, sure, I know what you're thinking. One should love to be with one's kith and kin. Well, I don't. I used to." She blunted her cigarette in the sunflower ashtray that someone had brought back from a vacation trip and picked up her purse. "Oh, don't look so sympathetic, Penny. I'll live through it. I always have. If I don't decide to jump off the Junietta cliffs into the Metonic."

Maybe this time will be better, Lottie thought as she unloaded the car on Friday morning. At least with the big blast today I'll have tomorrow and Sunday to recuperate. Unless one of the boys decides to stay for the whole weekend after all. Charles said he might. "Well, mother, where shall I settle you? Over by the big chestnut tree? I'll bring your pillows in a second. Want to take my arm? The ground is pretty uneven." Sixty-nine now. And I'm thirty-nine. How many more Evans picnics to bring her to? Eighteen when dad died. Hey, that's twenty-one years of servitude already. Sentenced for life, though.

"There you are. Now I'll take the food up to the pavilion and see who's here. Shall I?"

Shall I, shall I not. But nobody gave me any choice, really. Ever. She's so much happier with you, Lottie. So lucky to have a good job right here in Strettam. At your age, too. But we won't have to sell the old place with Lottie here to keep it up, you know. Mother's so much better off in her own house with her own things, Lottie. She depends on you.

Plastic cake plate. The big bowl of potato salad. Baked beans. Okay, pin on a smile. Maybe this time will be better.

Hullo, Charles. Lisabeth. Susan. Karen. Fine. She's right over there by the big chestnut tree. Fine. Where are you putting the cakes, Agnes? Hello, Bill. Tom. Timmie. Kathy. Tony. Fine. She's right over there by the big chestnut tree. Not better this time; worse. Karen's slim brown legs and short white socks. Tom's baby, chubby and cuddly in a yellow sweater. The teen-agers, *109* like so many handsome colts. Brenda's glossy dark curls. But they're not mine. Not mine.

"Where's Lottie? Oh, there you are, sis. I've been looking for you."

"Well, here I am." She edged the cake plate in between two pies. "What's on your mind, Jerry?"

"You remember Jill's sister, Becky, don't you, Lottie? We brought her along today."

Lottie looked down into alert blue eyes. Slim shoulders, slimmer waist, a dusting of white in crisp black curls. "Becky?"

"Becky Thomas. We were both bridesmaids for Jerry and Jill, once upon a time."

"Oh, yes. You were the one in the deep rose dress. Without that fluffy rose veil, you look a little different, you know."

"Not really?"

She has a bubbly kind of smile, thought Lottie. Doesn't look like a scab covering the kind of pus and garbage that my smiles stretch across.

"Lottie will look after you today, Becky," said Jerry. "Won't you, sis?"

"Glad to." Oh, of course. Lottie looks after everybody. Are you afraid she will fall into the river, or what?

"Get her to tell you about her job if you can," continued Jerry. "She's a nurse over at Murray State Hospital, and she really has some tall tales to tell, if you can pry 'em out of her. Why not come say hello to mom, Becky, before the crowd gets any thicker? See you, sis."

"Okay." Lottie picked up a knife and started sectioning the spice cake into segments. Murray State, huh? Ordinary nursing wouldn't be so bad, but psychos in a mental hospital? No, thanks. Hello, Tess. Hello, Jill. Yeah, I'm smiling at you. But I hate you, you know, with a fancy cerise-colored hatred. Cerise, with orange trimming. You have them, and I don't have them. And I suppose I never will. Not ever.

After dinner, boisterous Charles took over as the affable emcee for quips and jests and boasts about the progress of the year, as he always did. My family. Jerry's family. Bill's family. And Charlotte? Another year without getting hitched, huh, Lottie? Or do you have something to announce?

"Oh, of course. Married twice and divorced three times."

"No handsome millionaires beating a path to your window at the bank, eh, Lottie?" asked Bill. The brothers and the cousins laughed heartily.

Oh, but of course. Sixteen handsome millionaires per square mile in Strettam. Sixteen anybodies?

"Well, now," said Charles, "there's plenty of time like always for some naps and some games. And plenty of eats here for supper, 'specially if we crank up some freezers of ice cream. 'Bout six o'clock okay for supper? Now if some of you kids want to play volleyball—"

"What's your usual program in the afternoon, Lottie?" asked Becky. "Are you a volleyball expert?"

"Not exactly," said Lottie. "Not here, anyway. They usually have some rowboats out by Memorial Day. Want to look for one?"

"There isn't too much current in the river for rowboats, then?"

"Not on this side. It's more of a lake, and they have it all marked off with buoys. You couldn't have an accident if you wanted to. Which I usually do."

Becky looked at her keenly, but talked about black locust blossoms and wild blue iris.

"I'll row," said Lottie when they climbed into the boat. "I need the exercise." She pulled with long, smooth strokes.

"You're good, you know," said Becky. "If you're that athletic, I'd think you would be gung ho for volleyball. Especially with your nephews and nieces."

"Especially not with my nephews and nieces."

"Oh?"

"You sound just like a Penny Atkinson." She laughed, part of a laugh. "No, I'm not swearing at you. Penny's a woman I work with. She's a nice enough person, but she has a habit of saying two or three sentences in one monosyllable, the way you just did."

"Oh-h-h!" They both laughed.

"You work at Murray State, did Jerry say?"

"That's right." Becky's blue eyes were carefully alert.

"Psychiatric nursing?"

"All sorts. General duty. Intensive care. And, yes, I help the psychiatrists quite a bit." Lottie rowed silently for two or three minutes. Becky dipped her fingers in the water beside the boat and waited. "Want to talk about it?" she said finally.

The oars dipped, rose, coasted. Lottie swung them up on the edge of the boat. "Not much use," she said. She looked off into the trees beside the river. "One time—one time when I was a little kid," she mused, "we went out to my grandfather's farm. He had to kill a sheep while we were there. A poor old ewe. She had been mauled by a neighbor's dog, and before Grandad found her out in the pasture the wounds were full of maggots. He didn't want me to look at her, but I did. And I was sick for three days. Sometimes, any more, I think my mind is filling up with some horrible, crawly maggots, like those were."

"Because?"

Silence. Water plopped slowly against the metal surface of the boat. Silence. "You thought I'd want to play volleyball with the kids. Like any other fond auntie. Are you a fond auntie? Well, I'm not. I didn't want nephews and nieces and cousins. I wanted children of my own." Her voice shook a little. "When I was five or six, mothering my dolls was terribly real to me. When I was nine or ten, I started baby-sitting and daydreaming about having some children of my own. In junior high and high school, I never wanted to be a career girl as the other kids seemed to. All I ever wanted was to have a home of my own and my own children."

"And a husband?"

Lottie shrugged a little under the smooth texture of her blue blouse. "I always thought marriage would be pleasant, but mostly because of the children I was dreaming about."

"You're using the past tense, you know. You *were* dreaming?"

"Well, sure. I'm thirty-nine. Mom is sixty-nine, but she'll probably live for twenty more years. And there are no men on my horizon. Not if I'd use telescopes. And you know what Strettam is like, don't you?"

"Would it help any if you would get into a kindergarten classroom instead of the bank? Or is there a children's home in the area where you could work?"

Another part of a laugh. "That would be worse. I don't just want to be around children. I want to be around my own children. You'll say I'm sick, and maybe I am, but I've gotten so I hate to see a woman walk down the street with a fleecy little bundle in her arms. I hate my relatives for the children they have. I really do. I don't want to be a secondhand mother. I want to be a mother. Yes, I still want. Present tense. Every single kid up there on the swings is such a bitterness to me, I can hardly stand it."

Becky was swishing her fingers back and forth through the water. "Unless you can have a child, you'd like for all the other women to be sterile?"

"Yes. I would. People talk about apple pie and motherhood as things that everybody praises. I don't. Since I can't have my share of it, something just destroys me when I watch other women at their mothering."

"Would adoption be a possibility?"

"I doubt it. Not in Johnson County. I've made a few inquiries, off and on, for the last ten years. Maybe I should try again, try some more places. The people I've talked with obviously thought I was insane for wanting a child without a husband. In my wilder moments, I've thought about promoting an affair long enough to get pregnant. If I were fifteen years younger, I might try it. And you may faint now if you want to."

"Thanks. But no thanks."

Lottie picked up the oars again. "So that's what I mean about the maggots," she said. "Nice and squirmy, aren't they?"

"They're not really so different from anybody else's maggots," said Becky somberly.

Lottie looked sceptical. "Which psychiatric textbook do you find that in?"

"You've given them more encouragement than some people would," said Becky, "but they're not so different. I'm not thinking of the medical textbooks right now so much as of an older and better book, perhaps."

Lottie looked even more sceptical.

"Put a new phrase in the ten commandments," Becky went on. "Make it 'Thou shalt not covet thy neighbor's children.' "

"But I *do* covet them. For about twenty increasingly horrible years, I have been coveting. I covet the children, and I envy the neighbor who has them. And I'm getting so I hate every living person while I'm at it."

"But maybe coveting his children is a symptom and not the real disease. The maggots, all right, but not the dog that bit you. Or bites you."

"What do you mean?"

"Well—" Becky's blue eyes were looking deep into the foliage along the riverbank, and far beyond the foliage. "Well, different people get into different kinds of trouble when the Center isn't at the center. But there's always trouble if the old ego goes around wailing; if self-pity kicks up its heels."

"Self-pity?" Lottie's voice had little blue flames on it. "You think I should sing the doxology because of the raw deal that life has always handed to me, I suppose?"

"That's not such a bad idea," answered Becky quietly. "Because of, or in the midst of. Seems as though the doxology and the covets usually have a way of canceling each other out."

"So you think I should make like Pollyanna? Is that what you're prescribing?"

"No, not really. I'm not the prescriber. But Grace is. Grace always is—"

After Penny hung her new beige coat on the rack and tossed her flat tapestry-fabric purse to the shelf above it on Monday, she turned to look carefully at Lottie Evans' face. "Well, how was it? As bad as you thought?"

"Worse, but also better."

"Which is to say?"
"I think I am starting to asphyxiate some maggots."
"Oh?"

George McPherson

It amused them, that night, to squat in a circle in the graveled parking lot up at St. Mark's, like a pack of huge and ghostly wolves. Cigar-smoking wolves at that. It pleased Lechery to have three bushy tails, and it pleased Pride to wear an immense satin top hat perched over his long gray ears. It amused them to utter all their vowels in eerie wolf-howl and wolf-growl tones.

"Disgusting building, anyway," said Sloth as the smoke of their cigars drifted up around the shingled eaves of St. Mark's.

"Abso-o-o-o-lu-u-tely," howl-growled the other six.

"Always has been a menace, but it's getting worse," said Anger.

"Wo-o-ooorse," agreed the others.

"That verminous rector," said Pride. "He's a disgusting nuisance."

"Nu-u-u-uisance."

"We keep saying that," said Lechery. "Why don't we do something about him? Something really juicy and jolly."

Growls.

"Go ahead, Lech," said Pride. "You're the one. Right now he's braced against me, and you know he's never given Sloth the time of day. Nor Gluttony, either—"

"Nor me either," said Lechery. "But it could be mighty good sport for one of us to trip him up." His long wolf tongue licked against the edges of his long wolf lips, and he sniffed at the breeze. "Rector," he rumbled in his throat, "Rector, I think I smell your liver and lights."

ii.

"Another roll, George?"

"No, thanks. Well, yes, maybe I will. I burned a lot of calories on the hedge this afternoon."

"George, don't you think you ought to talk with the finance committee again? You're supposed to be the rector. You're not supposed to be the rector-cum-janitor-cum-hedge-trimmer-cum everything else."

"Well, doing the hedge is good for my waistline, Marge. I do wish we could get some secretarial help, though. If I could have someone to do the parish newsletter—and someone to type up some revised copies of my sermons, the whole file of them. I really would like to work up a book of Lenten meditations sometime from that series last year. Think I could?"

"Of course you could. You ought to. And soon. George, that reminds me. Maybe I have a secretarial possibility that the finance committee would consider. Something just now clicked at the back of my mind that I heard about when I was getting groceries this morning."

"Tell me more. You found some crisp green Strettam gossip among Mr. Wildeman's crisp green vegetables?"

She made a wry face. "His vegetables were no crisper than usual, unfortunately. Not gossip, but Mrs. Mason was groaning a little about her Terri, while she tried to find things Terri would eat."

"Terri?"

"Yes, you know. Christened Dorothy. Where she got the nickname, I don't know. Anyway, Terri came home several weeks ago, on doctor's orders. A lung problem or something. I didn't ask for a full diagnosis."

"You're a woman after my own heart, Mrs. McPherson."

"And you're interrupting me, Mr. McPherson. Anyway, Terri was supposed to have complete rest: Absolute and complete. But she's feeling pretty well now, and she's getting horribly restless, Mrs. Mason says. But the doctors won't hear of her going back to work yet."

"The doctors?"

"Yes. Dr. Bailey has been checking her progress, and he has been in touch with Terri's own doctor."

McPherson finished his pie and put down his fork. "Let's see. Where does she work? Keyesport?"

"No, somewhere a lot more remote, but I don't remember where. Dallas or Miami or St. Louis or Denver—I'm not sure. It took a bit of doing to fly her home when she got sick."

"I suppose. Now what is the point of this so far as our finance committee? What's Hecuba to me?"

"Hecuba? Her name's Terri."

"Wrong, you're wrong, my dear and lovely wife. By your own assertion, her name is Dorothy."

Marge smiled. "Then Hecuba just strolled in from a Shake-speare play, I suppose? Or something else you've been reading?"

"Straight from Hamlet, my dear!" George struck an attitude, hand on his heart and eyes rolling toward the ceiling. "O! what a rogue and peasant slave am I. And, as I was saying, what's Hecuba to me?"

Marge smiled again. "Well, I just wondered. If some part-time work were available here in Strettam, Dr. Bailey might let Terri start with that for a while before she's ready to go back to her own job."

"Sounds logical. She's a secretary?"

"Yes, and I gather a pretty good one. Executive secretary for the president of a clothing factory, or something like that."

"Should be able to organize files and copy old sermons then? Well, maybe I'd better talk with McNair and see what the finance committee would authorize."

iii.

Dear Mona,

Thanks for your note. I needed it. I'm absolutely perishing in this horrible, dinky town. Should've gone to Florida or California for the stupid recuperation bit. I honestly didn't remember what a dismal and petty place old Strettam is. When you're still in high school everything looks different. And by the time Dr. Knight got through prodding me, I didn't have much zingo left to make decent plans for a long vacation, did I? I'm still glad you were such a doll about reservations and all, Mona. Thanks a lot.

Here's a check for my part of the rent. Could you send me my green silk pajamas? Third drawer, right side. And my quilted housecoat, the white one? Thanks. Luv to the garbage men, and take care.

Terri

iv.

Dear Mona,

Thanks for the package. You *are* a doll. Things are looking up. Knight and Bailey—the local medicine man is a Bailey; tall and very dark and sort of arrogant. Looks foreign. I don't like him much, but he seems to know a thermometer from a stethoscope, and all that. You should see his office. Or maybe you shouldn't. It's not even two by four. Two by three. With the quaintest old farm journals on the magazine rack.

Where was I? Oh, yes. Knight and Bailey still won't let me set a time to come back to work, but they have given me a faint green light about working part-time.

But, yes, darling. For one of the local yokels. On the twenty-fourth floor of the Prudential Building. Ha. Actually, you won't believe it, but I guess I'm going to do some Girl Friday work for a preacher here. Cheers. Mom says he's Ivy League and handsome, but mom's judgment is not to be relied upon.

I wish you'd call Jackie or Teresa and sound them out a little about how things are going at Woodford, Inc. If you can. I don't really want Mr. Woodford to get along too well without me. See you.

Terri

v.

yes of course mr mcpherson in triplicate very my kind of man strong hands like tom had no i'm accustomed to an electric typewriter i'm accustomed to

but nice face thin face eyes ears nose eyebrows and yes in the box with the manila folders

should have worn better perfume and tomorrow other brassiere and yellow sheath and

but i will but you don't wife oh well where here car and my new nylon slip and to touch his hand like dry ice along the epidermis and do you want me to double-space it and do you want me and

vi.

"Oh, quite efficient. She's a fast typist, certainly. I'm going to have to make out a chart of my own private symbols. You know, I have never tried to make anything I've written intelligible to anyone except myself. I've always written an 'H' for 'history' and 'Xn' for 'Christian' and so on. Pretty confusing to a typist."

"More sherbet, George?"

"No, thanks."

"What sort of a person is she? As a person?"

"Must be about twenty-four. Quiet. She didn't say much except to ask about whether to double-space, and so on."

"And?"

"Oh, she has the usual number of eyes and ears. Looks like her mother. Or as her mother must have looked thirty years ago. Or—" He looked thoughtful and grinned. "Or as her mother would have looked thirty years ago if someone had taken her thirty-years-ago mother to a space age beauty shop. How's that?"

"Hard to imagine. It's hard to imagine Mrs. Mason ever being slim and young, isn't it? But she must have been."

"Who knows? Maybe she was even an infant once, in her younger years."

Marge laughed. "You do have an imagination, George. Know what? I'm glad I married you."

"Miss Mason—"

She looked up from the box of file cards and smiled faintly. "My other employer calls me Terri," she said. "If you'd prefer—" Two small lines deepened between his dark eyebrows. "I was about to say, Miss Mason," he said, "that if you were a few years younger I would telephone your mother about an appropriate skirt length for a church secretary. As it is, I presume your mother is no longer responsible for your wardrobe."

"She hasn't been for years. She certainly isn't now." Another smile, faint and derisive. "My regular employer likes his staff to look up-to-date. In fact, Mr. Woodford particularly commended this dress when I first got it."

"Then at the risk of judging a fellow-mortal, I might say that Mr. Woodford is probably something of a fool, or a lecher, or both."

"Indeed!" Another faint smile. "Well, while I'm here, I shall endeavor to please you, Mr. McPherson. In every way." An ironic edge touched her voice. "Though I'm not sure I can. I don't have much of a wardrobe here."

"Then buy a beach towel down at Dacey's and pin it around you," he said. "Now about this material on Isaiah—"

"Shall I bring a ruler so you can check me over every afternoon?" she asked innocently. "Oh, on these file cards. Do you want your topic headings typed in capitals throughout? Like this one?" She handed him a card, being careful to let her hand brush against his.

organ prelude ready yes Bible open on the lectern yes choir yes announcement bulletin ready beside the Bible yes neat and professional mimeographing for a change finance committee hope mr mcnair notices notices

too much to pay but it's not for very long but long sleek knees crossed yes holy holy holy dark pews

dear God she's here this morning didn't think she'd ever come dress green like fresh grass grass brass what did donne say my flesh is stuff not brass fresh curve of her breasts edge of her cheeks and with Your spirit let us pray like lost sheep too much the devices of our own hearts

shall i tell her not to come to work any more shall i flesh not brass the anthem will be does she know i know she's here but soon back to her other job not soon enough too soon too soon just one time to hold that body close no one would ever know fool fool fool let us hear the words of st paul my God my God how can i speak this morning with her sitting there lusting for my body but sermon in full manuscript can read it like an actor have done the things we ought not to have done not yet i haven't not yet now look in front pew at marge marge marge i love you truly truly dear

no one would ever know nice headlines in the keyesport paper strettam rector has affair with temporary secretary married man wife marge and three children

in my car up on the strettam woods road above town or for a drive with her down the metonic or

my God my God why hast Thou forsaken me

let us pray pray pray he that eateth and drinketh unworthily so let us blaspheme but let us pray but

amen

now unto Him that is able

amen

ix.

"George, darling—"

"Yes, Marge?"

"I've asked you three times if you want more coffee. Twice before I put the children down for their naps, and once since. Are you coming down with something?" She cupped her hand against his forehead. "Could be a touch of fever. Shall I get the thermometer?"

"No, dear. Do pour me some more coffee, though. Please. I know without the thermometer to tell me so that my head is throbbing."

"Is it, dear? I wondered, all during church. You seemed so preoccupied. And your sermon—"

"Yes?"

"You did better when we were in seminary, darling. When you were in seminary."

"Was it that bad?"

"Well, other people seemed to be impressed. But I'm getting hard to impress, darling. You've trained me to expect a lot from you."

He put down his coffee cup. "Sorry, my mind was off on a wild goose chase just then, I guess. What did you just say, Marge?"

"I said you've trained me to expect a lot from you. You have, you know. Look, it's a gorgeous day. Why don't you take the dog and go for a long hike up in the woods?"

"I was thinking about doing that very thing. Only not with Xerxes. Keep him here for the youngsters to play with when they wake up. I'll just take my own throbbing head. And my heart and soul and body."

"That's quite a crowd! Well, you'll be in good company. All of you."

He kissed her lightly. "Thanks, darling, for that vote of confidence."

x.

could go back to the church to pray but He's here too log for an altar rail if i make my bed in hell behold Thou art there

to the chief musician a psalm of david wash me thoroughly from mine iniquity and cleanse me from my sin thoroughly thoroughly thoroughly a psalm of david after he had gone in to bathsheba and cleanse me from my sin

my stuff is flesh not brass is flesh is flesh and make not provision for the flesh to fulfill the lusts thereof

ouch

hardness in this log for the hardness of your hearts moses because of the hardness of your hearts but I say unto you that whosoever looketh on a woman to lust after her hath committed adultery with her already in his heart

o God o God o God o God

singing birds singing leaves sweet stench of rotten leaves rotten rotten

as filthy rags

a clean heart o God and renew a right spirit

o God

high and lifted up and His train filled the temple undone undone a man of unclean lips lips thoughts blood mansex fingers and i dwell in the midst of a people of unclean lips

lips minds tv jokes hollywood everyone is doing it the new morality love love love if you really love a person a people of unclean lips

high and lifted up

Jehovah Jahweh I AM THAT I AM and God said unto moses taken away

and thine iniquity is taken away and thy sin is purged taken away with hyssop and i shall be clean

and thy sin purged

xi.

"You still look a little ghastly, if I may say so," said Mona. "Are you quite sure you should be back here?"

"Oh, quite sure. Airports always did wear me out, and today was rather worse—"

"Look. Climb into bed, and I'll bring you some supper on a tray. Okay? I thought about having some people in, but you don't quite look ready for the party bit."

"Well, a tray does sound better. Thanks. Any mail for me?"

"Naturally. Bills, especially. Mail here on your dresser. A couple of phone numbers here on the memo pad for you to call, but don't be in a hurry."

"Okay. M-m-m-m. It's good to be back in my own world, Mona."

"Even to leave that Ivy League number you wrote about two or three times?"

"Especially to leave that Ivy League number. He was an odd fish, Mona. Really an odd fish. Why are you smiling like that?"

"Just remembering a lecture I heard at the City Galleries last week; this fella from Oxford made quite a point of the fish being a symbol of the Christians, in the good old days of the catacombs and the lions. Was Mr. Ivy League a Christian symbol in the flesh?"

"Beats me. At first he was very cool, and then he was definitely warming up a little. And then—"

"Yes?"

"Something came over him. I don't know what. It was—well, like having a thin sheet of flame around him all the time—that would have scorched me, but good, if I tried to walk through it."

"You mean he was in a living purgatory, sort of?"

"No, not that. He was happy enough. Almost sparkly. But sparkly through plexiglass, if you know what I mean."

"I haven't the faintest notion. Sounds pretty weird to me. But look, cuddle down on your pillow, and I'll bring you a tray, like I said I would."

Dr. Harry Knightley

"Are you going to be in your study all morning, Tom?" asked Catherine, moving a dustcloth lightly across the piano edges.

"Probably, once I get there." He glanced at the clock on the mantel. "I'd better take these letters to the post office first, though; I see Mr. Layton's halfway down the block, so I've missed him. Betty, why don't you see if he left us anything interesting?"

Betty put down her book and loped across the room. She gets more like a young giraffe every day that she lives, thought Tom. Hope she stops soon. When she gets into her teens, she will.

"Nothing very neat," said Betty. "Three more book catalogs. You sure do get a lot of book catalogs, daddy. Oh, and here's a letter for you." She looked at the return address and groaned. "From Horrible Harry. Oh, mother, don't tell me he's going to come and stay with us again."

"From whom?" asked Tom.

"Knightley the Frightley," said Betty, tossing the letter to the desk where Tom was affixing stamps.

"Betty!" Mrs. Williams looked grim.

"Mother, I don't care. He is a horrible person, and I'd be just as glad if I never, ever see him again."

"Well, suppose you go look after Trixie's breakfast, anyway," said Mrs. Williams. Betty amble-bounced toward the backyard. Mrs. Williams put down her dustcloth and waited for Tom to open the letter.

"You're as apprehensive as Betty is," he smiled as he picked up a copper letter-opener.

"With more reason than Betty has, though."

He scanned the page and whistled a few notes from "Auld Lang Syne." "He's coming, Catherine. On the twenty-ninth. To be here three or four days and visit other men from here."

"From here? Oh, Tom. From our house, he means?"

"He certainly means. He 'trusts that this will not be an inconvenience to you and to your gracious wife, whom I look forward to greeting again.' You were too good a hostess last time, sweetheart."

"I wish it hadn't come this morning! I'm supposed to give devotions for a women's circle meeting this afternoon, and now I'll feel very undevotional, I must say. I'll be a piece of sounding brass."

"Well, I guess we'll just have to make the best of it. He is our D. S., darling."

"Yes. He certainly is." Catherine pushed dark hair back from her eyes. She looked tired and apprehensive.

"Well, I'd better get on down to the study, anyway," Tom said. "Now don't fret all day. He's neither a lion nor a bear."

"No, but I'm afraid Betty's impudent nickname has more than a little truth in it."

Tom picked up his letters. "What did she call him?"

"Knightley the Frightley."

After dinner that evening Tom built a fire in the fireplace and sat leafing through a stack of recent magazines. From time to time he glanced over at Catherine, whose knitting dropped often to her lap.

"Okay, Betty, off with the TV," Tom said toward the family room alcove. "Homework."

"Okay." She flicked the knob. "Daddy, why do we have to have that man stay here? Couldn't he stay out at Willefords or at a motel someplace?"

"Now, would that be courteous to the only District Superintendent we have?"

"Well, thank goodness he is the only one. Imagine having two or three like him around. Shudder!" Betty stretched and then amble-loped to her own room.

"The eagerness of this home to extend hospitality is overwhelming," said Tom dryly.

"Hospitality, yes," said Catherine. "Hospitality to Dr. Harry Knightley, I'm not so sure about."

Tom crossed his hands behind his head and leaned back in his leather chair. "In a nutshell, why do you dislike Dr. Knightley so much, Catherine?"

"Well, why does everyone? Why do you?"

"Don't evade, now. I'm trying to sort out my own feelings about the man. You're pretty sensitive about human relationships; always have been, since we were in college. I've been meaning to quiz you about your very adverse response to his last visit. It was adverse, you know. Now precisely why?"

"Well—" She put down needles and yellow yarn and folded

a half-finished sleeve. "He was so—so—pompous. No, pompous isn't quite the word. Dictatorial? Self-satisfied? So proud of himself. So sure that he has the right answer to everything in the world."

"And suppose he has?"

"Oh, Tom!" She unfolded the sleeve and folded it more tightly. "No, it isn't whether he's right or not; it's his—well, his grim ego. The way he—he—oh, I don't know; the way he intrudes his rightness. Like an old buffalo turned loose in somebody's rose garden. He's—Tom, I think he's a proud, proud man. And his pride hurts people like me when we bump against it. Is that wrong of me?"

Tom picked up the poker and adjusted glowing logs. "Pain has a way of hurting," he said somberly. Then he chuckled a little. "I wouldn't have thought of calling him a buffalo," he said. "But that's rather good. I'd have said his innards must be made of granite. There is a hardness in the man. I've noticed it in conferences and committees ever since we moved here, but of course we feel it more now that he's the D. S."

"A hardness inside," said Catherine. She unfolded the sleeve again and started looping yarn around long plastic needles. "Yes, that's it. A proud hardness. After he was here in September, I kept thinking, over and over, of how different I felt about Bishop Edmundson's visit. He was so great and good; you just felt it was a privilege to be under the same roof with him. Like having an Isaiah or a St. John present in the flesh. But there was something—oh, sort of gentle and teachable about him—"

"You wouldn't say Dr. Knightley is teachable?"

She was quiet for a long moment, and Tom looked up from the fire to see her reaching into her blouse pocket for a Kleenex. "He doesn't want to be taught," she said. "He knows it all already. And he doesn't want any helping hands reached out to him either. It would show that he's weak."

"You sound bitter, darling. Was he—"

"Curt and haughty. In a way that hurt more than I could really understand. I cried off and on for two days after he left."

"Why didn't you say so then?"

"Oh, I didn't want to bother you. And I was angry with myself for being so petty. There wasn't much I could really put a finger on. I had tried and tried to be what the books call 'the gracious lady of the manse' all weekend, and to develop some empathy for his papal majesty. I'd thought and prayed a good bit about my resentment of him; I really had. Well, just before he left I said, quite sincerely, that I would be praying for him and his responsibilities as he went on his way—"

"And?"

"And he sort of stiffened, in a way that surprised me, and said coldly that men ought always to pray and not to faint. And—" She hesitated and wadded the sleeve she had been knitting into a tight ball, kneading it like dough.

"And?"

"And he made a sort of disparaging remark about you, Tom, and actually intimated that I'd better spend my praying time in praying for your work rather than his."

Tom laughed, a cheerful and resounding laugh. "And that bothered you?"

"Yes. Very much. More than I could figure out. I felt like a third grader who had offered to shake hands with an adult and had been slapped with a ruler instead. He acted as though it would hurt his image of himself to admit being human and vulnerable and 'standin' in the need of prayer.' As though it were his prerogative to give out encouragement, but never, never to receive any.

"Now Bishop Edmundson—" She smoothed the yellow sleeve, looped the yarn, took several stitches. "Grandmother used to say that comparisons are odious, but sometimes they help me to figure things out. Bishop Edmundson would have thanked me, wouldn't he? Genuinely and sweetly. Probably he'd have sat right down at the kitchen table and asked me to say a little prayer right then and there before he drove away."

"Yes,. I imagine so. Shall I put another log on?"

"Oh, yes. It's a lovely bed of coals you have there, Tom."

"I'll have to bring another one in from the bin. Back in a minute." He returned, carrying a thick piece of birch. "Maybe it's a kind of hardening of the arteries," he said. "Not physical arteries. From what the other fellows in the conference say, Knightley has always been super-sure of his own theological rightness, and nobody could make him change his mind on prudentials. From that it has apparently moved on into being a bigger and bigger sureness of his own personal rightness in everything. His decisions just have to be right, and his judgment. And he *is* right a good share of the time, you know. He's a powerful preacher and a dynamic organizer. He's done a lot for the conference."

"Yes, I'm sure he has," Catherine said tonelessly. The needles moved quietly, and she shook another length of yarn free from the skein.

"Now what are you thinking about?" asked Tom finally.

"One thing you just said. His decisions just have to be right. I think—"

"Yes?"

"I think his self-rightness or ego or pride or whatever you want to call it has a family resemblance to the attitudes of a Hitler or a Mussolini."

"And what the old Greeks called 'hubris'? But that's strong language, Cathy."

"I know it is. And heaven knows he isn't responsible to me for his sins, past, present, or future, whatever they may be. But I was thinking of the evening in September when we had a little reception here for all of the preachers from the area who could drive over. Remember?"

"Yes. The night he gave Bob Woodford such a bad time."

"Exactly. After he got started telling Bob what was wrong with his sermons and his youth program and his parsonage and everything else, I kept trying to divert him by passing more refreshments or starting new topics of general conversation, but he kept coming back and yakking at Bob. Like—like a vulture coming back to a corpse."

"Bob is a pretty lively corpse."

"Oh, I know. At one point I even tried to suggest tactfully that Dr. Knightley take Bob into your study to confer with him, but Knightley couldn't be bothered. He almost seemed sadistic —as though he enjoyed making Bob squirm. Didn't he? I stayed awake that night thinking about him. It really troubled me. And the more I thought, the more I decided that it gave him a— well, a proud sense of power to chew away on poor Bob, and it gave him more of a proud sense of power to chew away there in the living room where he had an audience than in the study."

"Maybe you're right, darling. In fact, I think you are." Tom yawned. "Well, in any case, he's coming back to see us. On the twenty-ninth."

"Yes. And I'd better look up some verses on counting it all joy when you fall into divers temptations, and so on. He's really not so bad when you compare him with what the first century martyrs faced, I guess." She turned the sleeve over and held it up to inspect the nubby surface. "Oh, there's the phone."

"I'll get it," said Betty's muffled voice. Her door opened with a rush, and she loped to the kitchen extension. "For you, dad. Long distance. Nuts. Nuts. I thought it might be Diana."

Tom picked up the living room telephone. "Hello. . . . This is he. Why, yes, Dr. Knightley." He winked at Catherine, who sat rigid in her rocker. "Yes, I had your letter; it came this morning. . . . I see. . . . I see. . . . Then you aren't ready at the moment to reschedule? . . . Yes, of course. . . . No, quite all right. . . . Don't mention it. . . . All right, we'll wait to hear from you."

"He isn't coming?"

"He isn't coming. Something very odd. I don't know what to make of it. He just says there are some personal matters he must attend to, but he sounded shaken. Not like himself."

"Then he must have had a heart attack, at least. Oh, Tom, if he's in some kind of trouble, and we've been sitting here dissecting him like a frog in a zoology lab—"

He touched her shoulder lightly. "Don't collect guilt pangs, Cathy. We'd like to help the man. God knows we'd like to help him. And usually you can do more to help cure a disease if you know the nature of the disease."

"Does he have children? A son in the army or anything like that? Maybe there has been some bad news."

"Well, don't fret about it. Where did you put the evening paper? I haven't even looked at the headlines yet."

He told her not to fret, but he himself fretted for two days. He worked on sermons and answered correspondence, read parts of two new books, called on Charlie Wright when Charlie summoned him. But at the back of his mind he kept hearing the odd tension in Dr. Knightley's voice. Almost a brokenness.

"I think I'm going to Princeville this afternoon," he told Catherine at lunch on Thursday. "I told the committee I would get some quotations on new carpeting for the sanctuary. Maybe I'll swing on over to Cornwall and see if I can make a few tactful inquiries. I hope tactful."

"You couldn't do anything else, being you," she said. "You think there's something really wrong?"

"Could be."

"And that maybe you could give him a hand, whether he wants it or not?"

"Could be."

"Well, then, Tom, why don't you telephone Chuck Birkentree? Isn't he still at Wesley Memorial in Cornwall?"

"That's right. Good thought, Catherine. Maybe I will. In fact, maybe I'll call now, before I leave for Princeville. Where's my conference directory?"

"On your desk, isn't it?" Catherine started rinsing lunch dishes. She heard his voice in the living room and then a silence. A longer silence. "Was Chuck there?" she asked finally.

Tom came slowly to the kitchen door. "Yes, he was there. Very much so. Maybe it's both better and worse than it might be."

"Meaning?"

"Knightley is in trouble with the law."

"With the law!"

Tom picked up a dishtowel. "Thought I'd startle you. I wish I had a picture of your face right then, sweetheart. It would be one for the archives."

"Don't joke, Tom. Or is it really not serious?"

"As I said, could be better and could be worse. He was in Millerton on Tuesday morning and somehow made a wrong turn and started driving down a one-way street."

"Well, anybody could do that."

"That isn't all. He was also driving fairly fast down this one-way street and managed to have a head-on collision—"

"Oh, Tom! Was anyone—"

"Again, could have been worse. The other driver is in the hospital, and Knightley's insurance company is giving him a rough time. But wait until you hear this, my beautiful and devoted Catherine—"

"Admire me later!" she said with both pleasure and annoyance. "And save the kisses until later, too. Oh, Tom, stop! Tell the rest of it!"

"Well, it's just that Dr. Knightley must have given a rather crashing display of being—what did Betty call him?—of being Knightley the Frightley. Apparently he lectured the policeman and said the street wasn't properly marked and acted like injured royalty, rather than like a driver who had just goofed. And thereby he got himself charged with resisting an officer, or whatever they call it. And he got his picture in the Millerton evening paper. I'm surprised somebody hasn't telephoned me before now."

"Oh, Tom! Can you imagine what he feels like inside?" She patted the edges of the sink with a sponge and took the dishtowel from Tom's hands. "He can't bend to admit he's wrong or imperfect about anything. And then to have all of Millerton snickering about him. At least it didn't get picked up by the Keyesport paper."

"I'm surprised it didn't."

"So am I." She smoothed dishtowels across a metal rack. "Now what happens next?"

"There's a hearing of some sort tomorrow. Chuck says he supposes it will be a short suspended sentence or a fine. Can't amount to much. But Knightley himself—no, I really can't imagine what he feels like inside."

"If he knew how to bend with the wind," Catherine mused. "Most of us can say, 'Well, sure, I'm wrong this time. Sorry about that.' But he's too proud. He doesn't know how to be wrong about anything."

"Think I should still go by Cornwall?" asked Tom, glancing at his watch. "Think he'd rather lick his wounds by himself? Or would it be of any help to him if I dropped by?"

"I don't know, Tom. Why don't you pray about it as you drive to Princeville and see what impulse you have later on?"

"As usual, you speak wise words." He grinned. "Now may I call you my beautiful and devoted Catherine? And now may I kiss you?"

"Please do."

Three hours later Tom braked at the highway intersection. Back to Strettam? Does the old fellow need me or want me at all? A Christian brother as well as a superintendent. He flicked his turn indicator and took the Cornwall road. Maybe I won't mention this traffic court bit at all, unless he does. Maybe I'll just ask his comment on the building committee's plans for improving our sanctuary. If he's in.

They're away, Tom told himself minutes later. House looks closed. Blinds pulled upstairs. Well, give it a try.

He rang and heard a buzzer sound. Again. Again. Well, I tried anyway. He turned, saw the living room draperies move a little, and then heard heavy footsteps.

"Williams. Come in, won't you?" Knightley turned on living room lights. "Have a chair."

Ten years older, thought Tom. Hasn't been sleeping much. Face looks soggy. Like a King Saul when the morose moods were upon him. And am I a David, then, come to play upon my harp? Or to dodge a javelin?

"Good of you to stop by," Dr. Knightley said. "You've heard, I suppose, that I've been undergoing some rather unpleasant persecutions."

Persecutions? "I've heard a little, sir."

"You didn't see the attack in the Millerton *Journal?*"

Attack? My word and honor. "No, sir, I didn't."

"Very unpleasant. But I will say I have never felt a deeper bond of kinship with St. Paul. I haven't suffered shipwreck nor spent a night and a day in the deep—if you are speaking of the literal ocean deeps—but I feel as though I have been beaten with rods, I assure you."

"I know you must."

Dr. Knightley looked at him stonily, and Tom wondered for a moment if he had been taking too many sedatives. "You don't know, Williams," he said harshly. "Nobody knows—"

130   Tom waited.

"And I don't mean just the ignorance of the traffic courts nor the impertinence of the *Journal*," said Knightley.

He does look like a King Saul in torment, thought Tom. If he had a javelin handy, I'd move. What else then?

Knightley sighed. "Be discreet about where you mention it, my boy, but a much worse court action has been instigated against me." He paused. "In fact, the agitation concomitant upon this—this other matter was no doubt the reason for—for the beginning of the unpleasantness in Millerton on Tuesday."

He said on the phone that he had personal matters to attend to. His hand is shaking like a leaf as he keeps picking up that paperweight and putting it down again. A much worse court action?

"The fact is, Williams," Dr. Knightley went on, "I don't like to speak of it, and I won't often, believe me, but Mrs. Knightley has just filed for a divorce."

Tom felt as though his chair had lurched under him. Oh. That's why the blinds are drawn in some of the rooms upstairs. Why she hasn't been in to say hello. I thought the house was oddly quiet. She's already left him then. Quiet little woman with a complexion like ivory. Always seemed so devoted to him.

"I'm sorry, sir," he said quietly. "It must be very difficult for you."

"Like St. Paul's forty stripes save one, I'm sure," said Knightley grimly. "She has gone to stay with her sister in Minnesota for a time. I don't know what her—her arrangements will be. There is no other man involved." He spoke as though the words discolored his throat. "There is some small comfort to me in that. But she is charging mental cruelty, which is hardly more honorable to herself or to me."

"Will you wish to contest the proceedings?"

Knightley put back on the end table a small bronze lion he had been fingering. "I am still conferring with legal counsel," he said. "You will be discreet in mentioning this, my boy? I have spoken only with my lawyer since Doris left on Monday."

"On Monday just past?"

"Yes. A very gloomy and stormy day, as you may recall. I had been away for the weekend and returned at lunchtime on Monday to find that she had been gone since early that morning. She left me a rather harsh letter. In fact, I may say it was a *very* harsh letter." He smiled bitterly. "St. Paul spoke of his perils by his own countrymen and among false brethren," he said. "But Paul didn't know anything about perils from a wife."

"And you had been married for—for quite some time?"

"For quite some time, yes. Thirty-two years. Well, we'll talk   *131* on more sanguine topics when I see you again, Williams. It was good of you to drop by."

But you want me to go now, before you have an impulse to fling a javelin—or to fling that bronze lion at me? Shall I offer to pray with you? If we could both just fling ourselves down on our knees by your davenport and tell Deity about this mental cruelty you've shown to her. Shall I put an arm around those shoulders? King Saul—

"Good-by, Williams," Dr. Knightley was saying decisively. "I'm afraid I have an appointment downtown in a few minutes. I'll write to you soon about rescheduling that trip to Strettam. Or I'll call you, if I find that my plans move very quickly. Good afternoon."

Tom climbed back into the green Pontiac, turned the ignition key, and looked back at the windows with their drawn blinds; at the shrubbery with its edging of snow; at small icicles clinging to the eaves. Worse than I thought. Much, much worse. For thirty-two years she has been the buffer then. As he has become more rigidly right all the time, she has had to bend and bend and bend. Until she has broken. And he has broken, too, but he doesn't know how deep the crevasses are inside himself.

Three weeks later Tom came up the back stairs two at a time. "Don't hurry so fast," Catherine chided him. "There's still ice on the walk, isn't there?"

"I'm safe," he said. "Are you? Sorry I couldn't be here to see him off. People choose awfully awkward times to get sick and to want a preacher desperately."

"Is Mr. Wright so very ill?"

"Not so very. But don't evade, woman. Did this visit leave you as shaken as the other one did?"

"Not as shaken. I knew more what to expect. And I kept feeling such pity for him. I said he was like a buffalo in somebody's rose garden, remember? Well, this time I kept thinking of an old lion that can't roar and can't chew up his meat but keeps trying to and pretending."

"He didn't ever let you touch the sore places of his soul with your gentle fingers, Catherine?"

"No. And I tried. I really did." She smiled sadly. "Do you know, the very last minute was like a replay. I snatched my courage by both its ears and tried to tell him that I would be praying for him. And he said the very same thing he said before, that men ought always to pray and not to faint. And then he hoped we'll get a lot more accomplished for the Kingdom before he comes back again. You'd have thought he was St. Michael himself on an inspection tour. Or Lucifer. Wasn't he the archangel whose pride pulled him right down from the heights?"

"Well, that's the way John Milton told it, anyway. Darling, you'd better pray for Knightley anyway, whether he begs you to or not. I don't know when I've ever been sadder. He'll never be a D. S. again after this year ends."

"Oh, Tom. I hadn't thought of that. They won't put him back in, will they?"

"I can't imagine it. And no pastorate will want him now. I don't know what's ahead for him. But I hope there's a good hot lunch ahead for me. May I have it now, O thou soul of my soul and far above rubies?"

"Tom, you goon!"

"Now, is that a nice word to call your adoring husband?"

"Not very." She laughed. "That's why I used it. I'm glad you're so teasable, Tom."

"Teasable, and very fallible. Wait till I tell you the stupid thing I said to Marian Willeford this morning."

"He's fallible, and he admits it," she said, pouring tomato soup into waiting bowls. "For which let us sing the doxology."

Nellie Gaspereaux

One of the frequent recreations of the Seven Deadlies is to designate a current dishonor roll. Their epithets are profuse and florid as they name over their individual mortals who are currently most intractable. Often their rages overlap. On any given day, Anger and Avarice may deride the same man, or Lechery and Pride may rail against the same pretty widow. Envy and Avarice often agree, and their combined adjectives can be lurid indeed.

Some cooperative Strettam mortals are never mentioned at all during these ribald jibes; others are named over and over with venom and disgust. Sloth is inclined to come back to one name so often that the other six mock at him for his repetitiveness. But their mockery does not annoy him nearly as much as Nellie Gaspereaux annoys him.

The frenzy she provokes in him is one of the superb and unknown ironies of Strettam. If a census were to be taken and every person in Johnson County were asked to nominate people who could be expected to please Sloth either most or least, no citizen would think of writing Nellie Gaspereaux's name on the ballot. Nor would Nellie herself, though she couldn't write any name in ways that would be very legible to the census takers.

Actually most people in Johnson County and in Strettam itself hardly know that Nellie is still living, and still living in Strettam. If her name is mentioned to some of the older residents, they may look puzzled and talk about the accident and wonder whether she didn't die a good ten years ago.

Fourteen years ago everyone in Strettam knew Nellie. Then she was John Gaspereaux's young wife, comely and vivacious. She was Judge and Mrs. Herriott's daughter. She was the local artist with roses and tuberous begonias. She was the organizer whom other people turned to when vague moods suggested skating on the Metonic in January or blackberrying on the far slopes of Strettam Hill in early August or a group trip to Keyesport for shopping at any season. Or for concerts.

It was a concert trip that caused the people of Strettam to

mention Nellie with shock, and then with pitying sadness, and then with uncertain forgetfulness. She and John and the Herriotts drove over sleet-slick roads to hear a traveling choir. They were merry as they drove to Keyesport, in spite of the roads. As they returned they were in even brighter spirits, and Nellie hummed bits of the music they had just heard. Ten miles south of Strettam, where the Keyesport road then turned to follow the Metonic River, John turned a trifle faster than he intended and turned onto a pavement that was a glassy pond of ice. The Chevrolet skidded. John struggled with the steering wheel and felt himself oozing perspiration as though all his skin had suddenly started leaking. Nellie pushed stiff fingers against her lips, hard, to keep from screaming. In the back seat, Mrs. Herriott clasped the judge's hand and he gripped back. Then the car had whirled completely around and was in the wrong lane and was being pursued by a thundering transport truck.

Nellie glanced through the back window and saw the big truck and thought that it looked like a mastodon hunting down a squirrel. And she inside the squirrel. Then screeching noises and pain like fire and blackness. And other noises and other pain, like worse fire, and darker blackness.

She was in the hospital in Keyesport for seven months. When she first regained consciousness, they told her about the triple funeral and showed her clippings from the papers. She nodded. She could still do that. The paralysis was not quite total. They told her that her brother Gilbert had come back from New York for the funeral and had come again several times to see about her. She nodded.

When he came again, she noticed streaks of gray over his ears where gray had never been before, but she didn't try to tell him so. Whole sentences, sentences the listener was not expecting, were beyond her. Monosyllables usually succeeded.

"Well, Nellie," he said. "I'm glad you're awake this time."

She nodded and produced part of a smile.

"They probably told you I've been here several times?" She nodded again. He chatted nervously on random topics, but soon put them aside. "I've made a lot of inquiries, Nellie, about your further care," he said. "I didn't want to go ahead without your okay, since the doctors have kept saying they hoped you would eventually be fully conscious and aware."

"Yes," she said. But it came out, and not easily, as "aye-uh-ss."

"There are various state hospital arrangements that might be made," he went on, "but any state hospital is so—well, so institutional. It has to be. I wonder if you wouldn't be better off at Strettam. I've been over to talk with our cousins, you know, the *135*

Cannicott girls, and they are ready to make their guest room into a permanent hospital room for you. They'll hire a woman to help as a practical nurse. Do you think it might work?"

She looked at him so intently that he knew questions were forming which her tongue could hardly shape.

"I'll try to think what you want to know most," he said. "The doctors approve, yes. You should be here for a while more, but they don't expect any major changes now. You'll need almost total care, but it won't have to be from trained nurses. About expense: The insurance was generous, all the way around. We can invest your share of dad's estate in a way that will give steady income to pay the Cannicott girls. And of course I'll help out myself if it's ever necessary. All right?"

"All right," she said. Or almost said.

But it was not all right.

When the doctors talked to her with professional cheer, when the doctors released her from Keyesport, when the ambulance moved her to Strettam, when Bess and Myrt Cannicott settled her in the hospital bed they had bought, it was not all right. For weeks, for months, she wavered from intolerable despair to intolerable anger, from abysses of helpless boredom to volcanoes of helpless rebellion.

People came to call and struggled at conversation and forgot to come back. Myrt or Bess would move the lever to elevate her head in the morning and turn it the other way to lower the mattress again in the evening. Up and then down. Up and then down. My two great events in the day, she thought over and over. For me, one of the most alive people in Johnson County. Everyone always said so. Oh, if only the truck had killed me too. If only I hadn't talked John into going to that concert. If only we had come back by the other roads that the trucks didn't use so much.

She read a little. Books slithered out of place, even with the ingenious table-tray that Gilbert procured for her, and it often took minutes of fumbling before she could turn a page, or almost as long to make the practical nurse understand what she wanted. After an hour of reading, her eyes would ache and her neck would feel as though it were coming apart. Why bother? she would ask herself. I can't talk with John, or with anyone else, about what I read. Not even with the stupid practical nurse. If I could only do something. If I could only do something. Ever, during the rest of my life. My flowers. Never to touch my flower beds again. How long will I lie here like a vegetable? Like a soggy pillow with a mind fastened to it? If I could go to sleep tonight and never wake up again. Surely for a dead body like this it would be all right to let the mind die too. If I could even hold the bottle to shake out an overdose of sleeping pills. But these wretched sticks of hands will never do it.

Myrt and Bess were brusque, efficient women. When they were with her, Nellie wished them away. They bustled and talked about the garden, the grocery shopping, the washing—things she could never do again. Their very energy lengthened her passive hours into sour eternities.

It was Myrt, though, who secured the radio for Nellie's room, and the radio helped. After Myrt had searched the stores in Keyesport and Princeville and Cornwall and Millerton, looking for one that Nellie's almost helpless fingers could manipulate, she finally found one in the Dreiser Hardware, right in Strettam, that had big buttons to punch rather than little knobs to twirl.

For nearly two years that was Nellie's life: to have the bed raised in the morning and lowered in the evening or for naps. To receive the infrequent (and increasingly less frequent) call. To hear soap operas and newscasts. To sleep. To eat—or at least to let what a practical nurse put into her mouth slide down her throat. To sleep again. To hear weather reports, which embittered her because no rain or wind would ever splash her face again. And not even to see much weather, since the Cannicott's guest room window looked out on the asphalt alley and the back corner of the Baptist Church.

During that time, for nearly two years, Sloth never named Nellie to his associates. He knew she hated her dormant life, but he didn't mind. And he left her to Envy, who liked to sidle in and stand behind her, whispering.

One Thursday evening Nellie winced when a symphony concert ended and a bland announcer reported that the Hartman-Bailey Gospel Hour would now begin. She was not eager to hear the Hartman-Bailey Gospel Hour, but she was even less eager to change stations; even with the push buttons, her hand muscles were too disobedient for any movement to be easy. She tried to tune out her mind instead and started drifting off into a pleasant gray fog. Then quartet voices broke through the fog and anger blazed inside Nellie. "Work, for the night is coming," they sang bouncily. "Work through the sunny noon.... Work till the last beam fadeth, Fadeth to shine no more—"

Fools, said her mind. If I only could. If I could move. I'd rather drive a tractor than to lie here year in and year out; I'd rather work with a construction gang on a highway, or collect garbage.

The quartet was singing again, but she heard only a blur of chords. Work, for the night is coming. I wish the final night would come. The sooner the better. Work. While I lie here like a turnip. An organ interlude followed, and she let it seep through her anger. She floated on it, felt washed by it. Then the quartet was back, and she wished she had summoned the energy to punch the "off" knob. Even more lustily, with more strident vigor: "Rise up, O men of God, have done with lesser things. Give heart and soul and mind and strength to serve the King of Kings. . . ." Yeah. Strength to nod my head a little and to move these sticks of fingers a few inches, awkwardly, and to swallow what is put in my helpless mouth. Yeah, rise up. Of course, of course.

Again the organ. Then a resonant strong voice. A little like John's voice. Enough like John's voice that she remained passive and did not will her finger to push the "off" button. She heard resonance and masculinity and thought vaguely about John but did not notice words. Then her throat tightened until she felt as if she would strangle. "Now it may be," the voice like John's was saying, "that someone who is listening to me feels himself totally unable to follow the quartet's exhortation and to 'work for the night is coming.' Maybe you are ill, retired, handicapped, a shut-in."

Yes, it may be. It certainly may be. So?

"But there is more than one way of working. If you are alert enough to be listening to my voice now—" He paused, as if to select his next words with particular care, and Nellie felt small prickles run across her scalp. Yes? He almost seemed to feel her tenseness and repeated himself. "If you are alert enough to be listening to my voice now, then you have heart and soul and mind to serve the King of Kings. Have you not? And a capacity for strength in each of those, if not in the muscles of your arms or your back."

She had an uncanny feeling that he was standing right inside the little box of the radio, looking straight at her. "It may be that your work, my dear friend, is the hard and lonely work of an intercessor—" The strong, resonant voice flowed on, and she listened almost without breathing. Like a strong rope, a new hemp rope, and me drowning. Like coffee used to be, only better. Like a piece of a rainbow.

"—to offer your prayers for people you have never seen, and never will see," the voice said. "And because of your will, your energy, your resolution, to persist beyond persistence, to endure beyond endurance—"

More prickles ran across her scalp. Does he know about me? Did someone tell him how helpless I am and how hollow-idle my brain has been for—what? For three years now? Your work. The hard and lonely work of an intercessor. How? God, how? I can't kneel in a church or anywhere else. I can't even bend my knees for half an inch to pretend they're kneeling. No muscles. Nothing but a mind, and it has become as soggy as a dead fish. But he said heart and soul and mind. Are they different, then? Mind, and mind, and mind. "It may be that your work, my dear friend—"

Suddenly she realized that the voice had finished, had been finished for some time. A small fraction of her awareness said that commercials about Coca Cola and about detergents had come and gone also, and a newscast was beginning. She gritted her teeth and struggled to raise her right index finger enough to touch the "off" button. As always, she panted a little from the effort and lay quiescent. But not quiescent. Your work, my dear friend.

Well, how?

That night was almost eleven years ago. Nellie never described it to the Cannicotts nor to the practical nurses. Even if she had suddenly received full use of all her throat muscles for a whole day, she knew she could hardly have made them understand. They would not have understood what happened to Saul of Tarsus on the way to Damascus either. They soon knew that something was different about Nellie's interior climate and they were glad, in their kindly, bovine way.

They were soon curious as well as pleased. They pitied her effort and admired it, as she scrawled notes to them about what she wanted when she started thinking practical thoughts about her assigned work. "Bible" they understood quickly enough. "Bks— pryr" took longer. They sent someone to the rector at St. Mark's and got her a Book of Common Prayer. She received it gladly, but wrote more notes. On his next trip Gilbert found a new bedside table for her with a swinging shelf, and now the practical nurse rotates books on it week by week, as Nellie instructs her through arduous jabbing efforts at the memo pad. She still doesn't write easily, but holds the pen between her rigid index finger and the slightly crooked middle finger while it saws unevenly across the paper. While she groans and perspires.

She still experiments with schedules. Usually she has been fed and bathed and settled for the day by 9:15 or 9:30, and her present preference is to spend the next two hours or so with her books: reading, thinking, memorizing. Sometimes she grips the pen to make a squiggly "X" in a margin for emphasis. With effort, she keeps a notebook record of what she has studied in a condensed cryptography which would be meaningless to anyone else except herself.

By 11:30 or so, she presses a buzzer to signal for the Cannicotts or their hired helper to put any other books—George Buttrick, Andrew Murray, John Wesley, the Bible—back on the shelf and to hand her the Strettam telephone book. When she first scrawled that she wanted a telephone book and convinced them that she wanted to keep it with her, the Cannicotts were sure that her injury had finally affected her mind. "She'll never talk on any phone again as long as she lives; she knows she won't." She persisted, and now they merely think it is some mild idiosyncrasy that attends her helplessness. Many names in the directory are new to her. She doesn't ignore those, but she spends more time—more heart and soul and mind and strength—in her focus on the older names. The ones she went to high school with. The ones she and John skated with and partied with. Her parents' friends.

After the telephone book, lunch and a necessary nap. Turning pages and making her small cryptograph notes still wearies her almost unbearably. By 3:00 she rouses again and repudiates Sloth in a way that turns him gray with fury. He always stands whispering and suggesting, cajoling and threatening, at her bedside. Myrt or Bess or their helper raises her pillow again and hands her another notebook full of her own erratic squiggles. This one has a black "P" for "Projects" on the blue fabric cover. In it she has been noting hospitals and mission stations and children's homes and other "projects" for almost eleven years now. Once in a while she crosses out a hieroglyph that has become outdated. Oftener she adds a new one. The very first entry is a badly scrawled monogram: H-BGH. No one except Nellie could possibly decipher it, but no one else needs to. No other entry in her "projects" book has more smudges of ball-point ink to show where her pen has rested while she addressed Deity.

Supper, and sometimes callers. Not often now. If they come, she is alert, and the memo pad helps her gurgled monosyllables to communicate. Sometimes visitors amuse her very much, but she tries not to laugh outright. From their faces she has realized how much the gutteral cackle which is all the laugh she can produce must startle and dismay them.

Then the daily paper. Myrt and Bess were deeply perplexed when Nellie persuaded them that she wanted her own copy of the Keyesport *Herald*. "She could just 's well 's not read ours the next morning," said Bess. "Land o' Goshen. Hasn't she got all morning to read it in? 'Tisn't as if she had to know the weather forecast, either, so's she'd know what hat to wear. Poor thing."

But Nellie insisted. Often she has said to herself, though not to the Cannicotts, that perhaps her night shift was the most important work of all. My real vocation? My reason for being? Maybe the reason He didn't take me, too, as I used to wish so desperately that He had done?

Probably no one else in Strettam—no one else in the whole Keyesport area—reads the *Evening Herald* in the way that Nellie Gaspereaux has disciplined herself to read it, with pen in hand and metaphorical altar rails in front of her. Usually she lingers over the front page, putting a rough check beside names or circling them. Kings, presidents, dictators. Criminals, congressmen, labor leaders. After the front pages, she usually turns— moving the big pages with herculean efforts—to vital statistics and the society section. Bless them, Lord. Make them good parents. Divorced, Oh, God, Your hand of healing. Engaged. With Your tenderness, Father, teach them what You want their home to be.

Rather often Myrt or Bess will come in to settle Nellie for the night and find her already asleep, with the society page open before her and craggy check marks down its margins. "It does beat all what interest she finds in the paper any more," Bess will tell Myrt or Myrt will tell Bess. "You'd think in the evening she could just relax and listen to the radio, now, wouldn't you? But, no, she's occupied. She's like somebody hurrying to get the housework done before company comes."

And Myrt will answer, or Bess will answer, "Ain't it the truth? You'd think she was makin' preserves outa fruit that would spoil or somethin'. Poor thing. I don't understand her."

And Sloth will endorse the last sentence most grouchily. But the epithet he uses is not "poor thing." His has a much more sulphuric fume.

Mrs. Daimler's Staff

Mrs. Daimler put down her pen, flexed her fingers, and picked it up again. One more makes twelve. And that's the lot. Should have let Susie type them up this time, but it's more civilized, even in my scraggy penmanship. *My dear Miss Montgomery. Evening of August 29th, after the County Institute.... will be glad to see all of you in my home.... look forward to working with you during the new school year.*

She put the pen down again. Hope you'll like Strettam, Miss Montgomery. High time for a tranfusion. First new teacher I've had in three years, and then not new, but Sarah Lecky who grew up here. (And before that, who? Kathleen Morion?) Hope you'll be as brisk and poised as you were when I interviewed you in Chicago last spring. As chic as a mannequin from a Marshall Field window, but no mannequin. Too dynamic. Have a good summer at Cornell? Must remember to ask you about it on the 29th. Though they'll all hate you for it, I suppose, and dust off their one-upmanship routines. Oh, well. Not all of them; thank heaven for Beth Ann Frankel.

We're too small. Rub each other too much. Now if I had forty teachers instead of twelve— No, that wouldn't solve it; people are people-natured, whether you ship them wholesale or retail. The push and pull of the rest of it would be easier, so much easier, if they didn't envy each other so much. And they don't realize how they envy. (Who, me? Why, Mrs. Daimler, how ridiculous; giggle, giggle. Yes, you, Leigh Doyle. Especially you. Envy is your middle name, almost.) Maybe I've been a a principal too long, and cared too much, and tried too hard? Sometimes I almost hear their thoughts before they think them.

May Belle Rowan will arrive first with her subdued hostility, Type 1-A, I suppose. I should keep notes for the whole year and write a book. Envy, Theoretical and Applied. Envy as Practiced among the Aborigines of the Upper Metonic Valley. In Twelve Easy Lessons for the Classroom Teacher. But they'd all sue me, and nobody would buy the book, and then where would we all be?

So maybe I shouldn't have hired Donna Montgomery. Maybe I should have hired that fat little slob whose father brought her over from Princeville in April. Or the gum-chewing one, as dull as dishwater, who came in for interviewing just ahead of Donna? No. Hire the best you can and pour salve on the egos where you can. A $6.98 canister of salve, please, to be sent up from Martin's Rexall this afternoon?

Now, let's see. Both iced tea and my raspberry punch and those thin caramel cookies.

"Hello, May Belle. Do come in. Muggy, isn't it? Yes, you're the first, so any chair you want is yours for the taking. Quite sure? Yes, just the same, except for the fourth grade. Did you meet Miss Montgomery at the Institute?" Yes, of course, you'd make a point of it. If your curiosity has limits, I don't know what they are. "Oh, here's our new Miss Montgomery now with Beth Ann. May Belle Rowan, Donna Montgomery."

And I feel like a clairvoyant witch. Almost as though May Belle had two voices, one to say gracious inane pleasantries and one to say what's really in her mind: you're slim and dark and pretty and young; I bulge and I'm fifty and flabby; and I hate you.

Oh, May Belle, must you envy everybody else's appearance? All that resentment just deepens the wrinkles and crow's feet and makes your shapeless body sag worse. Still Type 1-A. Should I try to have another candid conference? I'm not a psychiatrist, though.

"Did you like that psychology man at the Institute this morning, Beth Ann? No, from UCLA, wasn't he? Really remarkable. Oh, excuse me. There's the doorbell. Hello, Leigh. I haven't seen you since June. Yes, of course, you wrote that you wouldn't. Have a good summer? Do come and meet the new member of our staff. Donna Montgomery, Leigh Doyle. No, just completed in June at Northwestern. And she had a summer at Cornell; it was Cornell, wasn't it, Miss Montgomery? A workshop on—what was it? French in the Elementary Classroom? Do tell us—"

Tell Leigh. She isn't listening. She's waiting to tell about her trip to see her cousins in Los Angeles. All right, Leigh, now cut in. And Disneyland, too. But she was listening, even though she wasn't listening. Six months from now she'll probably be in to talk with me about some French workshop that is bigger and better than Cornell's. Maybe in Quebec, where French is everywhere. And maybe she'll go to it, and maybe she won't, but she'll want to. She bought a newer house because she envied Beth's;

too often she buys clothes right after somebody else does (but better than theirs) like a Pavlov dog responding to bells. She's like a child that's spoiled but not hungry: 'I want some of *that;* Johnny has some; give me some.' Even while she's bragging about Disneyland and the Hearst castle, she's wishing she had done what Donna did during the summer. Monkey see, monkey do. I've been a principal too long.

"Well, Marvin. Nice to see you. Couldn't Jean come this evening? Oh, I'm sorry. How was the boys' camp? Wisconsin, wasn't it? You're looking wonderfully tanned and fit. Did you bring back quantities of new ideas for the playground?"

I'm glad you're back. Thank heaven I have a level head like yours in the sixth grade.

"Do serve yourself some punch, won't you, Marvin? And Beth Ann will introduce our new fourth grade teacher when there's a good pausing point in their discussion. Or did you meet Miss Montgomery at the Institute? Yes, from Northwestern."

"Oh, Wanda. Welcome, welcome. No, not everyone. How nice you look, dear, in that crisp plaid. Textured cotton, isn't it? Perfect for you. Have you met our new girl, Donna Montgomery? More punch, Miss Montgomery? Wanda, will you have tea or punch? It's that raspberry recipe, from my own berry patch. Yes, of course."

Wanda. Dear Wanda. Must you start comparing her with yourself and feeling inferior? You're pretty, child, even if you do happen to hate the red hair and freckled nose that Providence gave to you. You're excellent with first graders; what if you did finish college by the skin of your three front teeth? Be yourself, dear. You don't have to envy Donna's face or Donna's background. A canister of salve, please. The large economy size.

There is a salve, too, a salve labeled Grace. For free. But costing everything.

Oh, Wanda, Wanda. Does it hurt so much for you to meet a Donna? I must have a chat with you very soon. Such good reports about what you did with your reading program last year. You're you, and Donna's Donna. You don't have to measure yourself against her.

Nearly all here now. More cookies from the kitchen. And refill the punch bowl. But Frances Fleming isn't here. Maybe just as well if she'd forget to come. For so young a girl, so sharp a tongue. Flick, jab, cut, swish. Laugh, sneer, deprecate. Cutting the others down to her own size. I'd better talk with the superintendent again. She's poisonous to morale, unless she's mellowed; unless. Wish we could let her go. Tenure, though. Yes. So she's here until forever, if she chooses to be.

Why? What's at the root of it? (Please, please, a canister of salve.) Does she live on a diet of sour grapes? She doesn't have, she envies, and so she derides and deprecates? She'll find a way to hint that Donna's student teaching was inferior, or that Donna's clothes are too avant-garde, or heaven knows what. Yes, heaven knows. In Eden, envy wasn't. In Eden, Frances wasn't. Speaking of angels, which I wasn't.

"Frances, come in. How are you? Yes, nearly all here. No, only one. Have you met Miss Montgomery? Yes, of course."

And what stiletto will you choose, Frances? Or pinprick jabs, between your sips of raspberry punch? What will you find wrong with Donna? She's probably the finest first-year teacher that we've hired for these twenty years, but you'll be quite sure to keep her from knowing it, won't you? Where to buy some gentle human love? Suffereth long and is kind. And a clearance sale of all the envy, in assorted sizes.

"Oh, must you? Yes. Good night. Good night. Good night, Donna. Oh, don't mention it. Lovely having you. Good night, May Belle. Good night, Leigh."

"But there's nothing to it, Beth Ann. Just the punch bowl and a few plates, you know. Well, if you insist. I didn't really have a chance to say more than a 'hello' to you when you came, nor all evening either, for that matter. So glad you took our new Donna under your wing, Beth Ann. Yes, isn't she? Her recommendations are glowing. Most pleased. I hope Strettam can keep her. Oh, did you? No, I think I was in the kitchen when she was telling you about it. I'm very glad."

Very glad. And glad you're yourself. Like always, Beth Ann Frankel. Objective; not too subjective. Seeing Donna candidly, ready to admire her; not seeing her for painful or invidious comparisons with yourself. Vicarious, that's it: able to enjoy someone else's gifts or deeds or graces without whimpering after them for yourself. To admire without wanting. A postgraduate course in loving-kindness, that's what Strettam Elementary School needs, more than we need the Institute. Envieth not, seeketh not her own, is not puffed up.

Well, Donna's run the gauntlet once. How many signals did she pick up of their hostilities, their assorted envies? (Don't let their green complexions sallow yours, Donna Montgomery.)

"Oh, what happened to Sarah Lecky? I saw her this morning at the coffee break, and she said then that she would be here. There, that's everything. Thanks, Beth Ann. Thanks so much."

Rita Corbie

"Mary—" David Yeoman patted after shave lotion across his chinline and reached for the big tube of Pepsodent.

"Yes?"

He squeezed toothpaste onto nylon bristles and contemplated the orange plastic handle of his toothbrush. "Have you had any contact with Rita Corbie lately? Any real contact?"

He heard water gurgle in the kitchen sink as she rinsed breakfast dishes. He heard small, soft clicks as she put dishes into the dishwasher. "No, I don't know that I have. I talked with her for a minute last Sunday morning about Chrissy's robe for the junior choir. Why?"

He swished water across his molars, spat briskly, and put the cap back on the Pepsodent tube. "Because—" He moved to the kitchen doorway and leaned against the white enamel of the door frame, rubbing thoughtful fingers across his stubbly crew cut. "Because—well, she's with us and yet not with us. She comes regularly enough, but most of the time she seems a million miles away. At a conservative estimate."

"She's sociable enough when you talk to her," said Mary.

"Yes. She's cordial. But there's something—oh, I don't know— something synthetic even about that. Unless my imagination is working overtime. And—" He stopped. "And—" He stopped again.

"What's the matter, Dave? You aren't usually one to pussyfoot around." Mary flicked a dishcloth across the top of the stove and rubbed firmly against a small grease spot.

"I don't quite know how much to say, even to you," he said slowly, "but I've been picking up some awfully unpleasant innuendos about Rita."

"You have? About Rita? Where?"

"Oh, at the barber shop. At the filling station. At Gilson's garage. At Joe's Diner. Until yesterday I tried to think it wasn't her name I was hearing, and I haven't wanted to be a detective

146

nor a snoop. But yesterday outside the barber shop the name was clear, and the laughter was—well, pretty ugly."

"Oh, dear! I was thinking just a few days ago that I ought to have Rita over for supper again, or something. We haven't done as much as we might to help her handle being a young widow."

"Well, you can still have her over," said Dave. "If she has gone off a deep end morally, she needs help—real help—even more than she did before. If she hasn't, maybe you would counteract the wagging of some dirty tongues. And we know she has problems, whatever their labels are right now."

Mary sighed as she set the controls on the dishwasher. "I know she has problems. I'll think about it, Dave."

Mary thought all day. She thought while she made beds, while she used the vacuum cleaner, while she folded away laundry, while she hemmed a skirt for Karen. How much do I know about her, really? Must have been soon after we moved here two years ago that she came back to live with her folks. August, September. November, maybe? Two years in November. Just after her Colin was killed. Army, Navy, Marines? Air Force, that was it. Crash of a training plane. Never got out of the United States. Bitter about that. Chrissy, as cute as a button. Little black curls. Seven now. Five then. Cried for her daddy every night, Mrs. Folsom said.

A supper? Not much good for real rapport, with Karen and Dick chattering. Can't ship them away very well, though. Can't have her up for afternoon tea, either, since she works all day at the hardware. Every day? Thursday off, seems to me. Find out from her mother. And she'll angle for an invitation. Can't have her along with Rita. Oh, could, but she'd talk all the time. Not sure it would help Rita much.

"Any appointment made with Rita Corbie?" asked Dave that evening as he came from the basement with garden gloves and lawn clippers.

"Not yet. But I have been thinking about her, Dave. I really have. Oh, say, I've been thinking about something else. Could I use the car on Thursday maybe? The paper tonight advertises some midsummer clearances at Keyesport, beginning Thursday."

Dave groaned. "I knew it. I felt it in my bones. Ask Tom and George. I had coffee with them this morning, and I made a solemn prediction that you would be coming down with a shopping virus within five days."

Mary laughed. "Did you really? And did they have the same premonitions? Maybe Marge or Catherine would like to go along with me."

"Could be." He pulled a canvas glove onto his right hand and flexed his fingers.

"Oh-h!"

"What's the matter?" He glanced up from the clipper blades in surprise.

"I just had a thought. Rita Corbie is off work on Thursday afternoons, I'm fairly sure. Maybe she'd like to go to Keyesport with me."

"It's worth a try. Give her a call, why don't you?"

Mary picked up the telephone receiver. Yes, she would be off work, but no, she didn't think she had energy for shopping. Thanks, anyway. Mary sighed as she went to look for the rose spray. Well, that's that. Half an hour later the telephone shrilled, and Karen came to the back door.

"For you, mom. Sounds like Rita Corbie."

"Hello? No, nobody else. No, I've been out helping Dave in the yard and haven't even asked anyone. Oh, fine. What time? Wouldn't that hurry you? All right, fine."

Mary walked slowly over to the corner of the yard that Dave was edging. "Rita changed her mind. Send up a prayer, David. She made it pretty plain that she wanted to go with me only if no one else were going. Maybe taking her to shop was a good idea. I hope I can be a good listener."

As they drove toward Keyesport on Thursday, Mary wasn't quite so sure it was a good idea. Rita was rigid and silent. Words like "sullen" and "insolent" kept flitting through Mary's mind as she braked for speed zones or maneuvered her way past slow-moving trucks. Rita was slim and pretty, in a way that always made Mary think faintly of gypsies and of the opera *Carmen,* which she and Dave had seen once in Dallas when he was in seminary. Today Rita had on a red cotton blouse and long red earrings which heightened the resemblance.

Mary's comments on Strettam events and on scenery brought only murmured syllables. Her gentle questions about Chrissy, about the Folsoms, and about Rita herself drew monosyllables, too. Well, I tried, she told herself as she eased the car into the fifth level of the parking garage at Garrett's Department Store. And I was wanting to be a good listener. Life's little ironies.

"Let's see. They close at five-thirty," she said. "Want to plan to meet me here at the car, or shall I look for you in the lounge on third floor?"

"Oh, in the lounge," said Rita. "I don't have much to buy."

Not much to buy. Not much to say. But it was your decision to come along. What gives?

While she eased the Chevrolet down the ramp again, soon

after five-thirty, Mary took a quick look at her passenger. Rita seemed more rigid than before, and her eyes were staring at something much more engrossing than the concrete walls of the garage ramp. As though she were looking into a pit of snakes, for sure, Mary thought. Like what Dave and George McPherson were talking about the other night, of Dante's people in the *Inferno*. Shall I speak or shall I not speak?

"Only one parcel, Rita?" she said finally.

"Uh-huh. A dress for Chrissy." She paused, and her voice became metallic. "For a going-away gift, before I desert her."

"Before you—" Mary was glad she had to brake quickly for a red light. Her knees and ankles felt rubbery.

Rita laughed, and Mary thought again of *Carmen*. "I'm leaving Strettam this weekend," she said. "For good and all. Or for bad and all, you might say. I'm sick and tired of being schizo."

Dear God, help me now. To say enough and not too much. An unshakeable and unshockable faith: who said that? Eugenia Price, wasn't it? "Of being schizo?"

"Yeah. Schizo. All split up. On Sundays I take Chrissy to Sunday school and sing hymns with the rest of you. During the week I work for Dreiser's Hardware and set up my appointments as the local whore." She paused again. "You can let me out now if you want to, Mrs. Yeoman; I'll hitchhike home. Probably get there before you do."

"Don't be silly," said Mary quietly.

Rita giggled. "I think I'm going to be silly," she said. "Talking to you or hitchhiking. I was in a bar for an hour this afternoon, just getting ready to be silly. What's more, I'm going to be silly for the rest of my life."

"Where are you going when you leave Strettam, Rita? Do you know?"

"Sure, I know. To Chicago. A girl I knew when Colin was in the Air Force lives there. Her husband got killed, too, only hers was killed in battle. And she never did try living two lives. She didn't have any kids, and she went to business right away after her husband was blown to bits. So I'm going to stay with her."

Mary moved up behind a battered red VW, flicked her signal to change lanes, passed the VW, and steadied the car back in the right lane. Steady, Chevrolet. Steady, Mary. Dear God, help me now.

"Have you told—do your folks—"

Rita giggled again. "They don't know anything. Not one thing, I promise you, unless they're better liars and actors than I am, which I doubt."

"So—"

"So I'm going to flag down the bus at the bank corner on Saturday night, unless Glenn Fiedler brings me here to catch a train. That's one reason I wanted to come in today, to check on train schedules. Or Glenn might take me even farther, if he's in the mood for it. And I'll leave mother a note and explain that I just can't stand a little town like Strettam any more. Which I can't."

Mary held the steering wheel with her left hand while she rubbed a moist right palm against her skirt. Right hand, and then left hand. But how to wipe perspiration from the aorta? From the brain?

"Chrissy—"

Rita's pert chinline became more stubborn. "Chrissy will be miles better off without me," she said. "She is seven now, and she asks more questions every week. Too many. Mom will keep her in the straight and narrow. Mom and all the rest of you."

"You want Chrissy to stay in the straight and narrow, then, Rita?"

"Oh, sure. So far as wanting goes, I'd want me to be there, too. I'd rather be you than me. Don't kid yourself."

"Then why not end this schizo part of your life in the other way?"

"Be the Sunday girl all week?" Rita shook her head. "I wish I could, but I can't. I'm as weak as a kitten. When a man looks at me—the way men do look at me—I start planning for where and when. Even when Colin was alive, he wasn't the only one I slept with. He'd have killed me if he had known. Maybe it was a good thing for him that his plane went down."

Mary glanced at a "Merging Traffic" sign and then at the approach road. "Why did you come back to Strettam when Colin died?"

Rita giggled again. "Meaning that Strettam isn't exactly the town for a prostitute to set up shop? Oh, I don't know. You'd be surprised. I sure was." Her tone edged into bitterness. "I really came, I guess, because Colin's death had shocked me. It seemed like a divine judgment against me, or something. You know? And I thought a nice little country place like Strettam would reform me, for good and all. Boy, was I mistaken. I really must've been an innocent when I finished high school here and married Colin. You know? Within three weeks after I started working at Dreiser's, I was getting attention. Too much of it. Within three months in nice little Strettam I was being just as— as sociable—as I ever was at the Air Force base. Of course being a widow is—being a widow." She took a long breath and tapped her fingers together restlessly. "Oh, and I came back, when I came, because my folks live here, of course. And there was Chrissy, and I do have a mother's feelings for her. Believe it or not. Mostly you'll believe it not."

Mary thought she had never wanted so desperately to hurry off to some quiet corner and sob. "You said a minute ago that you can't be the Sunday girl all week, Rita," she said. "Have you ever been the Sunday girl on Sunday, really? Completely and entirely, no ifs and no buts?"

Rita looked out the window, and Mary wondered what kind of pageant she was watching. "Yes. No. I don't know, Mrs. Yeoman. I really don't. When I was ten or twelve, I was as pious as the next one, but I don't think I could have told you what it was all about. What the gang did, Rita did. Since then—oh, I don't know. Church has been like a social club to me, with a very complicated set of passwords. You know? And I could say enough of the passwords to keep people from bothering me."

Mary thought again of what Dave had said. Always a million miles away. "You have come pretty regularly, haven't you?"

"Oh, sure. For one thing, when Colin died, mom said I could bring Chrissy and come home if I would cooperate about attending church, and so on, and I promised." She snickered. "I didn't make any promises about some other things. She hasn't a clue."

"You're quite sure?"

"Oh, quite sure. It's getting harder, though. That's another good reason for me to leave now. I'm about at the limit of plausible reasons for implausible absences from the house. There's only so much you can do with shopping trips and hair appointments. I've fibbed a girl friend into existence over at Princeville, and I've visited her quite a few times."

Mary slowed for an intersection. Not too much farther, on to Strettam. Like trying to wake up during a nightmare. "Rita, why are you telling me all this?"

Rita cupped her chin on her fists, and her long, red earrings swung like small pendulums. "Yeah, why am I? Because I'm stupid, I guess. Partly I guess I wanted to shock you, or shock somebody. For too long now I've laughed inside on Sunday mornings, having people beam at me so piously and thinking how they'd look if they knew. I don't know. In a way it seemed as though I'd be a little more honest if somebody knew what the score really is. Somebody who wouldn't blab it all over town." She paused and moved her head and the pendulums swung again. "No, that's not it either. Not all of it. No. More like because my crazy, messed-up life is—well, it hurts like broken bones. And I sort of wanted somebody to sympathize a little, maybe. *151*

I don't want to do what I'm doing, and yet I do want to do what I'm doing."

"Oh, Rita." Mary glanced ahead, glanced in the rear view mirror, and swung the car off on the shoulder. "I should have stopped before," she said. "I can't think like this and drive like that."

"So you see?" said Rita stonily. "I got what I wanted. I wanted some sympathy. Well, anyway, you didn't make me get out and hitchhike."

"No, and I won't. Rita, it doesn't have to end like this. You can become a different person, but not in the way you're planning—"

"Not now." Rita's voice was dull. "If I had talked to you like this two years ago—but I didn't have that much sense. I never have had sense when I needed it. If you could work some magic for me, now—if you could work a neat little miracle or two, Mrs. Yeoman—"

Mary caught hold of Rita's hand. It went limp. Like Karen's kitten when it died in my hands, thought Mary. Rita shook her head. "Don't say it, Mrs. Yeoman. You can't work a miracle, but you know Somebody who can. But I—I'm not sure—not sure enough—that I want Him to. You wouldn't understand. I know that sex is a dragon that has me in its paws, but I like the dragon and I want to be in his paws. I—I can't live without sex, Mrs. Yeoman. I can't, and I won't."

Mary looked at the ridgepole of a farmhouse down the road to the right and realized how much she was trembling. "May I pray a prayer about your whole tangled circumstances?" she asked.

Rita tossed her chin and the earrings swung in tiny circles. "I can't stop you from praying, but, please, not here and now. I need to be getting home, if you don't mind."

Mary started the motor, although it took some effort to steady her hand on the ignition key. "David and I will be praying," she said. "For you, and for Chrissy too."

"As you like," said Rita. "It might even help Chrissy. Listen, you can talk to him, but if either of you tell anybody—and I mean anybody—one syllable of what I've said—"

"Don't worry. We won't."

Neither spoke again until the Norwich State Bank was in sight. "You want to go home, I suppose?" asked Mary.

"Yes—no, wait. Drop me off at the blinker light, would you?"

"By Joe's Diner?" Mary's voice was dubious.

"Yes, please."

Mary braked at the blinker and Rita opened the door quickly.

"Thanks. Thanks very much." She pushed the door shut even more quickly and hurried across the Metonic bridge toward Gilson's garage. What on earth? thought Mary. At this time of the evening. She looked up and down the highway and started to turn left to drive up Strettam Hill. She turned slowly, letting the Chevrolet act as numb as she felt. From somewhere nearby, just across the bridge, she heard a car door, a woman's shrill laughter, a motor. Little flames seemed to move across Mary's throat and face and to flicker from her ear lobes. She pushed the accelerator with a jerk, as though she were stepping on a very big spider.

If we had cared more when she first moved back to Strettam, she thought. If somebody had cared more. If somebody had asked me every day or two, as Dave did on Tuesday, "Have you had any contact with Rita Corbie lately? Any real contact?"

She parked the car, collected her parcels from Garrett's, and walked toward the house. The woods behind the Metonic looked very dark, she thought. Unusually dark.

Lechery thought so, too. "Just the right sort of darkness for a dragon to hulk in, don't you know?" He said to Envy. His tail was curled around an oak tree two blocks away, and he exhaled small puffs of smoke and curls of flame.

"You're overdoing something, old man," said Envy. "Why do you have to be bloated up as big as a freight train on this particular evening?"

"She said I'm a dragon, didn't she? So I can celebrate her progress by being a dragon, can't I?"

"Oh, I don't mind. Though you don't have to fill the whole hillside with your scaly paws."

"As a matter of fact," said Sloth from his vulture perch on Lechery's ridgepole spine, "as a matter of fact she didn't say *you* are a dragon, chum. She said sex is a dragon."

Lechery exhaled again. "Nobody uses my good ol' name any more, which is fine with me. When a woman like her says 'sex' the way she just said it, you can be jolly sure it's me she's talking about, and nothing conjugal; nothing in the Enemy's provinces. Same with some of my best pets that prattle so wisely about their 'situational ethics.' One of the fanciest nicknames I've ever had, eh? I just wish they were all as toothsome to nibble on as this one is." He grinned a broad dragon grin, settled his lower jaw against the hillside, and closed his dragon eyes. "Good chewing," he simmered. "Good chewing, for all the rest of her mortal years. And then—"

"Don't be too sure," said Sloth. "He has His agents in Chicago, too."

Lechery exhaled a thin plume of flame. "Very good chewing," he said.

Tom Vos

"Mighty handsome dahlias, Miss Cannicott," Tom Williams put his brief case down for a moment and touched wide yellow petals with respectful fingers.

"Thanks, Reverend," said Myrt, putting another six-inch blossom into her wicker basket. "I keep tellin' Bess that it's th' best season for dahlias we've had for years 'n years. Poor Nellie will have plenty of flowers in her room all fall, I guess."

"I'm sure that she will. How is she?"

"Same as always," said Myrt dourly. "Never the tiniest change, poor thing. Only lately she seems to be frettin' over somethin'. She keeps writin' somebody's name down on her little pad and actin' sorta worried—"

"A different name on different days?" asked Tom curiously.

"No, always the same. A real funny name. Her writin' is awful scratchy, you know, but it looks like 'Tom Vus' or 'Tim Vus' or 'Tim Vees.' Ever hear of such a person?"

"Doesn't sound familiar. But I haven't lived in Strettam as long as Nellie has. I'll ask around a little, if you like." He glanced at his watch. "I'm due at a committee, I'm afraid. Reverend Yeoman was expecting me a little sooner. Tell Mrs. Gaspereaux I'll stop in sometime soon with the portable Communion set."

Two hours later Tom pushed a stack of papers back into his nicked and battered brief case. "Oh, Dave," he said, "or any of the rest of you fellows, do you know a person named Tom Vus or Tim Vees or anything like that?"

Half a dozen heads made negative sounds or motions. "Friend of yours?" asked Dave Yeoman.

"Not yet," said Tom. "Small research item."

"Sounds vaguely familiar to me," said Jim Thurston. "Somebody who used to live here, maybe?"

"Could be. I haven't a clue."

"Maybe Ray Kendrick's insurance rosters would help you   155 out," said Jim. "Or you might ask McNair at the bank. He has contacts all over three counties."

A week later when Tom stopped at the Cannicott home with the Communion set, as he had promised, the mysterious name was still a mystery. He saw it on Nellie's scratch pad in the broken squiggles of her writing. "Tom Vos," it was surely. She had written it three times: once with a question mark after it, once with two question marks, once with a heavily penciled X.

"Someone you know, Nellie?" he asked.

She made the choked gutteral sound that from Nellie meant "Yes."

"Someone you're especially praying about lately?" Tom Williams knew more, and guessed more, than anyone else in Strettam about Nellie's vocation.

Again, the gutteral "Ay-ess."

"Anybody I've ever known?"

A negative grunt.

"Somebody I should get acquainted with, maybe?"

A vigorously eager "Ay-ess."

"Then I'll have to keep asking around, I guess. Can you give me any leads?"

Nellie's face was contorted with effort. Finally she lifted her right arm enough to touch a letter on the bedside stand. "A letter to you from Mr. Gilbert Herriott—" Tom paused. "Oh, that's your brother, isn't it? He can tell me about this other Tom, this Tom Vos?"

Again, a sound of "Yes."

"He's coming next week, Gilbert is, Reverend," said Myrt Cannicott, who had been watching and listening from the doorway. "I'll have 'im call you, first thing."

"Very good." Tom picked up the Communion set and started to open it.

On Thursday morning, he was writing briskly on his Sunday's sermon notes when the telephone rang, and a few minutes later Gilbert Herriott was sitting across the desk from him. "Yes, I know Tom Vos," he said slowly. "I can't imagine why poor Nellie has suddenly evidenced such a concern about him—unless the angels have been telling her something that the rest of us don't know. So far as I know there has been no change in his situation." His voice was tense and strange.

Tom wondered whether the tone he heard was pity, scorn, anger, grief, or something else. "Which isn't a happy situation, I take it?"

"Quite the opposite, unless he has changed. Look, maybe Nellie does know something I don't. I haven't seen Tom Vos for—

for close to ten years, I guess. Would you be free to drive up with me tomorrow afternoon? I'm sure it would please Nellie—"

"Tomorrow—Friday." He looked at a desk calendar pad. "Um—yes, that would be okay. I had a couple of calls scheduled, but they can be moved. Where is 'up'? Does Mr. Vos live far away?"

"Maybe twenty miles. Up beyond the Mill Creek intersection."

"Really? That close? How odd, then, that nobody in Strettam even seems to know his name. I've asked around quite a bit since Miss Cannicott first asked me."

"If he hasn't changed, maybe it isn't so strange," said Gilbert Herriott brusquely.

"Oh?"

"If you don't mind, I'll explain later. In case he *has* changed, I'd rather not make an inaccurate comment in advance. I don't have a car here with me—"

"At your service. The old green Pontiac behaves very well."

As Tom turned north on Highway 37 on Friday and followed the Metonic valley northward, Herriott was taciturn. They spoke a little of strikes and unions and living costs in New York City, but not of Strettam people. "Should be about the next right turn," said Herriott finally. "It's a bumpy little dirt road, or used to be. There. Just beyond the yellow fence."

"Looks as though it might lead to some summer cottages down by the river," observed Tom.

"Um-m-m."

The Pontiac bounced across ruts and tufts of wiry grass. "Better leave it here," said Herriott as they came to a narrower trail. "We can walk in from here." He picked up a brown paper parcel from the seat beside him.

"Doesn't look as though Tom Vos has much company," said Williams. "He must—" The breath died in his throat. They had turned a sharp corner and saw a tumble-down shack perched crazily at the river's edge. Four scraggly white chickens were scratching in the dirt. Piles of rusted tin cans drifted from the back of the cabin and out into the tufts of ragged grass. Old tires leaned against a half-dead cottonwood tree and pieces of broken furniture littered the yard.

Tom glanced at Nellie's brother. Grief, yes. Surprise, no. His face says that Vos hasn't changed. Like this for more than ten years, then?

A mangy dog ambled around the cabin, looked quizzically at them, and barked twice. Footsteps. Tom Williams felt a twitch of nausea as he looked at the dirty stubbled face, the grease-splotched T-shirt, the wrinkled trousers; the nausea did not lessen when they came close enough to catch odors of whiskey and perspiration.

"Well, whaddya want?"

Herriott watched him steadily. "The first cargo boat for Rio, leaving from this dock." Tom Williams blinked. Must be a private joke; an old salutation they used to use maybe?

"Huh?"

Herriott said it again, louder and with a forced twinkle in his voice: "The first cargo boat for Rio, leaving from this dock."

"Yeah?"

"Hullo, Tom. It's Gilbert Herriott. How are you?"

Vos looked suspicious and then belligerent. "You're who? Shep 'n me don't want no company."

"It's Gilbert Herriott, man. Your buddy from Curtis College."

Muscles and skin tightened in the slack face. "Well, son of a gun. Hairy ol' Herriott. Si' down, man, si' down." He pushed a broken rocker across the uneven floor of the cabin porch toward each visitor. "Jus' a minute, I'll get ya somethin' to drink—"

Herriott opened his brown paper parcel ostentatiously. "It's a picnic, Tom, a picnic on the dock. Here you go." Quickly he poured black coffee into a plastic cup and swung it into Vos's hand. The hand was not steady, but it held the cup.

"Well, son of a gun. Hairy ol' Herriott." He held up the cup and squinted at it. "Cheers."

They sipped and rocked, sipped and rocked, and watched the Metonic ripple past. "And this is my friend Tom Williams," Herriott said heartily. Too heartily. Williams felt another twitch of nausea. "He knows my sister Nellie."

Vos took a long swig of coffee. "Yeah, Nellie. Good ol' Nellie. Best singer in the whole college, wasn't she? Best singer in the whole state, maybe. Mighty purty, too; she always was. Why didn't ya bring Nellie along, 'stead o' this guy?"

"Nellie couldn't come. She thinks about you, though." A long pause. "Nellie prays for you, Tom Vos."

"Yeah?" He sipped coffee, slowly this time, and then rubbed his lips with the back of his hand.

Again a long silence, as they watched the ripples at the edge of the Metonic. Then Herriott repeated, more firmly, "Nellie prays for you, Tom Vos."

"Tell her thanks," said Tom Vos. "Tell her thanks a lot." His voice had become a little huskier, and maudlin tears welled up in his eyes. "Hey, I got an idea." He gulped the rest of his coffee, plonked down the cup, and strode into the cabin. For several minutes they heard rustling sounds. When he returned he was carrying a rectangle that looked like an unframed oil painting. "There," he said. "Give that one to Nellie. Tell 'er— Tell 'er— Oh, I don't care." He yawned twice. "Tell 'er whatever you want to." He yawned again and rubbed his eyes. "Come see me again, ol' Harry. Now I gotta—now I gotta get some sleep, if you'll 'scuse—" He sat down on the porch floor, leaning his head against the cabin wall, and soon was snoring.

Tom Williams lifted his eyebrows. Herriott nodded. "We might as well go now," he said softly. "He might be quarrelsome when he wakes up. You never can tell." They crossed the littered yard and started back up the narrow road. "It was more of a risk than I wanted to tell you; I wasn't sure what would happen. The last time I came he threw empty whiskey bottles at me."

"That painting—it is an oil painting, isn't it?"

Herriott held it at arm's length and surveyed it.

"Sure, it's a painting. Not bad, huh?" It was a surrealist landscape, dizzy with color.

"It's great. It's really great. Did he—is he—"

"He did, and he is. Or was. Hard to tell how recent this one is. In college we all thought he would be another Van Gogh, at least."

"So what went wrong?" They were back at the car. Herriott put his thermos and the painting into the back seat and waited for Williams to turn the Pontiac back toward Highway 37.

"Who knows? I caught some glimpses—too many glimpses— but I'm not entirely sure of anything. One doesn't like to guess at ugliness. But maybe you should know what I know, and what I have had to surmise. Preachers are old pros at listening to stories from the seamy side of life, aren't they?"

"Well, more or less."

"He was our budding genius at college," Herriott said. "We were all thrilled when he got a handsome fellowship to a big-name art school, and it sounded good when he wrote me that one of the profs had taken him into his home to live, to be his special protégé. But apparently some kind of a Potiphar's-wife situation developed. Only worse. Old professor, young wife; young wife seduces her husband's student." He paused. "When it's a man, you call him a lecher. Especially if it's an old man. What do you call her when a handsome young woman is the guilty one? Anyway, the story evidently went from bad to worse. He never told me in so many words, but I gathered that the professor's wife got pregnant, had an abortion, and died from complications."

"And—"

"And the professor knew. He didn't press any legal charges, but he had a lot of influence and evidently he used all of it, with plenty of vindictive anger dripping all through it, to make sure that any door that could possibly bang shut in the face of a budding genius would bang. They banged and banged and banged." He turned a little to look out across the shiny surface of the Metonic and to the hills beyond. "We had been like brothers in college, and Tom said enough that I caught some glimpses of the purgatories he walked through. He came back up here to the cabin—"

"Came back?"

"It was a family cabin. They had vacationed here for years. I had spent a lot of vacation time here with him while we were in college. Anyway, he said he was going to study on his own up here and hold himself to a strict schedule and become the Rembrandt of our age, or the Van Gogh anyway."

"But—"

"But he started drinking. And soon was drinking hard. That's one fact there's no possible doubt about."

They were approaching Strettam. Tom Williams braked at the blinker light and turned right. "Can you come along to my house for a bit? You're not in a hurry?"

"No hurry. Thanks, I'd like to."

In the parsonage, Tom plugged in a percolator and touched a match to kindling in the fireplace. "I'm glad it's cool enough to warrant the fireplace," he said. "Helps the cheerfulness quotient."

"Which Tom Vos's biography doesn't, I'm afraid," said Herriott. "Poor guy. A fool and a victim. If I have the story straight, that woman's lust ruined his life, and then her husband's anger smashed his career. Understandable anger, actually, but there you are."

"What does he live on? Does he work at all?"

"I don't know for sure; obviously I haven't been in touch in recent years. He may still do a little with odd jobs for the nearby farmers, and over the years he may have sold a canvas now and then. Like the one that's out in the car now. He has a lawyer brother over at Keyesport who is just about as proud as Lucifer—or did have; I suppose he still does. And I'd guess that the brother pays him a little monthly stipend on condition that Tom will keep completely out of his way."

"So. Her lust and the professor's anger and his brother's pride—"

"And then add on his drinking as a particularly nefarious kind of gluttony? A regular parade of the vices, isn't it? And Tom's sloth, too, heaven knows. For the last ten alcoholic years, and more, he has been letting himself vegetate out in that cabin. Or rot. He used to fish a little, hunt rabbits or squirrels, and grow a little garden. Maybe he still does. I didn't notice any semblance of a garden today. When I think of his tremendous creativity, just rotting away in that tumble-down cabin— It isn't as though he were a Thoreau camping at Walden Pond with his mind in high gear, you know."

Tom stirred the fire in the fireplace and filled their coffee cups. "It's hard on you to see him and think about him, isn't it?"

"Yes, it is. Partly because I feel so wretchedly helpless. He was another self to my self in college. There was an eagerness about him then that made all of us more alive. We'd never have believed *he* would be the one to become—an alcoholic. Never. It still burns my tongue, almost, to say that word about Tom Vos. And then—"

"Yes?"

"I'm not sure it makes sense, but Tom Vos's wasted life always seems to me to be some kind of a bitter corollary to my poor sister's wasted life."

"Put it the other way. Beside his, Mrs. Gaspereaux's is a life of sheer heroism, isn't it? And she didn't perpetrate her own downfall, as he apparently has done."

"Oh, I know that." Herriott put down his cup. "Right now I'm puzzling about why Nellie has had Tom Vos on her mind so much lately. Something must have dredged up old recollections and given them a new edge of concern. I'll tell her about today, of course, and she may be nudging you to go out and see him again. From what Myrt says, it hasn't just been a passing curiosity flitting through her mind."

"I'm sure it hasn't. Maybe she is sensing a particular responsibility to pray for him, as one of the blackest black sheep she has ever known."

"Though you wonder what poor Nellie's prayers could do for a man like him, don't you?" asked Herriott bleakly.

Some twenty miles away, Tom Vos was waking again. For ten minutes he sat rubbing his bristly chin and staring at the swirling water of the Metonic. "For me," he muttered finally to Shep. "Says Nellie prays for me. So she c'n pray; so I c'n pray. And then what might happen, do you s'pose? Now I lay me down to sleep— No, not that. Our Father, which—" His chin sagged against his right hand, and the right elbow propped itself against his knee; intermittently his voice rumbled on. Shep came to the edge of the cabin porch and whined. To have the voice speaking but not to any visible person and not in Shep-language either was an intolerable perplexity.

Slowly Tom stood up. He looked at Shep's alert ears and beyond Shep at a white chicken scratching in the dust and then at an oak tree beside the Metonic. Lines, curves, angles. For the first time in ten years he had a craving to sketch lines and curves and angles on smooth white paper.

Three

Dave Yeoman's Chevrolet eased to the curb, and Tom looked up from the crumbly earth he was patting into place around stiff-stemmed geranium plants. "Haven't seen you for eons," said Dave. "How about a seminar down at Joe's? I've been studying since six o'clock, and my mind is falling apart at the seams."

Williams brushed the loam from his thumbs. "Since six? My word and honor! Well, as a matter of fact, you came by at a good moment. I've just finished putting in everything that Catherine brought back from Princeville yesterday." He grinned. "I shouldn't, of course. Tuesday is my day off, and if I go down and talk with you guys—"

"Go wash your paws and come on," said Dave. "We can stop by and get George, to be sure he doesn't cut class today."

"Okay. Be with you in a minute."

"Well, what's on our mind today, Dave?" asked George McPherson a little later as he spooned sugar into a cup at Joe's Diner.

"I haven't decided," said Dave.

"And you up since six o'clock?" mocked Tom.

"Whaddya mean, *up* since six? Man, I was up at quarter to five. At six I was studying Romans."

McPherson whistled softly. "Are you well? Shall we take your temperature? Joe, do you have a thermometer over there behind the counter?"

"Knock it off," said Yeoman jocosely. "Who preached on sloth a while back? It's all your fault." He leaned back in his chair, sipped coffee slowly, and rubbed his crew cut with thoughtful fingers. "Tom Williams," he said, "something is on your Methodist mind. I can almost hear the mental machinery clanking. Speak!"

Tom put down his coffee cup and sighed.

"I said *speak;* I didn't say *groan,*" said Yeoman. "Shall we improvise a confessional over in the corner?" Tom's face didn't alter, and Dave's levity disappeared. "Something really wrong, Tom?"

"Besides the whole bent nature of the human race?" said Tom slowly. "Well, you said 'sloth' just now, and I had a pretty hideous case history of that particular villain's work put in front of me last week. Sloth and sundry colleagues of his, you might say." He looked vaguely into his coffee cup. He saw Tom Vos drowsing on his broken porch. He saw white chickens scratching in a yard and tin cans in drifts behind a cabin. He saw an oil painting in Gilbert Herriott's hands.

"Want to clue us in?" asked Dave.

Tom shook his head. "Not now. It's just that I met a man who might have been what he isn't, more visibly and more dramatically than one often encounters. Unless one works in Skid Row missions, I guess." He signaled Joe for more coffee and seemed to be flipping a key on one compartment of his mind. "That reminds me, though," he said. "Ever since you mentioned a while back that you were preaching on sloth, George, I've been meaning to get back to the topic. In fact, I had an impulse to call you the other night—or the other morning; two or three in the morning—"

"Well, why didn't you?"

"I felt more virtuous not to, of course," grinned Tom.

"And if you had summoned me from the depths, what would you have said to me? If I had been awake enough to listen."

"Well, after you talked about the idea," said Tom, "I went home and started digging a little in dictionaries and church history books and stuff. And when I went to a conference at Aldersgate a few weeks ago I did a little digging in the library at the seminary, too."

"Behold, the mighty scholar," murmured Yeoman.

"Yeah," said Tom. "Candidate for a D. D., and all that. No kidding, though, I found some ideas I'm going to be chewing on for a long time."

"Like what?"

"Like that those guys in the medieval monasteries knew a lot more about mental health than I've ever given them credit for. I've always thought of a slothful person as—well, you know, a lazybones who doesn't get his work done—"

"And?" George McPherson's face was like a tennis player's awaiting a serve.

"Well, I'm no linguist, but I shoveled out the idea that some of those ol' guys in the Middle Ages thought of sloth as including apathy and depression and gloominess and peevishness and a general 'don't care' feeling. Some of 'em classified sloth as 'the midday demon.'"

"George can feel another sermon coming on," murmured Dave. "He's getting that glint in his eye."

"There was one paragraph that was really vivid," Tom went on. "This guy was describing the clock-watcher sort of monk who wants suppertime to come before it does, and keeps leaving his cell to go out and check how far the sun has gone down, and thinks it's an awful slowpoke. Then he decides to go visit his buddies in the monastery hospital instead of keeping on with his studies—"

"Ouch," said Dave. "Now you're talking about us. Except I never do get through with my duties in visiting the shut-ins. Do you?"

"And what else did you dig up?" asked George. "Oh, Joe, would you bring me another of those frosted doughnuts? And more coffee, please? Thanks."

"Well, this same guy talked about the 'grass-is-greener-on-the-other-side-of-the-fence' type as being a victim of sloth, too. Bad mental health, see? Apathy, depression, gloom, more depression. And rather than getting himself fixed up on the inside, he wants to go somewhere else. Our kids would say he wants to 'split the scene,' I guess; is that the right slang? The book I was looking at had nice cadence to it. 'Being discontented with his surroundings, he vainly imagines that he would do better in some distant monastery,' or something like that."

"Um-hum," said George. "Um-*hum*. Like, if I were serving a parish in Detroit or San Francisco or Washington, D. C., now wouldn't that be great?"

"Speaking of great—ever hear of Gregory the Great?" asked Tom.

"Prob'ly, but I've forgotten," said Dave.

"Yup, friend of mine," said George. "Sent missionaries to our heathen ancestors in England, you know. Made one of the greatest puns ever, about *Angles* becoming *angels*. Angles as in Anglo-Saxon," he added as Dave looked puzzled. "Why?"

"Well, one of the ways old Gregory did his thing was in drawing up organized lists of kinds of sin. And sloth was one of 'em. He used the Latin word *tristitia;* other guys used another Latin word, *acedia*. That's what I felt like calling you about in the middle of the night the other night."

"Good grief," ejaculated Dave.

"What's the difference between the two?" asked George. "I used to know, I suppose, but I've forgotten."

"Just a minute," said Tom. "First, before I forget it—this fellow Gregory had one subdivision that really fascinated me. *165*

Under *tristitia,* he had one subtopic that has a whole lot of the twentieth century compressed into it. How's your Latin?"

"Fire away," said George. Dave looked quizzical.

"Okay. Here you are. *Vagatio mentis erga illicita.* Has a nice sonority, hasn't it? *Vagatio mentis erga illicita.*"

"Which being interpreted is?" asked Dave.

"*Mentis,* mind," said George. "*Illicita.* That's obvious. But *vagatio—*"

"Try 'wandering,'" said Tom. "Roughly, a wandering mind in respect to forbidden things?"

"Um-m-m-m. Yes. And for an age like ours that has tried to forget that anything was ever forbidden—yes. Now what about those two Latin labels you were going to tell us about? *Tris—* what?"

"*Tristitia.* Basically a sadness. The opposite of the doxology, and all that. Gloomy. Negative. No joy. Rather different from an activist's idea of sloth, isn't it? Maybe they had something. Maybe sometimes we try to excuse as a personality problem something that really is a *sin* problem, if you get to the nitty-gritty of it."

"Which we from time to time most grievously have committed by thought, word, and deed against Thy Divine Majesty," quoted George quietly.

"Now your other word," prompted Dave. "Time's a-marchin', friend. If I had known you were so wound up, I'd have left you in the geraniums."

"Next time you'll know better," said Tom. "The other word is equally worth chewing on. *Acedia.* Originally from a Greek word *ƙedos,* care, the dictionaries say."

"So the one afflicted with *acedia* couldn't care less?"

"Right. Exactly. And the topics on which he couldn't care less were God and immortality and his own soul. Not jobs and production quotas and mortgages and cars."

"At the risk of sounding rude," said Dave, "may I mention that it's almost lunchtime? I know it's your day off, Tom, but any definition of sloth under the shining sun would seem to suggest that I take you back to your geraniums and take myself to some things I've gotta get done."

"And miles to go before I sleep," said George.

"One more thing, though—" Tom's chin was on his hand and he seemed to be looking through the ceiling of Joe's Diner and off toward interstellar space.

"Shall we let him say one more sentence, Dave?"

"Okay. Reluctantly."

"Well, look. After all, is the taproot of the sloth business the same as the taproot of all other iniquities whatsoever—"

"Namely?" Dave was pushing back his chair and picking up his brief case.

"Well, selfliness. Inclining toward what *I* want instead of toward what God wants of me."

"That's a king-sized theorem to take along," said George. "Meanwhile, the miles to go before I sleep. Adios, Joe."

Elizabeth Dacey

"Aren't you ever coming to bed, Diana?" Cathy Welch came from the kitchen with a sandwich that oozed peanut butter around the edges. Her hair was on wide rollers and her face glistened with skin cream.

Diana looked up from the dining room table where books and papers were scattered at all angles. "Hey, I'm glad you came along," she said. "I'm about to quit. I just finished this character sketch for English class." She giggled as she started to pick up her books.

"I thought you started working on that right after supper," said Cathy. "And what's so funny?"

"I did start. I started last Saturday. Trouble is, I got going with a poem, but I don't dare hand it in. Somebody besides Mr. Hinman might see it; he might even want to read it to the class. And I'm afraid she'd be recognized."

"She? What she?"

"Well, I'll let *you* hear it. See if you can guess." She stood, straightened her shoulders, and held the paper at a dramatic angle. "It has a title," she said. "It's called 'In the Key of Grumbling.' "

"Oh?"

"Yes. Now listen:

Her theme song is
   'They ought, they ought.'
In the key of grumbling
   Her tunes stay caught.

With her in the room
   Throats will cough at rough tickles:
When she speaks, friends all swallow
   Sharp fishbone prickles.

Her lenses must be of a
   Filtering glass;
They see nothing for praising
   Arrive or pass.

If they'd give her a tour
　　Through the golden streets
She'd decry the design,
　　Scorn the rabble one meets.

She wears dark contempt
　　Like a fitted gown,
And she blackens the landscape
　　Of Strettam town."

Diana put the paper back on the table. "Okay, who is it?"

"Well, I don't know everybody in Strettam, of course. Or not very well anyway. Is it somebody who lives in Strettam?"

"Um-hum."

"Well, then, I s'pose it's Mrs. Dacey."

Diana laughed. "What did I tell you? Sure, it's Mrs. Dacey. But you see why I couldn't hand that in? It took me long enough to write, too."

Gracie Mermann

all flat just as flat as the Metonic River surface
flatter
nothing ever matters
house all clean again this morning vacuumed dusted and I
don't care I don't care I don't care
nicest house in the whole Metonic valley George says and
I don't care
forty-nine years old and I have done everything there is to
do in this dumb valley everything everything
blah
could make a dress but why bother
could write to my cousins but why bother
could make jelly
blah
blah in the morning and blah at night
blah to the left and blah to the right

sluggish
ruggish
buggish
sluggish

slothful
clothful
cheesecloth in my eye sockets flannel in my brain chest cavity
full of knitting wool
chest cavity heart cavity
empty empty empty
charge it up to my age bracket well partly maybe never paused
many pauses before
before
never cared though never cared a care not ever
George or not George
big house little house pigpen barn

so we do live in this split-level and I muddle around with
waxes and detergents
which I don't care about
for a man I don't care about
on a hill I don't care about
above a river that's stupid and gray
all day
all day
all day

blah

if I could have lived in New York or Paris
or even Keyesport or Princeville

if I cared two hoots about politics or civil rights or anything
anything anything
if I believed in anything hard enough to tell anyone else
about it
blah
who said lives of quiet desperation
o God o God o God o God

so they all think I'm happy and gay
what was it Jolene Thurston said last Tuesday at the Bartletts
your best friend won't tell you
your best friend won't hear you
screech screech scream
and they would all smile so politely and make the same old
jokes
blah

so I think
I will go
take a nap
in the Metonic
forever and ever
amen

And that afternoon Sloth went gyrating in triumphant hand-
springs up and down the hillsides that sloped toward the Metonic
south of Strettam.

Heinrich Dreiser

"Hi, Kevin."

"Oh, hi, Diana. What's new?"

"Well, let's see. Today, the twentieth of June. A new day—all new and never used before."

"On your way somewhere?"

"Just down to Dreiser's. Mom wants an extension cord and a spatula."

"On a gorgeous day like this, and your biggest adventure is to buy a spatula?"

They both laughed. "Well," said Diana, "Mr. Hinman says you can even dig ditches with grace and glory. S'pose I can shop for a spatula with grace and glory?"

"From Mr. Dreiser?"

"Why not? We're talking about how I buy the spatula and not about how he sells it. His store is about the gloomiest place along Main street, isn't it?" They both turned and looked down the street, past Joe's Diner and Wildeman's grocery and the Rexall and Dacey's, to the corrugated metal front of Dreiser's Hardware, with its rusty streaks across corroding ochre paint.

"He sure is a funny old geezer," said Kevin. "Remember the theme that Rick Hartford wrote about him? Dreiser sure would have had a fit if he could have heard how Rick imitated his accent."

"Actually his accent is sort of nice," said Diana. "And it's really funny to hear Mr. Dreiser put pieces of new American slang into his old German sentences. But I wish he were a more human sort of a human being. Buying something from him always makes me think a little of getting something from a vending machine. You're there to buy, and he's there to sell, and that's all there is to it."

"Business is business, *ach ja.*"

Diana laughed again. "Well, I'd better quit poking and go buy that spatula," she said. She paused, a very long pause. Up the street a customer was just entering Dreiser's store. (Was it Jim

Thurston?) He stopped to look at a decal ad which was on the plate glass door, a little red splotch that Diana didn't remember seeing before. He rubbed a curious finger across its surface, and Diana caught her breath. Bending over a little like that, he looks like Christ knocking at the door in the Bible story pictures, she thought.

"See a ghost?" asked Kevin.

"No." She hesitated. To say anything— No, even Kevin might think she was silly. "Now to go in search of a shining spatula. See you, Kevin."

Jim Thurston was the only customer, and he was about to carry away a pail of white paint. "Mr. Dreiser," Diana heard him say as she turned to a high counter piled with kitchen gadgets, "I don't think I've ever asked you where you attend church. We would be glad—"

Dreiser looked across his little steel-framed lenses and snorted audibly. Wide wisps of unruly hair above his ears quivered as he shook his head. "Church, *ach,* no," he said. "For church I haff no time. Sundays I make my orders, I make my inventories, I sleep. In Germany, yes, with my mother I went. For all the churches in America—" He shook his head more vigorously. "I could not care more *less.*"

Thurston picked up his pail of paint. "You're missing a lot, you know."

"I miss a lot, *ach ja.* I miss stupid sermons and stupid singing. I am not a *Dummkopf,* such stupidity to like to have—"

"We don't seem to agree," said Thurston mildly, starting toward the door. "Maybe you'll think differently one of these times."

The door closed behind him. Trying to choose between a spatula with a turquoise enameled handle and one with a copper finish, Diana heard Dreiser bang the cash register open and shut. *"Dummkopf,"* he snorted, half under his breath. *"Dummkopf. Du bist sehr dumm, mein Herr."*

"It isn't just going to church, though, Mr. Dreiser," she said.

"Verzeihung?" Oh, he's sorta mad. He forgets and lapses into German more when he's mad. She swallowed an odd dryness that had settled across her tonsils.

"Well, I mean—the important thing isn't going to church, you know," she said. "Mr. Thurston's or anybody's. God is important, and getting ready to live for ever and ever and ever is important."

He shut his lips so hard that his little gray mustache quivered. "You wish something to buy, yes?"

"Yes, please. This one." She handed him the turquoise-handled spatula. "And an extension cord, the longest one you have, please." Racks of chisels and hammers swam through her vision, and piles of plastic dishpans, and rows of garden tools. The old oiled floor had never looked so ugly and drab.

"Does it keep you awfully busy to run the store by yourself now, Mr. Dreiser, with Mrs. Corbie gone?"

"*Ja,* busy, always busy." He looked at her across his steel-framed lenses. Oops, she thought, he's still mad. "This store, *Fraulein,* this store is me. Me, Heinrich Dreiser. For your Gott and your heaven—I tell you, I could not care more less. Would He give me a store in heaven I could run for His angels? Here is your change. Two dollars, three, four, five. Thank you."

Diana looked at the red decal as she opened the door. An odd rough surface. No wonder Mr. Thurston wanted to touch it. Oh, it's on the inside, actually.

She walked slowly toward the blinker light. "Hey, Diana, wait up!" Kevin was just leaving the Rexall store with a Keyesport *Herald* and a copy of *Time,* and Diana obediently waited.

"Any new samples of gemixt English from Herr Dreiser this time?"

Diana nodded. Her eyes were on the point at which Highway 37 vanished into the northward horizon rather than on Kevin. "Yes. A sample that makes me feel as though I had some sand-burs in my aorta. Know what, Kevin? He said that for God and for heaven, he could not care more *less.*"

"Come again?"

"For God and for heaven—and for all the churches in America —he could not care more *less.*"

"Oh. Sort of inclusive, isn't he?"

Diana looked at Kevin, then at the magazine in his hand, and drew a long breath. "And it's just starting to hit me," she said. "Mr. Dreiser isn't just our Mr. Dreiser with a thick accent. He's about a jillion people all across the country. And all around the world. I s'pose not many would be so blunt about it, but when you come right down to it, that's the way they live. Isn't it? For God and for His heaven, they could not care more less."

"Or they care," said Kevin, folding *Time* under his arm and opening a little sack of peanuts, "but they don't know they care, and so they sell spatulas with all the more whangdoodle?"

Just above their heads, Sloth was turning slow, easy cartwheels along the Main Street storefronts. Above Dreiser's, he paused to do an elaborate and grotesque ballet.

Freddie Farless

He sat on a cushion of tough grass with his spine slanted against ridges of oak bark and a fishing rod braced against his left knee. Tiny ripples swirled against his line, and three crows cawed toward him from the next oak.

His Thursday off. His rod and reel. Peace shimmering on the Metonic. And anger burning, burning, in every corpuscle.

He thought he was alone, but four of Them sat behind him in the shape of giant vultures. At least one of Them was always with him, from alarm clock time to sleeping pill time. If he ever awakened at two or three or four, at least one of Them was immediately roosting on the foot of his bed.

This morning, again, the everlasting hassle. "No, I'm going fishing."

"Freddie, the front yard has *got* to have some attention. The hedges—"

"Well, why don't you hire someone to do it? You're making enough money to hire a full-time gardener, if it's clipped hedges you want."

"Oh, Freddie, just because I make more money than you do—"

"Okay, rub it in."

"Fred, let's not be petty. The office needs me—"

"Like heck. You need it, Clytemnestra. You need kingdoms to rule."

"Please don't call me names. If you're going to call me names, at that, you might at least use something I know instead of trying to show off your tremendous learning. Clytem-what?"

"Clytemnestra, my dear. She just happened to be the most unpleasant one I could think of at the moment."

She picked up her gloves. "I can't delay any longer. If you'd ever agree to move to Princeville, I would have a good half-hour longer to do housework every morning."

"Sure. As you've said sixteen hundred times. Move to some

box of chrome and glass in Princeville and sell this house which the Farless family has owned for a century—"

"Which your great-grandfather built from locally fired brick."

"Right. And you needn't sneer at it, and I'm not about to move out of it. Besides, it's nice to have my half-hour of peace after Queen Catherine the Great leaves every morning."

"Freddie, dear, don't be so melodramatic. You are going fishing?"

"Yes, drat it, I am going fishing. I am going fishing. I am going fishing. And I hope you draw all the crabbiest customers all day long."

"My, my, what a tantrum. Kiss me, darling."

His lips touched her cool cheek, and his imagination visualized snake fangs instead of lips. To bite, to pierce, to tear, to lash with poison.

To bite. Freddie realized that a weight was tugging at his line and started slowly reeling in.

When did everything start going so sour? So brackish? Such alum and quinine. For the zipteen trillionth time: I shouldn't have married her. I should have married Adelle Zorbic, before Glenn Fiedler came along to make such a fool out of her. I should have married Nellie Herriott, and then maybe there wouldn't have been a Gaspereaux wreck, and she wouldn't be a living corpse. And I wouldn't be a living corpse. I should have been a bachelor, with my guitar and my fishing poles and my books and my own old brick house. Without her, I could have written a book of poems every year, more or less, during evenings and weekends. None published, maybe, but I'd have been a happy man, with malice toward none and with nobody envied. As it is, what a collection of envies and covetings I carry around.

I shouldn't have married her.

But when she came to visit McNairs and I met her, she didn't seem like a steel and leather empress. Eyes so demure and face so demure. "And you write poetry, Mr. Farless? Oh, how thrilling. With a career in the bank, too?" And she was already casting me as a director of the bank, as a banker in Keyesport, as a banker in Chicago or New York. Expecting to push me up ladders so her own pride could climb ladders.

That horrible evening, after I told McNair not to use me for a vice-presidency and then told her what I had done. I never swore at a woman before. Was I sadistic to get so much pleasure from seeing her wince? But at a cost. Right then she started thinking about a career for herself. Started being more of steel and more of leather.

She's smart enough. Drive and energy enough. Too much. Wonder what she would have done in New York City. Or Hollywood. A TV executive? Lucifer's own daughter.

But all I ever wanted was a wife to wife me. To read with me, to fish with me, to hear my poems, to hold my heart in her two soft hands.

Fresh bait. There. To cast, now. Out, way out.

Caught. I swallowed her bait, and she reeled me in, and here I am.

Divorce.

Divorce.

She'd rather not bother. I'm still a convenience, sometimes. And she's too proud; doesn't want that sort of publicity. And maybe a wife has a prestige in her office that a divorcee wouldn't have? But if she gets her eye on someone she thinks will really do for her what she used to think I'd do, to fulfill *her* envies and covets—

The irony, that I still love her about thirty-seven percent of the time. If she didn't try to run everything, always. If she didn't try to glitter so at every party, or anywhere else. If she didn't always make me feel as though I were just the foliage and she the flower. Or, more, that she's the orchid and I'm the tree she kills by growing on it. My lovely parasite. If we go anywhere, even down to Wildeman's grocery, I start by admiring her and being fond of her and end by hating her egregious ego. Not that she'd have to build me up all the time, but if she'd say the admiring thing once in a while; if she'd step over into the supporting role now and then, rather than needing always to be the star in our small comedy—

Our tragedy.

It's the only life I'll ever have, and you're murdering it, Estelle.

There, another bite. Easy now. C'mon, fish, follow the reel. Oops, no. Gone. Gone. Like all my daydreams about being another Frost, another William Carlos Williams, another Wallace Stevens. Thirteen ways of looking at a blackbird. Who said that? And I'm lucky if I ever hear a blackbird any more, much less see him as any of the thirteen ways.

So I hate her kind of pride, and it drives me into a blue fury. Am I furious only because she tramples—with those elegantly styled heels of hers—on *my* kind of pride? So be it. A man does not lie still and smile while his own wife lifts a knife to castrate him. And in slow torture, not at one fell swoop. (Freddie, Freddie, how trite can you get? At one fell swoop.) With every month that we live, she makes me less a man.

So, one of these times it will come to divorce. Before that, I'm going to keep my maleness alive, outside of her tyranny.

If Rita Corbie hadn't moved away—

"Why, Mr. Farless, I don't know a thing about fishing." Giggle. Giggle. "Of course you're probably good at giving all sorts of lessons, aren't you?" Giggle, giggle. "Shall I sit here on the grass beside you, Mr. Farless? Will all of the fish just pop their eyes out watching me?" Giggle, giggle. Snuggle.

He lifted the pole and flung the hook farther out into deeper water. Nausea lurched through his midriff and he felt, again, as though he had just walked through a sewer. Rita Corbie was a slut and a tramp.

But to have an affair with a nicer girl. Someone who is not a computer and a dictator like you, Estelle. All girl but also all lady, and with enough mind to know tetrameter couplets from sonnets.

Sunset. Saffron and mauve. He stood, flexed his knees, picked up the creel. It's later than I thought. Estelle will be home, and dinner will be getting cold, and she will have a rare cache of poisoned arrows ready to shoot at me from the moment I enter the back door.

Well, it's really your fault, Countess. If you were more of a wife, you can be sure I'd be more of a husband. But you would rather set your records at selling real estate than to be a wifely wife to Adam himself in a bower in Eden—much less to a bank teller named Freddie Farless in the town of Strettam.

For which at this moment, my sweet Estelle, I hope that your attractive body will be eaten up, in due season, by particularly hideous and greedy worms. And that your dictatorial personhood will rot slowly in whatever hell can be found for it.

Other moments, other thoughts. Before bedtime, twenty different moods will come and go. If I weren't so fond of you, even you, during some recurring moments, I wouldn't ache and hate so much during other recurring moments.

He walked slowly toward his car, and the four of Them stalked slowly behind him like four giant vultures.

Matt Heiler

"Company coming," said Annette, nodding toward the big front window.

They watched a long white car easing up the lane past a bend in the road that looped around the knees of their big old oak tree. "That's a Cadillac, isn't it?" said Mavis. "Hope they're in a good buying mood that matches it."

A long-legged family emerged. "All of the clothes have Neiman-Marcus labels," said Annette.

"Sure?"

"Oh, quite. Maybe one Peck and Peck blouse. He's in oil, and she owns a radio station or two."

"As for their preference in sculpture, we'll soon see." The knocker clattered, and Mavis moved toward the door.

"This *is* Heiler's Studio? We weren't quite sure, from the directions they gave us—"

Authentic Dallas accent, thought Annette. Oil, let's hope. Maybe Matt's in luck this time.

"Yes, various pieces available for purchase," Mavis was saying. "This way, please."

Annette followed at a discreet distance. Let his wife do the sales talk; let her sister please not interfere. Great-aunt Adelaide's big living room isn't bad for a showroom, as I've always said. Take the bust on the mantel, Mr. Dallas. If you're smart. It's as good as a Brancusi. Or the tall copper Icarus over in the corner.

One of the colt-legged teen-agers peered up at the mantel and giggled hysterically. "Dodo, look at this. Did you ever *see* such a silly nose?"

"I think we have wasted our time in coming out here," said Mrs. Dallas. She was standing in the middle of the room and pivoting slowly. "There's nothing here that would go with my draperies and rugs. Nothing at all." But she and all her tribe lingered and looked and prattled and scorned for lengthening minutes.

"What in the world is *that?*" asked Mr. Dallas finally, looking at the copper Icarus. "Pheasant or rooster or dragon or what? Madam, we were given to understand that Matthew Heiler is a *sculptor*—"

"He is." Matt's voice was like a detonation of summer thunder. He had started down the staircase and stood glaring at the man from Texas. Like a Zeus, thought Annette. Like somebody posing for a statue of Moses ready to fling down stone tablets. How long has he been standing there? "Would you kindly get out of my house, you—you—you utter *fools?*"

"Well, I must say—" breathed Mrs. Dallas. But she didn't say; she strode, and her tall daughters and her tall husband strode with her.

"Fools," said Matt again. He turned, and they heard his heels thudding across the floor of the back bedroom that was now a studio.

"He's just as explosive as ever, sis?" asked Annette. "I thought maybe after a year and half out here among the tranquil fields and pastures he would be more placid. More bovine."

"No such luck," said Mavis. "I hope he hasn't stirred up too much adrenalin to get any more work done today. Let's go out to the garage and leave the house quiet while he recuperates. I'll do a little more sky in that new one I was working on last night."

"Okay, fine." Annette perched on a tall three-legged stool and watched her sister mix colors. "If he's like this over some empty-headed customers, the reviews of his one-man show in Rochester last fall must have given him five king-sized ulcers. He did see some of the reviews, I suppose? Or did you hide 'em all from him?"

"He did see some of the reviews. And his reaction was ferocious. Just ferocious. He calmed down after he got some letters from museum directors inquiring about purchase, though, and a fantastic letter from Mannini. You know, his major professor in art school. Then he was hard to live with for a while because he was so cocky. It was like being back in art school again, when his moods could go from jet black to orange in a few hours, depending on who praised him or didn't praise him and who praised somebody else or didn't praise somebody else."

"Well, that's the price of being a genius."

Mavis shook her head. "Not just of being a genius." She applied smooth brush strokes and stepped back to cock an appraising glance at the canvas. "A genius who happens to have morbid sensitivity dripping from every hair on his chinny-chin-chin. Or call it pride." More brush strokes. "I found a thing in

Dante's *Purgatory* the other day that really fits Matt. A painter named Oderisi, or something like that, was talking—from beyond the grave, of course—and said that 'ardor to outshine burned in my bosom with a kind of rage.' That's Matt all over."

"Ma-a-a-vis!"

Annette jumped again as her brother-in-law's voice rolled across the yard, but the voice didn't sound angry this time. Mavis wiped her hands on a paint-daubed cloth and stepped to the door of her garage studio. "Yes?"

"Let's have some coffee. Will you put the pot on while I go down to the mailbox?"

"Good idea. I'll be right there." She took off her painting smock and tossed it on a chair. "Let's fix a tray and take it into the showroom," she said to Annette. "He likes to sit and look at his children."

"It won't make him fume some more against those Texas yokels?"

"No, I don't think so. We'll risk it."

"Don't look now, but I think there's another hurricane blowing," said Annette a few minutes later, nodding toward the big front window.

"Oh, dear!"

Matt's heels clanked hard as he mounted the steps. "Of all the stupid idiots," he said. "Mavis, they've just made Tom Detlinger the Artist in Residence at Janisco College. Tom Detlinger!"

"Do I know him?"

"Sure. He was at the apartment sometimes. He and I were in a Life Drawing class together. He's stupid. He's utterly stupid."

"Were you counting on this appointment, Matt?" asked Annette. "Had you applied?"

"One doesn't go around applying for that kind of an appointment," said Matt harshly. "But the trustees at Janisco know about my work, of course. Their art gallery even owns one of my pieces. A welded metal heron. It's the best thing they have, by a long shot."

"I wouldn't have thought you'd want to move to Janisco," said Annette mildly. "You're hardly well settled in these studios here."

"I wouldn't have taken it," said Matt. "But they owed me the courtesy of naming me and giving me a chance to refuse. They've tacitly announced that Detlinger is a better sculptor than I am. The blithering idiots."

"Here, Matt, have some coffee," offered Mavis.

He took the cup, gulped twice, flung it back on the tray, and strode to the stairway. Three times, as he climbed, his left fist banged against the dented old mahogany banister. In a few minutes they heard the click, thud, crash, and tap of his tools from the north studio.

"Genesis of a masterpiece?" asked Annette. She settled her blue jeans more comfortably on the tooled leather hassock where she was sitting and leaned long blonde hair against the dark wainscoting.

"Maybe. More likely he'll ruin that beautiful piece of cherry that he's been so pleased about. His best work comes when the stone or wood or metal has been talking to him quietly, and not when he's raging. When his pride gets hurt like this, he's so furiously determined to get recognition that he slashes around and destroys his own ideas—and his own best materials, too."

"But maybe, long-range, this hunger to be famous drives him and sustains him?—drives him to his best achievement?"

"Maybe. I've been married to him for eight years, but I still don't really know how the landscape looks inside his mind. I'll never know. Sometimes I think it must be like the vicinity of a Vesuvius during an eruption, with hurricanes and tornadoes and earthquakes going on at the same time."

"Zowie! But something like that is what mom worried about when you married him, you know."

"I know."

"Well, like I said, maybe that's the price of genius."

"No. No." Mavis stacked the cups and went to stand by the mantel, diminutive against it in her pedal pushers and red cotton shirt. Her fingers traced the chin line, hair, and nose of the tall sculpture at which the girl from Dallas had hooted. "No. I've thought and thought about it for these eight years and more. I think Matt is a genius—heaven help him. Any genius does have a tremendous drive. That's partly why I know I'm not one; I'm a happy dawdler, and I always will be. Painting is fun, but so are a lot of other things. But the essence of being a creative genius is *creating,* not trying always to outshine and excel—" She paused and picked up the sheaf of mail that Matt had flung on the mantel. "Well. Here's a letter he didn't see. Must have been stuck inside a magazine. He'll want this. It's from his adored Mannini. Luigi L. Mannini."

"So do you interrupt his majesty's volcanic erupting to give him the letter?"

Mavis listened. "I don't hear his tools going, but maybe I'd better wait until he comes down."

"Like at dinner time?"

Mavis shrugged. "Maybe in ten minutes. Maybe for dinner tonight. Maybe tomorrow noon."

"Hey, he's on the phone," said Annette. "I didn't know he had an extension in the studio."

"Not in the studio. He'd die first. But there's one in the south bedroom, one he can detach when he doesn't want it to ring."

After a few minutes Heiler appeared at the top of the stairs. "Would you make me some more coffee, Mavis?" he said. "And how about some sandwiches?"

Mavis disappeared into Aunt Adelaide's old kitchen, and Annette watched her tall, bearded brother-in-law come down the stairs. Like a sleepwalker, she thought. Hey, what's he grinning about?

He sat on the wide ledge of the lowest step. "Mavis," he said loudly, "I've phoned a telegram to the president of Janisco that will blister his bald head. And a copy of it to half a dozen newspaper editors. Detlinger will wish he had never heard of Janisco, and vice versa." He laughed, a harsh roaring laugh that sounded like a winter surf against rocks.

Mavis rolled a serving cart through the tall doorway and pulled open the wrapper of a loaf of rye bread. She looked angry and frightened. "Well, I hope you'll be just as glad about it a year from now," she said.

Or a millennium from now? thought Annette. What was that Dante bit that Mavis had quoted? "The ardor to outshine burned in his bosom with a kind of rage." "Matt, you didn't see all of your mail," she said aloud. "Mavis says you missed something important."

Matt unfolded himself and reached for the sheaf of mail. Magazines and circulars fell to the floor when he saw Mannini's scrawl. "Hey, what day's today?" he asked after he had read a few lines.

"The twenty-ninth," said Mavis. "Why?"

Matt looked at the postmark, looked back at the letter, looked at the postmark again. "Stupid post offices," he said. "Wonder where they hid this. He's coming to see us, Mavis. May be here tonight. Says he's on his way to a conference, and this is right on the way. He'll phone from Princeville or Strettam or somewhere—"

"So I'd better take a sleeping bag and move out to the barn loft," said Annette. "I could just clear out and start home this afternoon, but if I vacate the extra bedroom, may I stick around? I'd like to let these china blue eyes of mine look once upon the great Mannini's countenance."

"Of course," said Mavis. Matt wasn't listening.

At midnight Annette took her flashlight and left for the barn loft. The next morning Mavis, scrambling eggs, smiled wryly. *183*

"You'd just as well have stayed in your bed," she said.

"He didn't come?"

"He came. About two. But he and Matt have been talking non-stop ever since. They probably don't even know it's morning. Ring the little bell there on the shelf over the sink, would you?"

"You think they'll stop talking to eat breakfast?"

"Maybe yes, maybe no. It's worth a try."

Annette went to the foot of the stairs, rang the little hand bell vigorously, and then stepped back inside the kitchen to be unobserved as the two men came downstairs. He looks like a cousin to Beethoven, she decided. Or like an uncle to St. Francis. Does an art school prof, and such a great one, subsist on ordinary mortal fare like scrambled eggs and toast? Do I dare to sit at the same table while he eats?

The great man yawned a little, burped a little, and smiled vaguely in Annette's direction. Both he and Matt seemed drowsy and tranquil after their night of talk. Local ornithology and the cloud formations of the morning absorbed their desultory conversation until Mavis, bringing fresh muffins, finally asked, "Well, Professor Mannini, do you find Matt's work improved by this rustic environment?"

"Environment or not, he is doing brilliant things," said the old man. "If he lives enough years and lets his soul grow tall, from heaven I shall look back, God willing, and see some sculpture worthy of the angels themselves."

Matt smiled a tight, unhappy smile. "Shall I tell that to Janisco College, Mavis? And to those creeps that were here yesterday?"

Mannini wheeled in his chair and faced Matt. "Now listen to me, my son. I have said if he lets his soul grow. If, if, if. I have listened all night to what you have not said. Now hear me. So long as you work to shine out above Tom Detlinger, or above Michelangelo himself, you condemn yourself to be a halfway man and a bungler. In art school always you were too much so: to be better than Detlinger, better than Morris, better than Casell. No. That is a poverty. To try for a medal, to try for a prize, that is a foolishness. To have a vanity over what your hands have done—it is to be so small." His veined old hands measured a space six inches apart. "When the fire of making burns in your brain, my son, then the creating hand of God Himself is resting on your head. He makes; you make. You hold the chisel, and His hand surrounds your hand. To have pride for that is a madness."

Please, Matt, don't explode, thought Annette. The skin on his face was tight, and his voice was so husky it sounded like someone else's. "You always told us not to be apologetic for our work," he said.

"Not to apologize, yes. When the mind of the Maker has put something into your mind, you must not droop down your eyes and say silly things about how poor it is. If your hand has obeyed your mind when your mind has touched His mind, you will be glad beyond gladness, and you will not speak a foolishness in pretending to be humble. But this is not the same as to rage when someone does not praise you, or makes a bad comparing, or has not eyes to see what you have seen. In God's name, live by what you are and not by the so-big space" — again his wrinkle-netted hands measured a space a few inches across — "between what you want to be worth and what any other man says you are worth. Not if the other man were Rembrandt van Rijn or da Vinci himself. And certainly, certainly not if it is some customer or some critic who maybe does not touch the mind of the Maker even once in columns of his writing."

"That's easy enough for you to say, with your temperament," said Matt resentfully.

Mannini smiled. "Oh? You think so? Matthew Heiler, to tell you these things I have walked through fires for this so long a lifetime. My soul has had blisters like goose eggs on its feet often enough, I promise you."

"Are sins of pride an occupational hazard of artists?" asked Mavis. "If all of the artists in the country were good Catholics, we'd keep the priests busy just hearing our confessions, I suppose."

"No matter," said Mannini. "No matter. Your husband is not responsible for the sins of all the artists in the country. But he'll have Matthew Heiler on his hands until the day of his death, God help him."

"And you really want me to be a namby-pamby milquetoast sort of a sculptor?" asked Matt in a flat, dry voice. "Not to notice what anyone else does, and not to try very hard —"

"Matthew, Matthew, Matthew. You have not always listened to me when you were in my classes, and you have not listened to me now. Other shows will come and go, but, so help you, God Almighty Himself is the jury who makes the verdict on your stone and wood and metal. Think of that often enough, and you'll try and try and try. More hard than yet you ever thought you could, I think."

I wish I were a sculptor, thought Annette. I'd like to do a big bronze of him, the way he looks right now, and title it "Jeremiah." Or maybe "John the Baptist, Preaching." "What you've been saying, Professor Mannini," she offered timidly, "is a lot like a poem I had to learn in fifth grade, about how 'each in his separate star' will—let's see—will 'draw the thing as he sees it for the God of things as they are.' "

"Kipling," said Mannini. "He has a good thought, yes. I like to think his thoughts, yes, but more I like another one. John Milton. He knew a man must live 'As ever in my great Taskmaster's eye.' Fame — oh, he was wise, that John Milton — fame, he said, is the last infirmity of noble mind. No little tawdry nothing mind is pushed around by wanting fame. But to want it is still an infirmity."

"So I'm *non compos mentis,*" said Matthew. "And if I were a Catholic, you'd be trying to haul me to a confessional somewhere, I suppose, like Mavis said. There isn't a confessional booth on this old farm, but I'd like for you to see what we have done with the garage. That's where Mavis paints. And my big studio is a corner of the old barn."

Annette carried a stack of dishes to the sink and pushed back a curtain to watch the men walk across the farmyard. "He's a great guy," she said. "Was Matt tuned in to hear him, do you think?"

Mavis shrugged. "Who knows? He used to come home quoting Mannini day by day in art school. Saint Luigi the Good, the guys called him. But so far as really hearing, to hook up some new connections in the electrical circuits inside his brain—I don't know. I just don't know. The professional art world is so horribly competitive —"

"What world isn't? Ever since our primal father Adam and his chum Lucifer, whose 'pride and worse ambition threw him down,' if Mannini's friend Milton can be brought into this kitchen once more this morning."

Mavis curtsied. "Good morning, John Milton. Nice to have you drop in again."

"Know what?" said Annette. "I'd like to see what would happen if Matt could plug in to the right power lines and live for a while by St. Luigi's code. I really would."

"I'd feel as though I had married a different husband, that's sure," said Mavis. "It's hard to imagine what his pride would be like if it weren't such a vain and touchy kind of pride. But living with a different model of Matt, built according to the Mannini specifications, is an experiment I'd be jolly glad to undertake just any old time."

Millie Killoran

"Two eighty-five, two ninety, three, four, and five. Thank you very much." As she pushed crinkled bills into the even more crinkled hand of a leathery little farmer, Janice Wilson glanced with annoyance at a bulky customer who was waddling up behind Martha Vincent, as Martha stood waiting behind the little farmer and his dowdy wife. Janice hated having customers line up to wait for her attention; they tapped fingers on counters, or hummed silly tunes, or fidgeted with their purses, and made her so nervous she wanted to scream at them.

"Mrs. Benedict is free, ma'am," she murmured in her glazed shopgirl voice. "She'll be glad to serve you." She nodded toward the adjacent hosiery counter where Alice Benedict was straightening boxes.

The bulky woman scowled a little and shrugged a little but did not move from her place behind Martha Vincent's pinched topknot of hair. Turning to pick up the little farmer's parcel of socks and garters, Janice caught a glimpse of Alice's face and was startled to see a look that she had never seen Alice wear before. Annoyance? Dislike? Pity? Or disgust?

"Yes, Mrs. Vincent?" She took a little heap of dishcloths and pot holders from Martha and stepped to her cash register. "Anything else today?"

Beyond Martha's shoulder, the bulky woman was looking stolidly at the battered old oak counter. She's trying hard not to look at Alice, but she's so aware of Alice she can hardly stand it, thought Janice. I feel it in my bones. When Martha took her parcel and left, Janice was half conscious that Martha was stopping at the hosiery counter to speak with Alice and that the two of them were moving over to the racks of ready-to-wear dresses. "You'd think *some* people could find another place to do their shopping," Martha was saying in a shrill sibilant whisper.

Janice felt suddenly queasy, as though she had been walking across a pleasant lawn and had suddenly stepped on garbage or on the half-eaten body of a dead rabbit.

"May I help you?"

"I want five yards of that denim over there," motioned the bulky woman. "And three pairs of them seamless nylons you've got on sale. Like's in the window. Size ten." Phew, thought Janice, there's something rotten in the shrubbery, for sure; it's hose she wants, and yet she wouldn't go near the hosiery counter when it didn't have a customer in sight and Alice Benedict was standing right there.

She stepped over to the next counter and riffled through the flat cellophane parcels in the sale rack. "Size ten? Here we are. What color?"

"That's okay, right there. I'm glad they're wrapped up in cellophane," she said, a little too loudly. "That way I know that dirty hands in this store ain't never touched 'em."

Muscles tightened in Janice's midriff. She feels — she feels — this slob of a woman feels about Mrs. Benedict sorta the way I used to feel about Joy McNair.

The woman took her parcel and waddled from the store. Martha Vincent finally left, too, after extended discussion of rainfall and aphids and what to do about cockroaches. Janice glanced around. Mr. Dacey was moving boxes of shoes at the back of the store, and Mary Odette was on her lunch hour. She strolled over to where Alice was straightening the rack of size eighteen dresses.

"Who was that fat slob that just left?" she asked. "I've seen her around town before, but not here in the store."

Alice's glance measured her slowly. "Let's not speak of Dacey's customers as slobs," she said finally.

"Okay, okay. But who is she?"

Another pause. "Her name is Millie Killoran. Mrs. Killoran."

"Oh. Ross Killoran's mother? The guy that works for a big appliance store in Princeville?"

"I believe she has a son."

"Does she —"

"Mrs. Dacey wanted you to make a towel display for the window," Alice said.

Okay, thought Janice. I know when I'm squelched. Prob'ly there's nothing I could ask that you'd want to answer. But I'd sure like to know — or maybe I wouldn't. Maybe it's something that smells even worse than a dead rabbit.

After dinner, Janice did not resist the temptation to ask her mother.

"Mrs. Killoran? Oh, dear, yes. Alice and Millie and I were in high school together. Millie was always crude, but proud, too. Terribly proud. She'd imagine insults where none were intended, and she had trouble forgiving anything. Like the mountain people who carry on their feuds for generations, I suppose."

"But why is she so mad at Alice? Ol' Alice gets my goat sometimes when she orders me around, but she isn't a bad egg."

"I wish you weren't so slangy, Janice. Oh, I guess it goes back to twenty years ago or so. How long has Alice worked at Dacey's?"

"Twenty-two years, she keeps telling me."

"Well, it's about that long, then. Several things happened that stung Millie's pride. About the worst was when Jim Benedict dated her a few times and then started going with Alice, and Millie was bitter about that. Then finally old Mr. Dacey — the father of your boss — used both of them during a Christmas rush one year and kept Alice on but didn't keep Millie. Millie has always said that Alice told lies about her and prejudiced Dacey against her —"

"Oh, that's silly. Alice is as curious as a cat, but she couldn't tell a lie if her life depended on it."

"I know."

"And if she has been stewing away in the juice of her offended pride for twenty years," Janice went on, "—hey, that's since before I was *born,* for heaven's sake! Why hasn't she applied some of that pride when she looked in the mirror? She's the fattest slob in this town, except for old Eliza Jarvis."

"I know. But you're not one to talk, child. You've gained ten or fifteen pounds since you started working at Dacey's, you know."

Janice opened her lips for a retort, but closed them again when she glanced at the big mirror over the mantel.

Half a dead rabbit. . . . And Joy in her coffin up there at St. Mark's cemetery. . . . And something dead inside my brain. . . . But when I gnaw on food, I feel a little bit alive, I guess. . . . Lazarus, come forth. . . . Lazarus, come forth. . . . In a town like Strettam, does any Lazarus ever come forth?

Dr. George J. Bailey, M.D.

Now that twig on the corner rosebush. And now that one. And another. Tom Williams put down the clippers, pulled off his gardening gloves, and flexed his right hand. Nothing like a Strettam dawn among Catherine's roses.

He glanced up at a footstep, the first of the morning except his own. Dr. Bailey: tall—six three or four, at least; clipped mustache; skin like tawny polished wood.

"You're out early," Tom said. "Summoned by the stork?"

Bailey shook his head somberly. "Not unless it was the stork that brought me."

"Brought you?"

A darker pigment seemed to settle across the doctor's face. "Today's my fortieth birthday," he said. "Makes you stop to think, and I've been thinking, with a vengeance. About fourteen personal demons have been kicking me around Strettam Hill all night."

"All night?" Tom frowned inwardly at himself for seeming able to answer only with a stupid repetition of the doctor's own words. Little Sir Echo, how do you do. "Catherine won't be up for half an hour yet," he said. "Want to come have some coffee and talk about the genus and species of these particular demons?"

The doctor hesitated, glanced at his watch, hesitated again. "All right. Still— No, I'd better not. I have office hours coming up, and I'm helping with surgery at Princeville later this morning. I'd better catch some minutes of sleep."

"Some other time, then?"

Again the doctor hesitated. "I hate to burden you with the maladies of my psyche, but I could probably use a prescription of the sort that you dispense. Maybe I'd be a bad patient, though, and refuse to swallow it."

How rich his voice is, thought Tom. Like Paul Robeson's. Like our records of Sir Lawrence Olivier—was it Olivier?—doing *Othello*. "This evening, maybe?"

"Not early, I'm afraid. Would nine o'clock do, or a little after?"

"Very good. Why not meet me at my study at the church? It's quieter than my pseudo-study here at the house."

"Right." Bailey took three steps and then turned back with a morose smile. "Does it have a good long psychiatric couch?"

"Well, no, but there's a big leather chair that always does its best to please."

All day Tom tried to sort out what he knew about the doctor. Moved here some three years ago, when Dr. Vancil wanted to retire. Just out of internship then. Good practice, even if a few people still say they will never go to a Negro. Though he's mostly white, obviously. They say he's good in diagnosis and treatment, but arrogant and brusque and sometimes even rude. Grew up here, didn't he? Yes, I'm sure I've heard that. Has a handsome blonde wife and a handsome big house. That big white colonial one with the pillars, up beyond St. Mark's. It doesn't really belong in Strettam. Too posh. Now what kind of demons? Marital problems, maybe? He's usually pretty taciturn. Usually too taciturn to tell anyone outright, I suppose, that he had been having a bout with demons all across Strettam Hill—whatever their species may be. Do we have any vestiges of the KKK around here? Something of that sort bothering him? Well, I'll be hearing tonight.

It was four minutes until nine, actually, when Bailey came in. He glanced appraisingly at the old leather chair, sat down heavily, rubbed his forehead and temples with stiff fingers. "Ah, an excellent couch," he said as he swung his feet up on the hassock. "Mind if I smoke? I don't usually, but last night's hike around the hill is catching up with me, and I'd like to remain more or less coherent."

"Go ahead."

Bailey filled a pipe, touched flame to it, and puffed quietly for a few moments. "Something inside me has been breaking loose, and I hope it's a therapeutic breaking," he said. "To start with, Dr. Freud, how much do you happen to know about my childhood?"

"Nothing, really. Someone told me you went to grade school here."

"And high school, too. That's all they said?"

"So far as I recall."

"Then the gossipers must stand in awe of you; there's a lot they could have said." He grimaced. "It was horrible, just horrible. I was a kind of Huck Finn without the humor and the glamour of a Mark Twain write-up. My folks lived in a shack at the edge of the river, two or three miles upstream. Dad — or the man I called dad — drank and gambled and caught a few catfish when he was sober enough. Nobody and nothing could ever make me think he was my own father. Mom — well, actually she was a sleazy prostitute, and I learned too much too soon about the baser elements of human experience, believe me. Both of them looked like Swedes or Norwegians—Nordic blond under their dinginess — but I didn't think much about looking so different from them until I started school."

"Here in Strettam?"

"Unfortunately, yes. There was a truant officer, and there was a school bus. There were ragged overalls and broken shoestrings and a piece of bread in an old syrup bucket for my school lunch. There were giggles and pointing, and a few times even beatings from the big boys. All very conducive to the learning process."

"But evidently you learned?"

"At least a little. Well, when I was eight, the shack caught on fire one day while I was at school, and mom and dad both disappeared from my horizons forever. There were some court actions that I didn't understand, and I was farmed out to an old Dutchman a mile north of Strettam, to be his chore boy." His face became bitter, and he puffed rapidly at the pipe.

"It was pretty grim?"

"Grim. Like a chapter from Dickens. I didn't mind the farm work so much, though it was long enough and hard enough, but old Jelwyck and his wife saw to it that everybody in Strettam knew about my antecedents and about their charity in giving me a foster home. They kept me dressed like a fifth-rate scarecrow, and they tried to pinch out every sprout of ambition that ever sprouted. For the rest of grade school and all through high school the kids tormented me and ostracized me. The older people talked about me and pitied me. Some of the old ones and young ones ridiculed my skin and called me ugly names."

"Does memory accentuate the ugliness, maybe?"

"Perhaps. But with all leeway for hyperbole, it was ghastly."

"Something better must have happened eventually? To help you change from *that* to *this?*"

"Several somethings. A teacher or two were like lampposts on dark nights. Not all of them. You know Mrs. Derwent, I suppose? I was the particular butt of her malice in high school, and, believe me, she had a quantity of it to pour out. The principal really went to bat for me when he decided I had at least two wits in my cranium, and he helped me to get a good scholarship for college —"

"The farmer, Jelwyck, let you go to college then?"

Bailey shrugged. "Luckily for me, he died at a very convenient time. His will didn't bring me any wealth, but I was emancipated from his pigpens. So — well, I won't bore you with all of it, but scholarships and sweat and summer jobs finally, finally saw me through." He paused and blew a series of little puffs from his pipe. "Finally. I was a lot older than most of my classmates."

"So?"

"Well, all of that is the overture to this particular opera. Or this soap opera. When all the men in my med school class were starting to look seriously for their places to settle and checking the openings in the journals, I noticed one day that Dr. Vancil wanted to sell his Johnson County practice and retire. And you might say that Mephistopheles himself moved into my room that night."

Tom lifted an inquiring eyebrow. "Was Vancil's practice *that* lucrative?"

"Oh, no. Average minus, as country doctors go. Adequate but not elegant, by any means."

"You had some fondness for placid Strettam, then, in spite of everything? But that wouldn't have been a mission for Mephistopheles."

"I hated Strettam and everyone in it." Bailey's fist thudded against a low filing cabinet, and Tom wondered if it would splinter. "I felt as though I had been degraded and avoided and laughed at here from the day I was born. Well, anybody knows that an American doctor, unless he's a blundering idiot in his practical affairs, is one of the most admired men in a community. Most places it would obviously be harder for a man with a little soot in his skin, like mine, to win his way, but the basic premise still holds. Frankly, that admiration principle had been a big part of my motivation in going into medicine. Well, it began to amuse me to think of coming back here to — how shall I say it? — to lord it over the very people who had always lorded it over me when I was a kid." Silence. A longer silence. "I've never put this into words before, and it's like opening a blood vein to try —"

"Take your time."

"Well, I simply determined to come back and be so efficient that I'd build a good practice, in spite of my permanent sun tan, and that I'd find my own sweet ways of being condescending to everybody who had ever taunted me or laughed at me or pitied me. I'd be condescending and even insulting. Sometimes they might know I was snubbing them, and sometimes they wouldn't. But I'd know it, and I'd gloat."

"And this is what you have done?"

"Right. I'm a good doctor. Anybody in the hospitals will tell you that. I haven't touched malpractice with a ten-foot pole. But at best I have treated the people of Strettam like so many machines to produce money and prestige for me, and at worst — well, anyone who could peer into my mind would say I have been flagrantly insolent to them. Often in covert ways they didn't even know, of course."

He paused and watched smoke spiral up toward the ceiling for long moments. "I suppose a lot of doctors really are pride incarnate so far as elegantly ostentatious spending goes, but I've been more deliberate about it than most. Everything I bought was to appease the miserable little guy I used to be and to make Johnson County kneel down. I won't try to say why anybody else buys what he buys, but I know that I carefully bought the biggest house, on the highest hill, because I wanted to outshine everybody else and do it publicly."

"And as a contrast with that old shack along the Metonic in your mental photo album?"

"Yes, that too." Tired lines were settling across the doctor's face. In the far distance they could hear the motor of a truck as it accelerated after the blinker on Highway 37. "And my life-style around town has matched my motivation about the house," he continued. "People think that I'm absent-minded, but I've often looked the other way and avoided a 'Good Morning' as a deliberate snub. Deliberate, but not too obvious, so as not to hurt the practice. Sometimes I've made appointments with the most important people in the county and then broken them, just for the sheer heck of it. Sometimes I've had a very malicious pleasure in finding something 'urgent' to do in my office in order to keep Robert C. W. McNair waiting longer in the examining room, or Ray Kendrick, or Charlie Wright, or just about anybody else that I knew when I was a kid."

Bailey stopped, and his eyes searched Williams' attentive face. "People I hadn't known before, too," he said. "I identified enough with black people, any and all black people, to have a surge of pleasure when I could show some covert malicious indignity to Whitey."

"If Whitey was in it," returned Williams, "you probably didn't ever let your office girls know about these assorted motivations for particular bits of conduct?"

"Right, I didn't. Sometimes they thought I was impossibly absent-minded and even arrogant, but they didn't know how deliberate it was. Nor that I was preparing these new poultices for my old scars."

"And your wife? Has she understood—"

"I don't think so. I hope not. Lois is a sweet person, and I didn't want to lose her, as I honestly thought I might if she knew the sorts of malice I had in me and what my real motivations were in coming back to Strettam. It has put a strain on our marriage, of course, for me to live in this much duplicity. Probably more than I knew. And it took some of the flavor out of a good many episodes not to be able to brag to anyone."

More white-blue puffs from the pipe. Bailey started to say something, checked himself, gnawed at the pipe stem. "Another thing," he said finally, "and this will make you say I've been really sick, or a clod, or both. If you were another M.D., you'd want to haul me before some committee of the A.M.A., I suppose."

"Well, I'm not. But if I were another doctor, I'd understand more of the subtle temptations a doctor faces, I suppose, whatever they are."

Four puffs. "We deal with human bodies all day long, obviously, and very early in the game they teach us to have a detached and professional objectivity. In med school and internship I lived that way. Here — well, I think I have been pretty good at role-playing as a respectful professional, but all the while I've had — well, a particular glee in what your Biblical language would call uncovering the nakedness of the town fathers whom I hated. And town mothers. And their offspring. Medical instruments plus some feelings of malice and revenge can be remarkably pornographic, I've discovered." A brooding expression of revulsion crossed the doctor's face. "There. I've said aloud what I didn't suppose I would ever say aloud. Want to kick me out the door and down the stairs?"

"Of course not." A long pause, while Tom Williams fingered the edges of his study Bible. "By the way, I notice that you keep using the past tense."

"Yes. I hope it's past tense. But I'm not too optimistic about my whole internal world spinning right side up at once. That's why I wanted to talk to you."

"I'm glad you came. Aside from the fact that life is said to begin at forty, is there any special circumstance that has started to turn you around in your tracks?"

The doctor emptied ashes from his pipe, refilled it, lighted it again. "Well, partly I've started wondering recently if this — this pornography bit was becoming a habit I couldn't break; whether it would stay with me in other offices. I've never thought I'd stay in Strettam for many years, and to think of carrying a mind away with me that would get its kicks from a Playboy stethescope for the rest of my life — well, it sickened me." Puff and puff and puff. "Partly the idea of turning forty really did get through to me." Puff and puff and puff. "Partly something else. It goes against the grain to say it, but your sermons have not been duds   *195* lately. Which is a nice, fat piece of irony. When we moved here, I persuaded Lois we should be a church-going family because I knew it would help my image, and I picked your church because it was the biggest. More people there to be impressed, and all that. But little by little I've been getting hooked, I guess."

"Well, I've heard worse news than that," said Tom with a grin.

"A couple of months ago when you preached on loving all the neighbors, it got to me," Bailey went on. "For weeks your shadow stood around in the corner of about every room I was in, shaking its index finger at me. And then last Sunday when you went hammer and tongs at this idea of loving your enemies, you were hitting me a jolt with just about every other sentence, you know. Me and my whole case history. So now —"

Tom felt as though he were watching a moth struggle to emerge from its chrysalis. It was like when Betty was born and they let him observe the delivery.

Dr. Bailey rubbed his eyelids with little circular motions and shook his head as though to stabilize some mechanism inside it. "Diagnosis, malignant, eh? So now, as I said this morning, I could probably use a prescription of the kind that you dispense. And, so help me, I will not refuse to swallow it."

Tom picked up the Bible he had been fingering and opened it slowly.

This time they were crows, sitting on the picket fence around the front yard at Welch's. They all watched silently as a tall man left the side door of the Methodist church and climbed into a sleek little foreign car.

"Well, there's mud in your eye," said Lechery to Pride.

"Beastly vermin," said Anger.

"He's not out of his mortal husk yet," said Sloth. "You still have plenty of innings coming with that one."

"We're talking to you, Brother Pride," said Gluttony. "The Enemy gave you an awful wallop tonight, but maybe the Bailey creature will still give you some good forage. Mere nibblings compared to what he has been giving, of course —"

"Shut up," said Pride. "All of you. This revolting Bailey one is bad enough, but he's only an insect. If all the dark ones in this country that Anger and I have been needling about their accumulated hurts were to imitate this Bailey bug — or if even a few of them did — the implications are horrendous."

"But so are we," reminded Gluttony. "Especially you. You know how the rest of us all get our courage from you, Brother Pride."

"Always have," said Lechery.

"Always will," said Anger. "Always, while mortals are mortal."

"Are mortal," echoed all the others, in a refrain that was like a chant. Like a caw. Like a curse. "Are mortal. Are mortal. Are mor-r-rtal."

Jennifer Aldrich

Keeping the bag of groceries balanced on her left hip, Katherine Aldrich struggled with the latch and finally held the key firmly enough to push the door open with one hand.

"Well. You're home?" She flung the heavy brown paper bag on the cluttered drainboard, watched it sag to one side, watched four white onions roll impatiently from it.

"Looks like it, doesn't it?" muttered Jennifer. She sipped noisily at the last of a chocolate milk shake.

"I thought you were going to Keyesport with the other kids. Isn't this the day for that choir festival you've been yakking about for two weeks?"

"Yeah, sure."

"Well, then?"

"I decided not to go." Jennifer muttered into the milk shake glass as she shook it over her tongue for three more drops.

Katherine pulled the grocery bag upright with an angry twitch. "Well, why not? I gave you the dollar, didn't I, after all that begging? Where's the money? You didn't lose it?"

"Here." Jennifer reached into her jeans pocket, tugging a little. The fabric was stretched tight across her wide hips. She flung a crumpled dollar bill on the table.

"Well, then, why didn't you go?"

Jennifer took a doughnut from a half-empty cellophane bag. "Just because," she said flatly.

"Jennifer Susan Aldrich, you tell me the truth. I'm not putting these groceries away and I'm not cooking supper until you tell me what's going on. And your father will be coming pretty soon, unless Mr. Wildeman keeps him overtime again —"

Tears were collecting on Jennifer's lashes and starting to roll down her plump cheeks. "Well, because every other girl in the whole choir had a date," she said sullenly. "There were plenty of guys, too, because Filer was taking the boys' glee club. Filer didn't want it to be a date affair. But it turned into that. And nobody —" She picked up a paper napkin and wadded it against her eyes. "And I wasn't gonna be the only —" More tears. More use of the paper napkin.

"Is that all?"

"All? Mother, it would've been horrible. It's horrible anyway. At noon in the cafeteria I heard some guys talking about me. 'You could still ask Jennifer,' said one, and the other one just howled. 'That fatso?' he said. 'That'll be the day.'"

"Well, you *are* fat," said Katherine. "Your dad would never have looked at me twice if I had been as sloppy fat as you are. I keep telling you —"

"You sure do."

Katherine started putting tin cans on the pantry shelf. "Keep a civil tongue in your head, young woman. Here, why don't you peel some potatoes while I start the chicken? If you'd ever go on a diet and stay on it —"

While Jennifer peeled the potatoes, an occasional tear dripped into the sink, and she reached more than once for another paper napkin. Flipping the switches on the stove, Katherine eyed her daughter crossly.

"Crying won't help, stupid," she said. "Did you ever talk to Mrs. Overton like you said you were going to?"

"Oh, sure. After Phys. Ed. class a couple weeks ago. She's as skinny as a garden snake, and she doesn't have any idea what it's like to be like this. Don't eat so much, she says. Count your calories, she says. Get more exercise, she says. As though it would be just as easy as — as — as blowing your nose."

"Like I've always said, you sure must take after your father's side of the house."

"Then I wish to hell that you had married someone else." In one motion Katherine swung the chicken skillet over to the side of the stove and spun around to face Jennifer. "What did you say?"

Jennifer looked like a young bull with blood on its horns and pawing. "I said I wish to hell that you had married someone else."

Katherine took one step toward her daughter, lifting her right hand and then her left to strike a harsh thud against each of Jennifer's plump cheeks. "I told you to keep a civil tongue, and I meant it. I won't stand profanity in this house from anybody. I can't help it if you're determined to be a glutton all the time, but some things I won't stand—"

Jennifer flung down the paring knife and ran for the stairs. She banged the door of her room behind her and flung herself on the bed to cry in a paroxysm of blubbering sobs. Sobs subsided into sniffles, and finally she dozed.

The room was half dark when she wakened to a loud knocking at her door. "Jennifer! Jennifer? Come on down. Supper's ready." *199*

"Okay, dad."

He was waiting for her at the top of the stairs. "Mom says you had a rough day. Don't worry, baby. There's a lot to life besides silly high school boys."

"Is there?" She blinked against new tears.

"Of course." He laughed, and she thought faintly of Christmas programs when he had romped into a room with that same laugh. "Right now there's supper, for instance. Now you dig right in, baby," he continued as they sat down at the kitchen table, "and forget about all your school troubles. See?"

Katherine looked at him crossly and put a bowl of mashed potatoes down with an extra bang, but she didn't protest. Not until Jennifer reached for the potato dish to give herself a fourth serving. "That'll do, Jenny," she said sharply. "Enough is enough, I always say, and too much is too much."

A pout on her face, Jenny shook a potato hillock from the serving spoon to her plate. "Next time she won't be so hungry," her husband soothed.

"Too much is too much," muttered his wife.

Jennifer planted a pudgy elbow on each side of her plate. "It's so unfair," she said drearily, looking at the empty gravy dish as though it were a fortune teller's crystal bowl.

"What's unfair, baby?"

"Life. And everything."

"Like what?" he persisted. He leaned back to loosen his belt and belched comfortably.

"Mom says too much is too much. Okay. I eat too much and it shows here —" She thumped her thick waistline with both fists. "— for the rest of my life. I even *smell* too much food and it shows on my hips. There's lots of other things you can do too much of, but does it make you any different to look at? No."

"Like what?" he asked again.

"Oh, kids are always saying their folks scold 'em for sleeping too much, or going to shows too much, or watching TV too much, or playing tennis too much, or hot rodding too much. Why is it so much more of a huge big sin to eat too much? You and mom watch TV too much, don't you? The yard's an awful mess ever since we got a color TV, and you know it —"

"Now, now, baby, don't tease your ol' dad."

"I'm not teasing. It makes me mad enough to spit. I eat too much and everybody laughs at me, and no boy would take me to the concert tonight. Not even the dumbest, pimpliest twirp in the whole choir. And then I come home and mom calls me a glutton. Okay, so I am. Well, why doesn't somebody yell 'glutton' when you watch the late late shows on TV until your eyes just about fall out and you can hardly get up to go to work the next morning, I'd like to know? Why doesn't somebody scream 'glutton' when Earl Junior smokes too many cigarettes and Uncle Earl drinks too much beer —"

"Now, listen here," interposed Katherine, "one swig of beer is too much, and one puff of Earl Junior's coffin nails is too much. And don't you forget it."

"Okay. So why don't you scream 'glutton' at Earl Junior as soon as he smokes the first one when they're here, I'd like to know? Last summer Aunt Edith worked herself sick when she did too much housecleaning. You know good and well she did. But did anybody snicker and scold and yell 'glutton'? They did not. They acted like she was all holy and righteous and the finest person that ever was. A martyr, that's what everybody made *her* out to be."

"Jennifer Susan Aldrich, that's just about enough out of you. Will you shut up now and get your dad some pie?"

Jennifer glared at the gravy bowl for long seconds before she went sulkily to the cupboard and brought back half a cherry pie.

"And furthermore," she went on, still with an angry pout laced through her lips and eyebrows, "I just thought of something else. Old Martha Vincent called you up last night, didn't she, and talked for one full hour about everybody and his brother and his brother's pet dog? Okay. Everybody in this town knows that that old biddy talks too much. I wish it showed in her wrinkled old body when she gobbles down the gossip, the way it shows if somebody like me eats a few calories too many."

"A few calories," mocked Katherine. "Heavens to Betsy!"

Mr. Aldrich was chuckling. "I can just see it," he said. "Boy, I can just see it." Laughter started deep in his middle and rumbled up to his lips. "Boy, if Martha's chin got longer and longer with exercise, the way she wags it every day — boy, oh boy!"

"You make me tired," said Katherine. "Both of you. It doesn't make our yard look any better because Martha Vincent's yard is full of weeds, and you know it." She started stacking purple melmac cups and plates, thumping them together with unnecessary clicks and clacks. "So Uncle Earl makes a mess of his life in one way; that doesn't take any inches off from Jennifer's waistline, does it? And whether you like it or not, Miss, people that run to the table like pigs runnin' to a feedin' trough are always gonna get laughed at. They always have, and they always will. And they're gonna get called gluttons because that's what they are."

"Well, I still say it isn't fair," said Jennifer. Anger smoldered in her voice and in every cell of her fat body.

"Good show," said Anger. Each, genie-huge, was astraddle a different housetop in the neighborhood, but all had been watching Jennifer while Anger prodded her with his baton-like wand. "Best performance that one has ever given me!"

"For which you can give full thanks to me, you know," said Gluttony from across the street.

"I do, fervently, Brother Glut," said Anger. "But I'm warning you: keep an eye on that one. She already knows more about your devious tricks than most of them ever suspect. Knows in reverse, you might say. If the Enemy once gets His hooks in her, she'll really be a caution."

All Seven stared at her malevolently. "A caution," they muttered in slow unison, "a caution . . . a caution."

Alden Owens

Was it morning? He turned heavily and pushed his chin deeper into the pillow. Simultaneously he had become aware of a faint musty odor from the mattress, of cold feet, and of a deep visceral sense that something was awry. Something ghastly. School? Budgets, salaries, the new Student Council constitution? No. Consciousness moved closer, and he remembered whistling when he left the office the day before, with the desk much cleaner than usual. Whistling "Finlandia." And Miss Rycoff mentioned —

Yes. He groaned and pulled the blanket up over his chin. To sleep a little longer before coming back to face last night again. Before facing Louise's puffy face across the breakfast table. Wonder how long she cried. Why did she make me so unusually angry? When her vapid mind and her stupid curiosity have been embarrassing me at just about everything we have gone to for these twenty years, why did she gall me more at this particular party for those particular teachers?

Why did she keep on asking Jean Filer about her sister's illness when Jean clearly didn't want to talk about it? If Louise scents gossip, she's like a hound after a rabbit. If she weren't so blamed inquisitive. If she didn't have to ferret out every single thing about everybody she knows and all their kinfolks. And people resent it. Jean Filer was mad enough to spit tacks, and so was Lisa Tremain. If Lou's voice weren't so shrill and her manner weren't so relentless, people wouldn't mind her so much. And heaven knows I wouldn't mind her so much.

He turned over, punched the pillow with his fist, and thrust his chin into it again. Or if she collected facts in order to do something constructive, to help people through their emergencies, I wouldn't mind so much. As I've told her roughly a thousand times.

Her voice is getting more like sandpaper all the time. Like fingernails across chalkboards. How could I ever have thought she was sweet and confiding and had a voice like a twittery bird? That summer at Northern State, about a millennium ago, when she met me and determined that she would capture me, and somehow camouflaged how crass and mindless and selfish she was.

To sleep a little more. He flipped over and pulled his knees up under his chin into a foetal position. If my Linda Lee hadn't gone home from Northern for that summer, if she had stayed for summer school too. If I had married her — or any of a hundred soft-voiced and sweet-souled women I have met since then. Othello to Iago: "Her voice was ever gentle and low, an excellent thing in women." Linda. Linda Lee. Oval face and dark eyebrows. Voice like a distant and very gentle French horn. Very gentle.

For the thousandth time, he summoned up the daydream; Linda Lee appeared through drowsing mists beside him. She touched his face with her fingertips and brushed her soft brown hair against his cheek, and he slept.

Then an alarm clock shrilled, and a radio blared, and he heard water running somewhere in the distance. Distance? Oh. Wide awake now, he remembered — with an ache that jangled through every separate nerve ending in his body — the raw anger and the abrasive words of the previous night. And finally I came here to the davenport for the rest of the night. In a minute she'll be yelling at me to get up. Or else she'll keep a haughty, frozen silence, and I'm not sure which will be worse. He sat up, stood up, folded the blankets, pushed the davenport cushions back into place.

She came to the top of the stairs and looked at him bleakly as she started down. "It's seven, Alden."

"I know."

"Do you want eggs or pancakes?"

"Neither. Just cereal."

She pulled her fuzzy coral robe together more firmly over her drooping nightgown and went to the kitchen. Andrea del Sarto to Lucrezia, he said to himself as he reached for his slippers. "My serpentining beauty, rounds on rounds." Was that the way Browning had Andrea say it? Rounds on rounds. Yes, you still have the rounds, Lou, even under that old robe. And your rounds do still accelerate my corpuscles a little the way they did when you'd come into the Venetian Lounge at the Union Building and look around to see if I were there. Rounds on rounds. But Andrea to Lucrezia in another tone of voice: "Had you, with these the same, but brought a mind! Some women do so."

Why *couldn't* you have brought a mind, Louise? Not so much of a dowry, is it? Some women do so. Linda Lee would have. Adelle Fiedler would have. To sit across a breakfast table from Adelle's luminous eyes, to have Adelle talk to me in that low throaty gracious voice — Thou shalt not covet thy neighbor's wife. Glenn Fiedler's hardly my neighbor, though; he's too seldom here.

He turned off the cold needle spray of the shower and stepped onto the bathmat, resolutely turning his mind toward the office. Memos blew through his mind like autumn leaves: the Pep Assembly; the band; Mr. Filer's next trip to Keyesport with the choir, since the last one went so well; all those job applications for next year.

Breakfast first. In the kitchen, his stomach muscles tightened as he eyed her puffy face and her tight lips above the Cream of Wheat saucepan. "You could apologize, Alden," she said. Her voice made him think of a guinea fowl's harsh squawk, and his nostrils prickled as though he were smelling the odors of an uncleaned henhouse.

"Yes, quite. I could apologize to Jean and Lisa—"

"Oh, Alden, don't be so high and mighty. It was just a conversation, like any other conversation—"

"Precisely. And exactly. Any of yours." He spooned sugar over Cream of Wheat and gulped tomato juice. "Or I could apologize to myself," he said.

"To yourself?" She looked almost angry enough to pour the coffee on his head instead of into his coffee cup, but she splashed it at the cup.

Alden didn't answer. He reached for a magazine from a rack beside the refrigerator and started leafing through *New Yorker* cartoons. When he rose and reached for his brief case, she put her fuzzy coral robe firmly between him and the garage door. "What did you mean, Alden Owens, that you could apologize to yourself?"

He smiled vaguely. "Oh, never mind, Lucrezia. I'm due at the office."

"Lucrezia? *Lucrezia?*"

He brushed past her. "Good-by, Lou. Have a good day." Putting the key in his Buick, he smiled a little more. He felt as if he could almost step into her mind. (Like stepping into a rumpled room all full of unmade beds and dirty sheets.) She'll wonder first if I'm losing my mind. And then she will wonder if I have been going out with some other woman. And she'll probably inquire delicately whether I have any secretaries or teachers or pretty seniors named Lucrezia. Delicately, yes, as delicately as an old milk cow in the lettuce bed. And then she'll have a small fit because I'm always making obscure jokes. Obscure, forsooth. "Had you, with these the same, but brought a mind. Some women do so."

He slowed to pick up Joe Filer at the end of the Filer lane   *205* north of Strettam and talked rapidly about bands, choirs, tubas, and drums for the rest of the way to the teachers' parking lot at the high school. But in the midst of a sentence about tubas he saw himself sit down at a breakfast table across from Sue Ann Filer, and the passing telephone poles flipped a refrain into his mind: "No shrew is Sue . . . no shrew is Sue . . . ." So there, too, and Burma Shave. The taming of the shrew. But no taming of Lou. Sue never needed taming. She has poise and verve and more knowledge of Liszt and Chopin than Joe has. That time we all went to Keyesport for a string quartet, she said wiser things as we drove back than the review in the *Herald* carried the next night. I hope you know how lucky you are, Joe. Thou shalt not covet thy neighbor's wife. Is Joe my neighbor or just my employee?

He swung his brief case from the back seat, flicked the key in the car door, and walked with Joe across the graveled parking lot. I hope you know how lucky you are, Joe. To swap with Joe— While he pulled firmly at the brass door latch and walked into the high school corridor, his mind leaped back from what it had almost said as though it had stepped on a cobra. Wife-swapping. No, oh, no. Not the lewd games you read about in the newspapers. Not to go to bed with Sue Filer. But to have a wife that wasn't always buzzing at me like a swarm of wasps, and buzzing at everyone else. To have a wife that could talk about Liszt and Chopin. Thy neighbor's wife, or his ox, or his ass, or anything that is thy neighbor's.

Moses wrote it for people near the stone age, didn't he? The cave man type, grabbing up his neighbor's wife as a chattel and hauling her by the hair to his own fire-blackened ring of stones in the cave he called his.

"Good morning, Miss Rycoff. Any important message from the White House?"

She smiled at his old joke. "The usual number, I believe. And the usual number of memoranda from teachers. First, though, you may want to go through these job applications." She handed him a manila folder. "Mr. Swainton said he'll be in around ten to talk about prospective teachers, and this morning's mail was a real harvest for a change."

"Any glittering diamonds? Oops, I'm mixing your metaphors. Any good wheat, or is it all chaff?"

"That's for you to say, I guess. Nobody in biology, I'm afraid."

"Shucks." He started riffling through the papers.

"There's someone who wants a part-time spot in Social Studies," Miss Rycoff said. "Sounds quite good. Her husband is going to retire, and they'll live in Princeville."

"Um-m-m." He moved into the inner office with "Alden

Owens, Principal" stenciled on the glass paneling of the door. Seated at his desk, he continued riffling through the folder. Suddenly the typewritten paragraphs of one letter squirmed like slim black maggots and perspiration beaded across his face. Linda Lee Manire. She did marry a funny name like that. And it has to be her signature. It has to be. The same curly loops on her L's. The same slant. The same firm clean strokes.

The black maggots were crawling more slowly, and he squinted to slide them into coherent words. "retiring now, with the rank of lieutenant colonel . . . his boyhood home in Princeville . . . so that I could be available, perhaps half-time . . . ."

Alden Owens walked slowly to the window and stood looking out over the graveled parking lot, a blur of black and beige and red splotches. Linda, available. Available. Does she know I'm here? He stepped back to the desk. No, not even addressed to Swainton by name. Just to a Superintendent of Schools. Which doesn't say that she's totally unaware of my whereabouts, though.

To see my Linda Lee in these very corridors . . . .

The old daydream came into focus again: Linda Lee beside him; Linda Lee touching his face and his hair. By now, though, she's a plump matron with a blue rinse on her hair; I don't want to see her again. That's a crazy lie. I want to see her, to talk with her. I've got to. Swainton will have to have her come for an interview, at least, and I can maneuver to take her out to lunch or something. And from there—

Could we possibly hire her? Swainton mustn't know—anything. Swainton won't want to hire anybody in Social Studies unless we nudge old Mrs. Cantrelle into retiring or push Jeffries over into Language Arts. Which we could do. Must. He looked out at the parking lot again: black and beige and red boxes; black and beige and red.

I could let Swainton ignore the letter, and maybe never see her again myself. Or seldom see her, like at county fairs. Oh, I refuse.

I could get her on the staff and keep it all very impersonal and cool and distant. "Good morning, Mrs. Manire. Good afternoon, Mrs. Manire." I could ignore her and avoid her and say frosty little nothings to her. Like heck, I could.

I could see her and adore her and let her know it. Oh, Linda, Linda. My Linda Lee. Sometime, sometime, for a weekend in some cabin, when Lou thinks I'm at a principal's meeeting. While Manire is dipping his fishhooks in the Metonic. Your face is a blot and a blur and a blank, Colonel Manire, and I don't mind if it stays that way. But Linda, Linda, Linda. After all of the sawdust I've eaten, to taste of some fruit—

Black and beige and red.

Will I? Will she?

Black and beige and red.

The intercom buzzed at his elbow. "Yes?" he said to its black surface.

"Mrs. Owens is on line two," said Miss Rycoff. Was there a tight wariness in her voice? Probably. So Louise is crying, probably.

She was crying. She blubbered words of tenderness, from which he recoiled, and words of apology, at which he grimaced. He soothed a little, wheedled a little, and hung up feeling as though he had walked into a bank of soggy, spongy foam. She's viscous. She'll always ooze over into everything I ever do. Always.

Hopeless.

I despise her, but that doesn't release me from her. Willynilly, I'm attached to her for always. Always? Other people get divorces easily enough. Shall I? Shall I talk with a lawyer? Or am I always to despise her and to envy other men for the wives they acquired? Always glumly to covet some neighbor's wife.

He walked back to the window. He looked again at rows of tires and windshields. He did not see them, even while he saw them.

Glumly coveting, vaguely coveting. But maybe now with Linda, not just to covet, and not just vaguely. Will I? Will she?

Louise. Had you, with these the same, but brought a mind. Some women do so.

Automobiles, black and beige and red. He did not know that he was facing Covetousness, eye to eye, as Covetousness hulked outside the window like a tall genie from a bottle. He did not know that Covetousness grinned and licked his lips and snuffed hungrily at him. He did not know that Lechery stood waiting at the other window.

He did not know.

On the Bench

At the northeast corner of the Norwich Bank stands a sturdy bench made from oak planks and painted white. It has been there longer than anyone remembers. Day by day it hears quantities of nonsense and quantities of wisdom. Farmers pick up their mail at the post office next door and then sit down on the white bench to discuss prices and rainfall and the policies of the federal government. Charlie Wright comes in to the bank to deposit rental funds from his farm property and lingers to tell any available listener of his newest information on the oldest Methodist customs. Men who live in seedy little cabins across the Metonic and north of Strettam walk to town to buy tobacco at the Rexall or tinned milk at Wildeman's, and before they tramp back across the Metonic bridge they sit on the Norwich Bank bench for a while to talk about the foreign wars they fought in.

Young girls protest, sometimes, against doing errands at the post office. The old men who sit whittling and smoking and sometimes spitting make the girls self-conscious. Actually the bench sitters have more interest in old wars and the weather and their rheumatism than in the self-conscious children who flutter past them like so many insects.

Bill Dolan and Mac Fletcher are two who frequent the bench most constantly. Bill lives halfway up Strettam Hill with his niece and her husband. They tolerate him and try to be kind, but he knows that Julia is glad when he isn't underfoot during daytime hours. Mac has a tiny house of his own just beyond Eliza Jarvis's. His little home never evicts him, but the mild sociability of the Norwich Bank corner is his clubroom, and he relishes the days when weather lets him linger there. Both Bill and Mac are among the inveterate whittlers; neither is among the smokers or the spitters. Each finds the sunshine a little more mellow when the other is beside him.

On a Tuesday in June, Bill and Mac were both whittling in amiable silence when Edgar Gentry's old Ford wheeled to the curb across the street in front of Dreiser's Hardware.

"Him again," murmured Bill.

"Yup." They watched him amble into Dreiser's. They watched him toss a parcel into his Ford. They watched his blue overalls go into the post office and come out again.

"Worse 'n usual," said Mac.

"Mebbe," said Bill.

Gentry greeted them glumly and settled himself on the white bench.

"What's the news?" asked Mac.

"Nothin' much that I know of," said Gentry. "Same as always. The rich is gettin' richer, and us common ordinary folks gets poorer and poorer." He paused, and the others whittled quietly. "Lookit them blamed fancy cars, whirlin' through Strettam all day long. And me with my old Ford that I've had for twelve, thirteen years already. Lookit that one, now." A long red convertible was resuming speed after the blinker light pause. "And that one." He pointed to a Chrysler with a California license plate.

"Which do you want, Ed?" asked Bill, flicking a tiny piece of wood away from his knife with a thumbnail.

Gentry grunted. "Any of 'em. Any's better 'n mine. That big red one, now—"

"Go ahead," said Mac. "Buy you one."

"Sure, half a dozen. Just like I'll buy Doc Bailey's house. And the bank too." Bitter wrinkles around Gentry's mouth deepened. "Like I always say, some people get the breaks in life, and some people don't. 'Tain't hard to see why them guys in Chicago and New York takes to crime. You see these people with big farms and these big cars and their fancy homes, and you want your share of their things, believe you me."

"Like you always say, some people have all the good luck?" prompted Mac. A quizzical smile fluttered across his genial old face.

"They sure do," said Gentry. "People like ol' McNair and Doc Bailey and Charlie Wright — I plumb hate to be around 'em."

"How's the family?" asked Bill.

"Fine. Jus' fine. My boy is gonna take the farm next to mine, I guess. Gotta talk with McNair one of these times about a mortgage. Man, I'd like to buy something once, jus' once, without mortgagin' my soul. If I could buy one or two of those farms ol' Wentworth don't need no more, now he's dead an' gone—" He rose and dusted off his creased overalls with the palm of his hand. "Well, I'd better be gettin' along. The wife will be lookin' for me."

210   Dolan and Fletcher whittled in silence for five minutes. "Give

him every farm in the county, though, he'd still want more, now, wouldn't he, Bill?" asked Mac finally.

"Prob'ly."

"Wanting's a queer thing. His kind of wanting sure has a flavor of poison in it. Always."

"Yeah, I guess." Dolan looked at his friend, a long shrewd look, and then resumed whittling. "He envies and wants and thinks *he* has the bad luck. With his wife at home cooking dinner for him right now."

"I know," said Mac. Pocket knives flicked, flicked, flicked. Each knew the other was thinking of Mac's wife Elaine. Of the agonizing months while her sanity wavered and broke. Of his weekly trips, for years on end, to the state hospital. Of her grave, where the grass was not yet growing. And, like a double exposure film, they thought also of Bill's wife Esther, whom he finally found when she was forty-two and lost in childbirth eighteen months later — and the child stillborn. "I know," said Mac.

"Ever bother you for McNair to own the bank and not you, Mac?" asked Bill.

Mac grinned. "Every time Eddie Gentry comes by, you ask me that same question, Bill. Answer is still no. But I'm glad for McNair to run it, so's we can sit outside it."

"No ambition," mocked Bill.

"Too late in the day for that. We had our turn. There's a time for ambition; it comes and it goes. There's a time for acceptance, and the time is always."

"Acceptance?" Bill smoothed the back of the rabbit he was whittling on. Each knew the other was thinking again of Mac's wife Elaine.

"Yes. Part of the human situation, isn't it? The human situation if it has a divine dimension." He tipped back his head and looked southward where the sheen of the Metonic was visible between houses. "Ambition for a while. Acceptance always. Envy like Edgar Gentry's — never, never." He looked up to see Freddie Farless and Mannie Mitchell leaving the bank and starting briskly across the highway toward Joe's Diner. He waved, and his eyes followed them up the street. "Think they envy us our peace and leisure, Bill?"

Mannie, in fact, was saying lightly, "Does it make you want to retire, Freddie, seeing them?"

"Oh, I guess not. But I keep thinking that I'll sit down and chat with those two old fellows some time. They always look like a village variety of the old Greek philosophers, don't you think?"

"Greek philosophers, my eye," said Envy to Covetousness.   *211*

They were lolling against Dreiser's plate glass window, watching the bank bench with extreme distaste.

"Don't underestimate philosophers, buddy," said Covetousness. "The Enemy uses them against us, too."

"Anyway, I hate these two old lice that the Enemy has made such pets of," said Envy. "I'd like to throw them into the river, pocket knives and all."

"Or into more homelike cauldrons? You know, other mortals wouldn't say He has made pets of them. They're poor and old and lonesome; they both live on next to nothing, as other mortals count nothing—"

Envy snarled. "Other mortals, piffle. They both adore the Enemy, and they'd say He reciprocates, and we can't touch 'em."

"Well, there's still our boy Edgar Gentry."

"Yes," said Envy. "That one is remarkably good to chew on. Always jumps when we prod. Never talks anything over with the Enemy, never. If we could only keep 'em all from doing that—"

Lucy McNair

After she had served the McNairs their dinner, Mattie O'Toole put a platter of very choice beef in front of Bert Killoran. "There now, lad, eat up. Part of yer salary, no thanks to him in there. He thinks I'm giving you hamburger instead of the same roast he's eating. Worse luck to him."

"You really hate him, don't you, Mat?"

"I'm gettin' to it at a downhill gallop," she said grimly. "Honest, do you like being his gardener?"

"I've had worse jobs. He doesn't bother me. It's easier clippin' hedges here than lookin' after Charlie Wright's Herefords like I did on my last job. And you're here, Mat; I'm not fergettin' that." He put a big hand on her knee.

"Go 'long with you."

"I mean to go along with you, right up to your room, as soon as you get them dishes done." He started to laugh, a bellowing, bull-throated laugh.

"Shut *up!* Want to get yourself fired? They don't want no noise from the kitchen while they're eatin' their hoity-toity dinner with their candles and silver and all."

He chewed noisily on a big bite of beef. "Mat," he said finally. "Them McNairs. You see 'em both more'n I do. Are they happy, do you think? With all their money an' this big house an' all—"

She rolled her eyes toward the ceiling, swore long and heartily under her breath, and then shook her head emphatically. "Happy? Man, I bet they're the least happy folks I've ever cooked for. They leave the house all prissy and smilin' as though they were the king and queen, like everybody in this dumb town treats 'em. But I'm telling *you,* Bert Killoran, one of these fine days yer gonna be out of a job when they close the house because one of 'em has shot the other one. You mark my words." He dropped his fork, and it clattered to the floor. "Shut *up,*" she said again in a throaty stage whisper.

"You — you're joking, Mat?"

"I am not. I've got other things to joke about if I wanted to joke. Maybe it won't be shootin'. Maybe he'll throw her in the river, or maybe he'll hang himself—"

"You've gotta be kidding."

"I am not kidding. Not fer a second." Her buzzer sounded, and she picked up a coffee carafe to refill cups. When she returned, he was staring blankly at his plate, and his fork was still on the floor beside his chair.

"You shouldn't say it, Mat — not even to me. You're no prophet."

"No, I'm not. But I've cooked fer ritzy people ever since I wuz thirteen. I've seen some plain an' fancy kinds of hate among 'em, but not often as much as is buildin' up over that dinin' table right now."

"Oh, come on. You're a worrier. Here, gimme a dish towel."

Actually at that moment the conversation was suave and genteel. The Kendricks were dining with the McNairs, and Robert McNair as host was as debonair as the tiny white rose in his lapel, as gracious as the matching roses in silver bowls on table and buffet. Lucy was chic in a slim blue sheath, with bouffant blonde curls impeccably arranged. Bert Killoran, or anyone else, might have called them one of the most ideal couples in Johnson County.

Later, when the Kendricks had gone, Bert Killoran or anyone else might have felt gooseflesh at hearing Robert McNair denounce his pretty wife for flirting with Ray all evening.

"Darling!" She tapped his lips with her fingertips. "That wasn't flirting. Invite a real man to dinner sometime soon, and I'll give a good demonstration of the real thing. Now don't get angry, dear boy. Or do, if you like. It only gives me another opportunity, you know; you aren't forgetting the bargains I make."

He looked at her with fury and desperation, uttered a vicious oath, and strode toward his room.

"Oh, my dear Robert, how very coarse of you," she said. She went to her own room and sat for long minutes looking at her face in the mirror of her dressing table. "We look very angelic, don't we?" she whispered. "How very, very nice for us." She smiled, and at least four of Them touched her face to help her smile that particular smile.

A few days later she was reading a movie magazine when the telephone rang. "For you, Miz McNair," reported Mattie stolidly.

"Yes?"

"Lucy," his voice said, "do you remember I told you that one of the big Keyesport banks wanted to send an apprentice out for us to train here?"

"Of course, Robert. Why bother me with it?"

"They've just been on the phone again. One of their top men—"

"Well? Do come to the point, darling."

"Well, this young man is the son of the chairman of their board, that's all. And Ames more than hinted that I invite the kid to stay in my own home, hotels and motels being absent from the scene."

"They *are* absent, aren't they?" she purred.

"So is it all right if I confirm with Ames to have the boy come?"

"But of course. I'll get the guest room ready right away. . . . Next week? . . . Well, I'll have a look at the guest room now while I think of it. How long will he stay?"

"We're not sure. Two weeks, anyway, I suppose."

She smiled a little as she went to the linen closet, and her hands caressed her body quickly. Soon, Lechery was whispering into her hair. Soon.

"Telephone again, Miz McNair," said Mattie loudly. She let the kitchen door bang smartly behind her. Mattie looks like a sick fish, thought Lucy. She's too accusing, with those eyes of hers. As if she were a puritan herself. If she doesn't relax, I'm going to fire her, in spite of her fantastic recipe file.

"Yes? . . . Oh, Glenn, darling. Yes, this afternoon is safe enough. As usual, up in the woods? You could come here; I'm just making up the guest room bed, darling. Be my guest! . . . Oh, I'll tell you about it this afternoon, my dear and handsome hero. . . . Well, all right, I'll see you under the greenwood tree." She laughed, a malicious little laugh. "Where does Adelle believe you to be selling today? . . . Oh, lovely. . . . Yes, darling, of course."

"Any interesting mail come today?" asked Robert that evening.

"Yes, dear. On the mantel." Interesting mail, interesting male, she thought. On the mantel; that isn't the half. "What's the big formal invitation? I hope you notice how dutifully I didn't open it."

He flicked open the envelope. "It's an invitation for that mayor's reception at Keyesport. On Friday night. Odd to get it so late."

"Some secretary made an error," said Lucy. "We're already invited. And I'm wearing my black dinner dress with the sequins."

"I wish you wouldn't." He scowled. "It makes you look like a cheap chorus girl, Lucy."

"I know. That's why I want to wear it. Chorus girls have so much fun at receptions, don't they? Remember the kind of fun I was having when you first found me?"

He groaned. "That was twenty years ago. And you are now a   *215* respectable citizen and a committee woman at St. Mark's Episcopal Church—"

"And your wife. Yes, yes, of course." She lifted her fingers in an obscene motion.

"Woman, are you going mad?"

"No, no," she said pertly. "You are the one who goes mad. You go on a mad-mad-mad binge, and then Lucy has a right to be a playgirl one more time, in just any way her little heart desires. You should know the rules of the game by now — the rules I made up three years ago."

"Her little heart," echoed Robert. "God help us!"

"Oh, do you think He might?"

"Don't be blasphemous," roared McNair.

"I will if I want," she said. "And I will wear my black sequined dress on Friday night. And then I'll come home and help the ladies at St. Mark's to plan the annual Sunday school frolic, just like always."

"Listen," he said. "Wear that show girl outfit if you must. But if you misbehave, I may do something violent. I'm warning you."

She giggled. "If I misbehave! You make me sound at least thirteen, daddy dear."

She misbehaved. When he thought of leaving, he looked for her all through the mayor's mansion and finally found her on an upstairs porch, cuddled against the dress uniform of a navy officer. And he swung a heavy fist at the officer. The officer parried smoothly and pretended to think Robert both drunk and mistaken. He escorted them both to the door and kissed Lucy's hand with disarming gallantry.

While Robert whirled the car around corners in angry silence, Lucy settled herself yawningly and pretended to be asleep. Seeing Glenn Fiedler again—and tonight—and a bright young lad coming to stay with us for two weeks, she thought. Maybe Strettam isn't such a desert. She breathed with careful regularity, and soon her feigning was not feigning.

She woke, confused, to find herself alone in the car. It was parked in their driveway. Dawn was shimmering through the trees over beyond the Metonic, and robins were starting to twitter. She yawned, stretched, and went upstairs. Robert had nearly finished his toast and coffee when she came downstairs. "Darling, did you forget you had me with you?" she pouted. "Why didn't you waken me?"

"If I had touched you, I might have broken some bones," he said grimly.

"Oh, dear, he's angry," she said in the same pouting treble.

"They'll have a bad day at the bank, won't they, darling?"

"Lucy, what *is* the matter with you lately?"

"Lately? I've always been me."

"You weren't this way when Joy was alive. Thank goodness, Joy isn't around to know what her mother is like now."

"I wasn't *me* when Joy was alive," she said lightly. "Now there's a *me*. It's what I was, and I am, and I will be."

"Not necessarily what you will be. People change. Ask Billy Graham."

"Oh, Billy Graham!" She laughed her most malicious laugh. "Have you become a friend of Billy Graham?"

"We could find worse friends." He glanced at his watch. "Lucy, I do love you—"

"What a dreadful pity," she said with a yawn. "And what a bore." She touched the buzzer. "Bring me some coffee, please, Mattie?"

Jim Gallion, the apprentice from Keyesport, arrived on Thursday, and Lucy appraised him all evening. Handsome, courteous. A mere boy. Deferential, but guarded. Very guarded. She was annoyed when he pulled a small tinted photo from his billfold and introduced his fiancée. She was annoyed again when she went to put fresh flowers in his room the next morning and saw a Bible on the night stand. A big study Bible with chipped and frayed edges. Oh, that's your sort, is it? Well, that may just make things interesting.

And Lechery, always padding behind her, smiled benignly.

On Wednesday, Jim asked five times and finally persuaded Mary, the receptionist, that his errand was urgent.

"Yes, my boy?" McNair picked up a cigar. "Sit down, sit down. Care to smoke? Lucy doesn't like the fragrance in the house, but here I can indulge."

Jim sat down silently.

"Something about our procedures bothering you? Any of the tellers can explain just about everything we do."

Jim shook his head. "It isn't as simple as that. I wish it were. Sir—" He gulped twice. "Sir, would you mind if I voice a prayer before I — before I go on?"

McNair blinked. "Sure, go ahead, if it will help."

Jim bowed his head and spoke a few intense sentences. Terribly upset over something, thought McNair, and the wary gooseflesh crept up his arms. Oh, my God. She hasn't. She wouldn't. *My* God? Jim Gallion's God, anyway. Wish I could ever feel as filial toward Deity as he seems to feel.

Jim's voice stopped. His face was grimly apprehensive. Like a man asking for a thirty thousand dollar mortgage when he knows that fifteen would be too much.

"Sir — is there — is there any basement storeroom or anything here at the bank where I could stay, without anyone knowing it?"

Again gooseflesh crept up McNair's arms. "No, Jim. It wouldn't do, if we had."

"There's no hotel or motel in Strettam, I know. Shall I go on back to Keyesport before I am expected? Or is there any reasonable reason I could give for moving to some other home in Strettam? To Mannie Mitchell's maybe?"

"Now wait a minute. I'll trust your word, Jim. What, exactly, is the trouble?"

"Must I?"

"I think you'd better."

"She — she comes into my room. At night, sir. Three times now. There's no lock on the door, you know. Last night I had to push her out bodily, and she thought it was terribly funny. You — you didn't hear—?"

"I probably thought it was a nightmare if I did. It is a nightmare at that. A huge one."

"I'm sorry, sir. Awfully sorry. So now what should be done with me?"

McNair groaned. "The obvious thing would be to call a carpenter and put a Yale lock on the door, but everyone in town would soon know I had done it. In a town this size, the gossip can be deadly."

"I can understand that."

"There are several nice homes you'd enjoy," McNair went on. "And they'd enjoy you. But I think Ames would resent it pointedly if he learned that I let you move to another spot after he especially commended you to my hospitality. And I doubt whether he's a person whom I'd want to explain anything to—"

"Right. I doubt it very much."

McNair squared his shoulders. "Well, there are twin beds in my room, you know. We'll just announce to her that we're going to be ready to talk shop whenever you're awake."

"Yes. All right." Jim Gallion rose to go. "Now I'd better get back to the accounting procedures, hadn't I?"

"Very well. One thing, though." McNair crunched out the tip of his cigar in a big copper ashtray. "You talked to God a while ago as though He's someone you know."

"Yes. He is."

"If you don't mind, we won't talk *shop* during every waking moment while you're here."

Jim smiled, his first real smile in four days.

Mattie O'Toole heaped ham with raisin sauce and au gratin potatoes in front of Bert Killoran.

"You're awful quiet tonight, kiddo," said Bert.

"Am I?"

She sat down, picked at a bite of ham, sighed, and sighed again.

"Hey, what's goin' on?" he asked.

"That's eggzackly what I'd like to know," she said. *"Egg-zackly."*

"Meanin' what?"

"I've told you about this young fella they've got stayin' with 'em? Well, he's a queer fish — some kind of a holy roller, I guess. They're sittin' in there at the table readin' Bible verses along with my lemon chiffon pie. Now, I ask you, Bible verses?"

"Sounds like a good idea, if they're both as close to bein' trigger-happy as you said the other night. Bible verses never did hurt nobody, I s'pose. Mebbe you oughta go back in and read along with 'em, Mat." He started to chuckle loudly.

"Oh, shut up."

Robert McNair sat on the edge of his bed. A dark satin dressing gown was looped loosely over his plaid silk pajamas. His hair was rumpled, and his left hand was rumpling it more as his right hand turned pages in a black-bound book. He stopped at one page and looked at it for long moments. Absent-mindedly he heard the shower stop running, heard Jim Gallion whistling "Swing Low, Sweet Chariot," heard Jim coming back into the bedroom.

"It's all marked up," he said. "You do take it seriously, don't you?"

"Yes, I certainly do."

"Even though nobody else does any more?"

"Nobody? Actually a great many people take it seriously, sir. What about your rector, Mr. McPherson, for instance?"

"Oh, sure, that's his job."

Jim smiled. "Well, if nobody else on earth took it seriously, I'd still have to. It speaks to me."

"So I'd gather from the way you have underlined things all over the place." His left hand smoothed strands of hair and then rumpled them again. Smoothed and rumpled. "Look. This sentence you've got circled in red and with stars in the margin. Do you really believe that?"

"What sentence is it?"

"About the only one you've got marked that much. 'Therefore

if any man be in Christ he is a new creature: old things are passed away; behold, all things are become new.' You believe that?"

Jim perched on the arm of a tapestry-covered wing chair, his chin in his hands. Two of Them loomed behind him, and one of Them reached its paws across his face to muffle his lips, but he spoke very clearly anyway. One of Them put other furry paws across McNair's ears. Jim's voice still came through to the eardrums, but as if from a greater distance. From across a chasm.

"Yes, I do. I've seen it happen, sir. It happened to me. And I've heard or read about the millions of people it has happened to down through the centuries, ever since He was here on earth."

"What do you mean, it happened to you?"

"Just that. Until I was a junior in college, there wasn't a religious hair on my head. I fiddled around with a folk rock combo, flunked out once and got readmitted, quarreled with my dad, and got invited to leave home. Even tried pot a few times."

"And then?"

"Well, there was this Christian coffee house near the campus, and some people I had thought were religious nuts took an interest in me."

McNair yawned and glanced at his watch. "We'd better get some sleep," he said, "but I'm not saying that in order to give you a brush-off."

Jim sat quietly for a moment. "You said you might take me fishing on Saturday afternoon," he said finally. "Shall I take that along?" He nodded toward the black-bound book.

After a slow silence, McNair nodded. "Yes. Yes, I think you'd better." He swung over on his back and clasped his hands behind his head on the pillow. "At least one of us in this house has got to become a new creature, one way or another," he said heavily, "or there's wreckage ahead."

Jim waited.

"I'm not just being melodramatic, like some character in a Grade D movie," said McNair. "You've probably heard some legends about my horrible temper. Unfortunately, anything you have heard is probably quite true. For your sake and Ames' sake, and my own, I've been hoping against hope that the volcanoes inside me wouldn't blow up while you're here, but there's no guarantee. And Lucy is — Lucy. More so all the time. In ways I don't understand at all. If something doesn't change— Something is going to change, either toward improvement or toward a smashup. I'm sure of it." He closed his eyes, and some dark shadows moved over his face. "I suppose I love her and I hate her, with too much of both emotions. And it seems as though they both are growing at compound interest. Sometimes when anger explodes inside me, I'm very much afraid that I could kill her. And sometimes I think she dislikes me enough to kill me as she would an ant or a cockroach."

He turned over and switched off the table lamp. "Go to bed, son. If you can stand to. Having heard all that, would you rather take a sleeping bag out in the backyard? I've got one there in the closet."

"No, sir, of course not."

"I hope you can sleep."

"Well, if I can't, there'll be other nights for sleeping. First — first I want to talk to my Father for a while." McNair looked startled and glanced at the telephone, then nodded a small nod as he saw Jim kneel beside the big leather chair by the window.

In November, Lucy looked up from the russet chrysanthemums she was cutting for the dinner table when Mattie called to her from the back door.

"Yes, Mattie?"

"Telephone, ma'am."

"Could you take the number? I'll call back in twenty minutes or so."

Mattie disappeared and returned. Again her shrill braying voice reached to the chrysanthemums. "He won't give no number, ma'am. Says he'll hold on for twenty minutes if he has to."

She put the clippers and an armful of flowers into her basket and left the basket nodding on the grass. "Who is it, Mattie?"

Mattie looked as though she had suddenly caught an odor of decaying fish. "He wouldn't give no name."

Lucy looked at the telephone receiver for a long moment before she picked it up.

"Hello? . . . Oh, yes, I heard you were back in town. . . . No, Glenn. I told you in September: not today, and not ever. . . ." She laughed easily. "Unless you want to bring Adelle and join our Bible study at three this afternoon? The rector and his wife are coming, and a few other people. . . . But I do mean it. Listen. Robert and I are having Mrs. Heiler — the sculptor's wife — make a lovely lettered panel for our north bedroom wall. It's going to have a quotation on it, a Scripture verse. . . . Yes, that's what I said. Now, listen. This is the verse we've chosen: 'Therefore if any man be in Christ he is a new creature: old things are passed away; behold, all things are become new.' . . . No. . . . No. . . . Well, it's me and not me, Glenn. As if you'd take a horrible, dingy, old gray dress and dye it fuchsia, maybe. . . . Well, there are hymns like that, you know. 'Washed in the blood of the Lamb.' . . . No. . . . No. . . . Look, Glenn, I've got some things to do." His voice was still resonating inside the receiver, but she put it on the hook.

When she started back through the kitchen, Mattie stopped her. Glazed rolls were cooling on the oven top; a greased casserole and rows of spices stood on the work table in front of Mattie.

"Yes?"

"Miz McNair, I wuz wonderin'. Is that big picture you've put in there over the buffet gonna stay there?"

Lucy smiled. "Well, I don't know. Probably. We might like to try it in the living room over the mantel sometime. Or in the library. Why?"

"But it's gonna stay in this house, where I'll see it all the time?"

"Well, I think so. My husband did speak of taking it down to the bank for a while. But now he has another one to try at his office. You know, the big Sallman one that we had on the mantel last week. Why?"

"It gives me the heebie-jeebies," said Mattie. "Those eyes. They're creepy. They follow me all around the room. Last night I sez to Bert, 'As sure as my name is O'Toole, that picture is gonna go out of this house or I'm gonna go out of it.'"

"Would you rather we had put up a crucifix? Would a cross give Him more honor?"

Mattie looked stubborn as she picked up a box of paprika and her measuring spoons. "No, ma'am."

"I hope you won't be in a hurry to go, Mattie. Mr. McNair really appreciates your cooking, you know. And so do I."

"Well, like I sez to Bert, 'As sure as my name is O'Toole, that picture is gonna go out of this house or I'm gonna go out of it.'"

Lucy laughed softly.

"I'm not makin' no jokes, ma'am," Mattie said resentfully.

"Maybe you are, though," Lucy said very softly. "It just occurred to me that the easy solution, then, would be to change your name from O'Toole to Killoran. Then you could ask Him for a benediction instead of running away from His picture. Couldn't you?"

A dark red flush mottled up across Mattie's thick neck, and she seemed to be gulping vainly for words. "I'd better finish my flowers," Lucy said. "Bert has done a wonderful job in getting them to blossom this year."

Bert sniffed as Mattie put a pottery bowl in front of him. "What's that?"

"Turkey casserole. They like it special." Mattie nodded toward the dining room.

Bert took a wary bite, and another, and another. "Baby, you

sure can cook. If I wuz smart, I'd make you marry me so's they couldn't ever fire me without firin' you. And they won't ever fire you."

A dark flush mottled up her neck again, and Mattie felt as if she were choking. "Bert — Bert, let's — let's get married."

He stopped chewing and his mouth hung open. "You mean it, Mat?"

"If you — if you want to."

"That's what I wanted the first week I was here, ain't it? But you snorted at any idea of settlin' down in double harness."

"I know. I feel some different about it now."

"Well, glory be."

The buzzer sounded, and Mattie picked up the coffee pot. As she passed the picture above the buffet, she genuflected ever so slightly. "—be to the Father and to the Son—" her mind murmured.

Out in the backyard, Lechery was lying prone on the grass and pounding it with paws and heels and head and tail, like a two-year-old in a seething tantrum. Then he rose to the forty-foot height of his current guise and walked around the McNair house, kicking it at every other step. Four of Them, each seated on one of the brick gateposts, cheered him on.

Sunset Point

"Sure, I'm game," said Kevin Thomas. "What time, Cathy?"

"Well, not too early. It'll be cooler. Leaving here about seven, maybe?"

"Okay. What'll I bring?"

"Oh, just yourself and your bike. Diana and I will bring the wieners and stuff this time. Maybe you could bring matches, though, and be the vice-president in charge of starting the fire. I'm not much of a Girl Scout. Okay?"

"Okay, sure thing. Who else is going?"

"Depends on who else I can get hold of. So many of the kids are working somewhere else this summer. Andy Metcalf for sure. Sarah Sellers prob'ly, and maybe Rick and maybe Steve Bates. Hey, I'd better hang up now and try to get Sarah while she's home for lunch. Okay?"

Seven bicycles, careening down Strettam Hill, swerving right at the blinker light to cross the bridge and turn left on the cracked and pitted asphalt of the old highway.

"We could stay on new 37, you know," said Rick Hartford. "Must be a mile closer to Sunset Point that way."

"A mile closer to Sunset Point and a jillion miles closer to the mortuary," answered Kevin. "Boy, that road is for the birds, with so many semi's using it now."

"So's this one," said Cathy Welch, swerving around a badger hole. "For the birds and the beasts."

"Makes you feel more remote from all the clutter of civilization, though, doesn't it?" said Diana. "I really like it back here on this road."

"Think you're riding into fairyland or something?" asked Kevin.

"Well, not exactly." Diana chuckled. "Who ever rode into fairyland on a red bike with wieners in the basket?"

"Why not?" asked Kevin. "Better with wieners than without wieners, seems to me."

"Just be sure you keep the wieners in the basket," said Andy Metcalf. "Especially on the next slope. Remember these curves? Boy, did I ever have a fancy crash on this one when I was about in sixth grade. Remember that, Steve? I think it was an all-day bike hike with Scouts."

"We used to have a lot of bike hikes along about then, didn't we?" said Kevin. "We ought to do it more often. This was a good idea, Cathy."

"It was Diana's idea, really. She said we hadn't been to Sunset Point for at least a year, and I guess she's right."

"We're getting old and sedate before our time," said Kevin. "Too bad about us."

"Not so old," said Diana. "Just busy. Study and work and band and piano and church and all the rest of it. We don't stop to hear—"

"To hear ourselves think?" finished Kevin.

"That wasn't what I was going to say, but it's true." Her pixie face was tilted toward the bars of sunset light that streamed through wild grape vines and walnut trees.

"So what were you going to say?"

"Oh, I don't know. To hear the trees grow. To hear the stars in their courses. To hear the Big Dipper dipping."

Kevin's freckled brown face was very thoughtful for a moment. "Hey, you ought to write that down," he said finally. "Somebody could set it to music, like a Bob Dylan lyric."

"Can't write now," said Diana. "Too many potholes. Man, this road is really falling apart."

"Before it ever gets to fairyland?" teased Kevin.

"Not if Sunset Point is fairyland," said Diana. "Which I almost think it is. Look, around one more bend, and there we are."

Seven bicycles turned, braked, halted. Seven murmurs of satisfaction. Steve and Rick flexed muscles and grunted. "Still the same old Metonic down there," said Kevin. "Hiya, Metonic. How ya doin'?"

"Anybody would think you had been away for twenty years," said Sarah.

"Oh, haven't I?" returned Kevin. "Maybe it's just nineteen. Anyway, where do you want the fire, Cathy?"

"Over here in this stone fireplace, don't you think? It's flat enough so we can watch the fire and still watch the scenery."

"Anybody would think," said Andy, "that you expect the scenery to disappear if you don't keep checking on it; it won't go away. It's been here for centuries."

"Yes," said Diana, opening a package of wieners, "and it will be here for a lot more centuries, if they don't blow our favorite 225 planet up with their bombs. But we won't be here for a lot more centuries."

"So?"

"So, having the Metonic spread out down there below you on one neat August evening when you're a junior in high school, you'd better look at it!" cried Diana. "Look, and look, and look. Use your eyes while you still have them."

Rick folded his long legs and eased his six-four body onto the plank bench beside the table where the girls were spreading out buns and relishes. "Because my purty brown eyes are going to be shut up in a coffin one of these days?" he asked. "Look, we're on a picnic. Let's be cheerful."

Diana put down the mustard jar and looked thoughtfully down toward the river. "I didn't mean you have to think coffiny thoughts, Rick," she said. "Though nobody knows when our turn's coming. Like Joy McNair. She didn't know. But if we all live to be a hundred and two, that's still only a hundred and two years to look at the Metonic. Or maybe some of us will get to look at the Seine and the Thames and the Nile and the Amazon—"

Kevin came over from the fire he had just started. "Diana's about to start quoting something," he teased. "I feel it in my bones." He touched his right index finger to his tongue and held it up. "Good breeze from the southwest," he said. "Good direction for poetry to blow in from. Go ahead, Diana. What did Mr. Hinman tell you?"

Diana's green eyes were glinting with mischief. "Everybody is now about to quote something," she said. "No poetry, no hot dogs. You start, Kevin."

"Hey, no fair. I'm weak as a cat from biking up that last hill and worn to a thread from the labor of starting your fire. How can I think?"

"Oh, come on. Not a whole poem. Rick, start him out."

"Well, naturally, after what you just said about seeing the Metonic while we can: 'Gather ye rosebuds while ye may.' I don't know the rest of it, but that's enough, isn't it?"

"You'll do. Sarah?"

Sarah Sellers pushed red curls behind her ears and made a thoughtful face. "I didn't hear all you and Rick were talking about," she said, "but Mr. Hinman's favorite one about the cherry trees ought to fit in somewhere."

"Can you say it?"

"Let's see. 'Loveliest of trees, the cherry now is hung-de-da-da on the bough.' Doesn't fit with August, does it?"

226   "Diana, this fire is getting really nice for hot dogs," interrupted

Cathy. "Shall we start? Steve, did you guys get enough wiener sticks cut for one apiece?"

"Sure, plenty of sticks," said Steve. "Here, catch."

"Well, Diana—" Kevin started to exult at not having to quote anything, but he softened his tone as he noticed how intently Diana was watching the river surface. "Seeing any steamships coming up the river?"

"No, not yet."

"I'll read you a whole stack of poems some other time," he said. "How's that?"

"Thanks, Kevin. Know what I was going to quote for mine?"

"What?"

"Something from Fra Lippo Lippi."

"Fra who?"

"A painter Browning wrote about. Browning has him say, 'This world's no blot to me, nor blank. It means intensely, and means good. To find its meaning is my meat and drink.'"

"Hey, that's great."

"Come on, let's get our wiener sticks," said Diana.

After the wiener sticks had become marshmallow sticks and in turn had become slim glowing coals among the other glowing coals, Steve Bates looked up at little puffs of orange cloud. "Boy, you can sure see why they called this Sunset Point, can't you?" he said. "I s'pose the Indians used to use it for a lookout point, didn't they?"

"Prob'ly," agreed Andy. "We talked about that in American history last year, and everybody thought so. Somebody thought if we'd dig around, we'd probably find arrowheads."

"Penny for your thoughts, Diana," said Kevin.

"Just a penny?" she retorted. "Not a quarter?"

"I'll give you mine for free," said Sarah. "That breeze feels like September, and that means school, and I don't want the summer to be over."

"Neither do I," said Kevin, "but I still want to know where Diana's imagination has gone galloping off to."

Diana smiled, "You sure?"

"Sure, I'm sure."

"You'll be sorry."

"No, I won't. Go ahead, shoot."

"Well — oh, I guess I was thinking of sixteen things at once. The way a person usually is. Andy said if we'd dig around we'd probably find arrowheads, and I thought if you dig around in anything you find something. Like — oh, like why people do what they do. Like all the wretched people in the world, and if you dig around a little you find out why they're wretched. And then I was starting to think about what Rev. Williams said last Sunday. You know, about sin, big S, and sin, little S, being — what did he say? — being at the core of every human sadness?"

"He really got going, didn't he?" said Kevin.

"I wasn't there," said Rick. "He preached on sin and he's agin it, huh? Like my dad's old story about Calvin Coolidge."

"It was more than being against it," said Diana, poking at the embers with a cautious toe. "He really helped me figure some things out."

"Such as?" prodded Rick.

"Well, like sin, big S, being — what did he call it, Cathy? 'A basic bentness in our moral being.' How's that for a mouthful?" She said it again, savoring the alliteration. " 'A basic bentness in our moral being.' And then there's sin, little S, which comes in fifty-seven varieties, like Heinz pickles. Or more."

"Like stealing and gambling and beating your wife and getting drunk and all the rest?" asked Rick, leaning back against a tree trunk, with crossed hands behind his head.

"He didn't spend much time with that sort," said Cathy. "You ought to borrow his notes sometime, Rick. He'd probably let you."

"Well, thanks. You mean I need some special instruction on the fifty-seven commonest kinds of sin? Thanks a lot!"

"Silly," said Cathy. "I mean he had done an awful lot of thinking, and it comes out pretty mangled when we try to hit the high points for you. You know what I mean."

"Okay, apology accepted," said Rick easily.

"I think," said Diana with some intensity, "I think we all need some special instruction, Rick. And Strettam does. And the whole country does."

"Oh, come now. Our nice little ol' Strettam?"

"It's little, and it's old," said Diana evenly, "but human beings live there. Which means it isn't all as nicey-nice as it might be. Like Rev. Williams said: There is a basic bentness in our moral being. Or, in plain, ordinary language, we're just naturally out of kilter with God."

"With fifty-seven different ways of being out of kilter?" said Kevin. "But some people are more out of kilter than others."

"Well, sure," said Diana. "Only prob'ly some of the ones that we think are pretty neat from what we see of 'em may not look that way to God. Like—oh, you know. Like a lake can look all clean and pretty on top, but you drain it and find old tires and rotten shoes and rusty tin cans and all kinds of stuff."

"And those are the fifty-seven varieties?" Kevin asked, taking his turn at poking the edge of the dying fire with a sneakered toe.

"Yes, sort of. Only some of them are the granddaddies of the others. Like pride. If a person could really understand all there is to know about pride—"

"He'd be mighty proud of himself for knowing so much, I imagine," said Andy.

"Rev. Williams did say something about pride being on some special list, didn't he?" asked Sarah.

"Hey, Sarah was listening," joked Kevin. "Put it on the bulletin board for MYF."

"I always listen," said Sarah. "Anyway, he did talk about a list, didn't he?"

"Sure," agreed Kevin. "What he says they used to call the seven deadly ones. Sounds like the snake section of a zoo, you know."

"Maybe that's not so far off," said Diana. "Seems to me that some of the ones he named off — you know, the seven deadlies — are the ones that most of the others hatch from."

"And they're the kind that are always ready to trip up what we'd call the good people, as well as the bad people and the in-between people, aren't they?" said Kevin. "If you can sort people into bins like potatoes. I mean, like he mentioned pride and envy and — what else? Sloth? Do you s'pose there's anybody in Strettam who doesn't get prodded around by *that* kind of impulse just about every day of his life?"

"Know what?" said Diana. "I was sorta thinking, just about like that, while I was ironing this morning. Unless you want to be a good example of a bad human being, which I don't s'pose anyone really does, it's awfully discouraging to think of so many different kinds of wrongness that you can trip over. Like roots across a path in the woods, you know. You dodge around one and you're going along fine when wham, bang, another one trips you up. And then something hit me. I want to talk to Rev. Williams about it. There may be fifty-seven kinds of sin, little S, or there may be a hundred and fifty-seven. But there's a single, unified, individual, one Grace to be the antidote. The alternative."

"Hey, slow down," said Rick. "You lost me."

"Single," said Diana, and paused. "Unified." Pause. "Individual." Pause. "One." Pause. "Grace. There, how's that? Was that the same thing I said before?"

"Listen," said Cathy. "It's going to be completely dark in about two minutes. Shall we get the stuff packed up?"

"Wait a sec," said Kevin. "I'll turn my bike light on so you can see the table."

"Thanks," said Cathy. "Hey, I didn't ask when I was phoning around — I hope everybody has lights on their bikes."

"Mr. Hinman wouldn't like you," said Sarah.

229

"Why not?"

"Does everybody have a light on *his* bike? His, singular."

"Okay," said Cathy, "but I always hate being a 'his.' All aboard for Strettam. Is everybody on *his* bike?"

Seven bicycle lights curving through a woods path over broken asphalt. Seven bicycle lights turning right at the bridge and crossing the Metonic again.

"Good night, Steve."

"Good night, Sarah."

"See you, Cathy. Boy, was this a good idea! Thanks a million!"

"Good night, Diana. Oh, and here's the penny."

"The penny?"

"For your thoughts."

"Oh. Thanks, Kevin. I'll put it in my scrapbook. Good night, kids. Good night. Good night."

Postlude

"Sleepy Strettam" is the nickname it receives most often. Cadillacs and Buicks and Chevrolets on Highway 37 pause at the blinker light. Drivers glance left toward the smooth, wide surface of the Metonic River, ahead toward the "Speed Limit: 30" sign, right toward the row of storefronts facing Main Street and facing the river. Having glanced at Strettam, most drivers proceed to ignore Strettam. By the time they accelerate at the "Resume Speed" sign, three blocks beyond the Norwich State Bank corner, they could not say the name "Strettam" if three kingdoms depended upon the saying, nor if next year's income tax were thereby to be canceled.

Once, four years ago, a Dodge from Arizona was so attracted by the tulips and lilacs in Simon Wilson's yard that it turned right at the blinker light and drove slowly up the sloping streets, all the way to St. Mark's Episcopal Church at the very crest of Strettam Hill. The Dodge even stopped for three minutes in the graveled parking lot beside St. Mark's before it ambled back down to Highway 37.

Sleepy Strettam. Merest microcosm, Strettam. But a cosmos, though micro-. At the last census, only 1,797 people. But for them, 1,797 different centers of the universe. Everyman lives in Strettam. Strettam is Babylon and Nineveh. Strettam is Gomorrah. Strettam is Oxford and London, New York and Rio.

Strettam is one of the sixty or seventy surrounding towns that metropolitan Keyesport tends to consider as her vassals and outposts. But Strettam is also vassal and outpost for contending eternal cities.

Welcome to Stre
Population 1,7

The roadsign could have read, "Just another American town."

In this novel, a cross between Thornton Wilder's *Our Town* and C. S. Lewis's *Screwtape Letters*, Elva McAllaster paints the spiritual portrait of a small American town.

Strettam may seem like a sleepy little burg as you drive by on Highway 37, but it is a battleground where lives—and souls— are ultimately lost or won.

The people of Strettam are strangely familiar; they experience the same temptations, loves, hates, failures, and desires that all of us do. But only the reader can go behind the scenes to see the workings of the Seven Deadlies (the sins of Pride, Envy, Wrath, Sloth, Covetousness, Gluttony, and Lechery) as they fight for the souls of the townspeople and battle Tom, George, and Dave—the town's three ministers who meet at Joe's Diner to plan their spiritual strategy.

Strettam is realistic, urbane, entertaining, touching, and always challenging, for Elva McAllaster is one of those masterly writers who, by telling a story, can tell us even more about ourselves.

Elva McAllaster is a professor of English at Greenville College in Greenville, Illinois. She has written several books, including *Heaven's Reveille* and *Here and Now*, and numerous articles and poems.

BL388
9783p
ZONDERVAN PUBLISHING HOUSE
FICTION
ISBN 0-310-26491-X

0 25986 26491